A WALK THROUGH WINTER

SHANNON BUCHBACH

A Walk through Winter

Text copyright © 2015 Shannon Buchbach

Cover image by artist Lucky Gumbo; copyright © 2015

ISBN: 978-0-9944242-1-1

www.ShannonBuchbach.com

DEDICATION

To my family for their love and encouragement.

To Glenn for his love, sheltering and support.

To all those who encouraged this dream; particularly Leanne, Sarah and Del.

CONTENTS

A WALK THROUGH WINTER

"We must be willing to let go of the life we have planned, so as to have the life that is waiting for us." – E.M. Forster

PROLOGUE

The house was eerily dark and quiet. Lance flicked on the light as he stepped into their spacious apartment and, from habit, called out to his wife.

There was no response.

Amanda should have arrived home from work hours ago! Perhaps she has gone out shopping; although, she would normally leave a few lights on . . . Lance thought.

Moving to the laundry, he emptied the remaining dog biscuits into Tobby's bowl.

Looks like I will have to buy more tomorrow as Amanda certainly won't take time out of her busy socialite schedule! he thought, as concern turned to irritation.

"TOBBY!"

His voice was swallowed by the walls of their open-planned first floor. Again, there was no response. Lance's concern returned. Why hadn't Tobby bounded up to him, full of energy and anticipation? Perhaps she had taken their beloved border collie for a run . . .

Lance sighed. Tobby seemed to be their sole-remaining, mutual love.

Unsettled, Lance left Tobby's bowl to prepare his own dinner. He pulled a plate of leftover Chinese Sang Choy Bao out of the fridge and placed it in the microwave to reheat. The microwave's humming sounded out of place in the stillness of the apartment. Tension hung over him, its source remaining unknown.

Lance breathed in deeply and then expelled the breath, relaxing his broad shoulders as he did so. A fractious marriage left no room for a welcoming house. Their apartment was chic, yet loveless. They had purchased it for its hospitality potential; those ambitions remained unfulfilled.

With a "ding" his dinner was ready, forcing Lance back into the present. He carried his plate over to the table. Then he saw it. A rectangular, A4 envelope sat alone on their glass-topped kitchen table.

"Lance." His name was neatly penned on the outside in Amanda's handwriting. Ripping open the tab, he slid the contents out.

His insides turned to ice as he read the small Post-it note stuck to the papers:

Lance,

I think we both know that it can't go on like this – that we can't go on like this.

I've taken Tobby with me. I need his comfort. I'm sure you understand.

Please find enclosed the divorce papers. I've given mine to the lawyer already.

Will be in touch.

Amanda.

Lance noticed a single blot at the bottom of the page. She had been crying as she wrote her good bye.

PART 1 – WINTER'S FROST

Blessed is the man who walks not in the counsel of the wicked, nor stands in the way of sinners, nor sits in the seat of scoffers; but his delight is in the law of the LORD, and on his law he meditates day and night. He is like a tree planted by streams of water that yields its fruit in its season, and its leaf does not wither. In all that he does, he prospers. (Psalm 1:1-3)

CHAPTER 1

Lance awoke knowing that there was another day of business meetings ahead of him and groaned. He rolled over and stretched out an arm to turn off the buzzing alarm clock. Pushing back his soft, ash-brown hair he read "06:00". At least that gave him enough time for a short run before breakfast. Always an active man, Lance found that he required physical activity before meeting-filled days, or he became distractible and inattentive, which was not the best front to put on when attending an international networking and planning conference for your company.

The air was crisp as he left the hotel. Winding his way down the sloping roads, he passed under a railway bridge and through to the beach beyond.

Lance drank in the vision. It was a picturesque setting. Rimmed by rugged mountain ranges, the wide bay was as a bowl, its surface dancing as diamonds in the rays of the rising sun. To his right, a row of colourful changing huts sat beside a grassy picnic area; to his left, the curving path became obscured on its journey to the neighbouring town of Muizenberg, a beach-side suburb of Cape Town, South Africa. There were two brave swimmers in the chill water. Near the tip of Africa, the waters of the Indian Ocean at St James were mingled with those of its icy neighbour, the

Atlantic Ocean. Lance shivered. Even as a surfer he would not easily be enticed into the water without a full-body wetsuit.

Lance's muscular legs responded enthusiastically as he broke into a gentle jog. Breathing deeply, he revelled in the sensation of the cold morning air as it filled his lungs and cleared his head.

Lengthening his stride and drinking deeply of the crisp air, Lance thanked the Lord for the retreat his business trip was providing. It was a change of setting from life in Manhattan: No more lawyers and away from an empty home. Free from the depressing phone calls of well-meaning relatives and the equally depressing silence from some of their mutual friends.

Ten minutes later the path ended, panning out into a gravel car park. The road ahead would take him to beach-side shops. Instead of taking to the road, he veered to the right and bounded down a short flight of stairs. Hitting the sand, he dodged a stranded jelly fish and continued along the beach until the Muizenberg River obstructed his path. Heading away from the surf, he slowed to a walk and made his way onto a pedestrian bridge and back down to the road. He longed to continue – to try to outrun his life – except, it was time to head back.

Lance was tempted into an elegant French patisserie by the buttery smell of baking pastries, as he passed a small group of shops, and treated himself to a fresh croissant and coffee for breakfast.

Lance savoured the crisp croissant, eating it slowly, as he nursed the coffee in his other hand and slowly made his way back to the hotel. Both his treats were finished before he arrived back at the elegant Richmond House. The converted mansion loomed before him and Lance realised that is was only now, after a run and a coffee, that he was ready to endure the day.

Was his job that draining? he wondered. Did he really look upon his job as something merely to endure? When did it begin to drain him, rather than excite? Responding to the questions of his heart, Lance determined that after the conference concluded he would utilise his accumulated leave and take time off to rejuvenate.

Entering the lavishly furnished foyer, he was greeted by his American co-worker exiting the formal dining room. Tom had a genuine smile, was well-liked by colleagues, and could effortlessly ease the tension from even the most highly-charged corporate meeting. His business suit appeared in stark contrast to Lance's sweat-marked running attire.

"Morning, Lance," Tom chirped.

"Hi. You well?"

"Yeah. You went for a run? That requires more energy than I have at this time of day, I'm sorry to say. You better be quick if you want to get breakfast in before we start," he said, all his words tumbling out of his mouth in fast succession.

"I grabbed a bite at a bakery down the road so I'm set," Lance replied. "See you shortly."

"Yep. Oh, and Lance?"

"Yes?"

"Please make sure you take a shower before the meeting!" Tom quipped, pegging his nose between his right thumb and index finger.

* * *

The day of business turned out to be a positive affair. Being from the same company and aware that they weren't required to secure a new investor for their company, or make a sale, created a casual atmosphere. As the men relaxed, their personalities began to peep forward from behind the masks of professionalism. Ideas were traded about bettering the company image and strategies were developed for expanding into the Asian Market.

Lance found the exchange of ideas intellectually stimulating and rewarding. The day was far more interesting than the one before it, where they had exchanged statistics on their various sectors in the global market. However, by the end of the day, despite the positive atmosphere, Lance was unwilling to keep the same company for another hour over dinner. The hotel's rigidity placed him in a cage, from which he was restless to escape, and so Lance asked Tom if he would prefer to go out for dinner. Tom readily agreed, preferring to relate to people on a one-on-one basis, rather than in large groups.

They parted company briefly to collect jackets, before heading out into the cool of evening. Retracing his steps from the morning, they made their way to Muizenberg on Tom's suggestion that they try a gourmet pizza restaurant, which he had heard praised by one of the hotel staff.

Lance enjoyed Tom's company, finding it easy to relax in his company. The man was of a serious, yet positive, disposition and able to keep conversations flowing smoothly.

As they walked, Tom asked how Lance was coping after his divorce.

"That seems to be the question of my life at the moment," Lance joked half-heartedly. "I'm not sure. I guess I'm getting by. This trip is a well-timed break from it all; a time to clear the head."

"And here I come bringing it up again?" Tom suggested.

"I don't mind. It's harder when I'm talking to those at home who know her well. I don't want to influence how they see her. The truth is: we were both guilty of walking towards the divorce. Whilst knowing this in theory, it would be welcome on occasions to lash out in a verbal tirade - listing all her faults, flaws and the (perceived) ills she did to me - but I can't do so with my family; it wouldn't be fair."

It was evident Lance was emotionally drained, despite the jest in his voice. He tried to process the events in his sluggish mind. He was tired and unable to force the effort required to analyze his emotions. It was as if he had become a zombie; dull of heart and head.

"It's not like I blame her," pent up words began to come out, slowly at first, but progressively picking up momentum. "We both stopped making the time for the other. We fell in love quickly; our marriage coming as the result of feel-good emotions, rather than a thought-out life commitment. Whilst I would love to use the excuse that we were both too young when we married, we weren't young by the time it ended. We chose the easy way out.

"We fought all the time. Over petty things. It wasn't like we were arguing deep theological issues: Who left the milk on the bench? Why hadn't I mowed the lawn? It was her turn to take the rubbish out. Eventually, all the little accusations mounted up and the house became more of a hell than a haven. I began working later hours and she began to suspect me of having an affair." Lance choked on the last words.

Tom remained silent, giving his friend space to share his heavy burden.

"I think that may have been the pivotal moment," Lance continued. "There was a day when I came home from work at around one A.M. – it was during the Franken merger. She was quietly sitting against the front door, waiting for me. I was instantly concerned and fearing the worst. A stream of thoughts ran through my mind: Had someone died? Who was in hospital? Did she have an illness? All those kind of things.

"I remember she stood up, resembling the calm before a storm. A visible shift in emotions swept across her face - from sorrow to rage. It scared me. I went to take a step forward – to hug her, or something – when our eyes met. They burned with fire. I now know the look of a woman scorned and I tell you what, Tom: don't ever go there. Truly, there is nothing to match it! I have never been more afraid of someone in my life than I was at that moment –

"What the neighbours would have thought doesn't bear considering! There we were in the communal hallway, having a verbal sparring match! I think a neighbour, or two, may have opened their doors - not that we cared what they thought.

"The words of accusation flew from her mouth: Did I think she was stupid? She knew I was sleeping with another woman. Who did I think I was to treat her like that? Had I really thought I'd get away with it?

"I yelled all kinds of horrid names at her in reply. I was caught up in my own defensive; I was far too hard-hearted by then to try a compassionate approach. How I wish I had responded in love. I wish I had taken her into my arms and dispelled her fears and assuring her of my commitment to her."

Lance took a deep breath into his lungs and released it slowly before continuing: "Eventually she stormed inside and slammed the door. I took off. Just got into the car and drove. I spent the night driving aimlessly. Man, I must have looked a wreck at work the next day."

They arrived outside the restaurant, breaking Lance's nostalgia as they slowed their pace. Silence held between them as they entered the dimly-lit pizza cafe. Being a Tuesday night, the restaurant was nearly empty with only one lonely customer sitting at a table to the right of the door.

The Italian restaurant had a small, indoor dining area. A few wooden tables with long, cushioned benches sat on each side of the doorway. It was dimly lit and the radiating heat from the wood oven accentuated the homely vibe inside. There was more seating outside, but it was less welcoming, sitting on a barren lot and surrounded by a razor-wire fence. They opted for the intimacy and character existing indoors.

"Anyway, enough about me and my woes. How've you been going?" Lance asked, as they slid onto the padded, red benches of the corner table.

The focus turned to Tom, who gave glory to God for the recent provision of a pay increase, gratefully received as his wife grew round with their first child.

Lance and Tom continued to chat happily of family as they drank strawberry milkshakes and shared a gourmet pear and camembert pizza. Lance was joyous for his friend despite his own unfulfilled desire for children; he wasn't one to begrudge others their blessings. Watching Tom talk animatedly of his family plans brought a genuine smile to Lance's eyes and lifted his spirits. He forgot about his own disappointed hopes for children as he was dragged into Tom's next life adventure.

The evening out had brought wonderful freedom for Lance. His head had cleared and a tentative hope had appeared on the horizon. The small glimmer of hope proved to be a mirage, as it called him to once more open his heart to God.

* * *

Upon entering into his hotel suite Lance had been assailed by an urgency to seek God's presence. Overpowered by the call, he had collected Bible and journal from his bedside table and proceeded to the small courtyard adjoining his room.

Beneath a host of stars, Lance cried out to God in anguish of spirit:

Father, when will you bring me back to a place of rest? When will I once again gain a sense of security? Will this pain in my heart ever end, or even ease? It hurts too much. It is as though first the rug was pulled out from under me, then the carpet, and now you are ripping up the very floor boards I stand upon. When will it cease? Where do I search to find firm ground?

You say your way is easy and your burden, light, so why is the weight of the yoke cutting into my shoulders?

When Amanda and I divorced, you promised me a future and a hope. You promised me healing. All I have known is pain, disappointment and despair. My heart remains in shards. I have fought to keep my heart open to you, but I can feel it starting to seal its self in an act of protection. All I desire is to fall into a dreamless sleep, never to awaken. All I long for is to be emotionally numbed.

His chest constricted and anxiety mounted up within him. Countless months had now passed, trapped in a constant inner struggle. He desired intimacy with God, but feared what it would bring to the surface; he was tired of the unknown future, yet afraid of receiving sight and fearful of the pain that the path of healing would inflict upon him.

He ached for security. He longed for comfort. So far, God had granted him neither.

Looking up at the night sky, he prayed:

Knowing there are people in worse circumstances does not make this place of brokenness any easier! Will depression swallow me? Is that my end? Drowning my mind in the bottle is growing in appeal, no matter how abhorrent such an act of despair may be. At least it would dim this endless ache. God, I am tired of this place!

I've already tried wearing my body to the point of exhaustion, but it did nothing to exhaust the pain in my chest. Work gives me no satisfaction. Our - my - home is empty. Where can I find reprieve? Why does nothing satisfy? Where are you in my life? I want to experience your presence.

Come to me, Jesus. Comfort me. Where are you in this?

His shoulders slumped. Despair crept deeper into his heart. Blackness threatened to engulf him. Would he fight, or would he surrender? If he fought, would he conquer?

Kneeling to the ground, he raised his hands in surrender. God was God and there was no other.

I don't know where you are in this, God. I don't know what your plans are. I cannot see your goodness now. Still, I will trust you. Despite all of this, I surrender my life once more into your hands. I entrust my heart to your care.

A stabilising centre formed amidst his swirling emotions and the heavy weight pressing on his chest began to ease. Slowly, the turbulence stilled. The peaceful quiet spread out from his mind, to his body, and finally, into his heart.

Lance drew the night air deep into his lungs, pushing out his stomach, and listened. A single thought took root in his mind. It filled his awareness. Lance knew it was God sowing the words, so far was it from his own thoughts in that moment:

"You cannot serve God and money.

"You cannot serve God and money.

"You cannot serve God and money."

Lance's body froze as his mind considered the command. God had been growing his dissatisfaction towards work in order to bring him to this revelation: even though he had been serving God since he was fifteen years old, he had been trying to serve money, too.

11

Lance had wanted the worldly comfort attached to money. He and Amanda had lived comfortably, they had acquired significant finances between their two jobs and, with no children, their wealth had continued to grow. But what had it given to him?

Lance could not say. The aesthetic beauty of his house was slighted by its emptiness; there was no life within its walls. No children laughing. No wife singing. Nothing. No, he thought, money had not brought him happiness. It had not even offered contentment.

Lord, I give it all back to you. It was never mine and I am sorry I tried to keep it for myself. The Law demanded a hefty tithe from the Israelites. When Christ came, He amplified it further - to one hundred percent. You demand everything and that is what I give you tonight.

Maybe if we had lived more generously our marriage would have turned out differently; then again, maybe it wouldn't have.

Lance's thoughts moved him back to his marriage.

I put you on to the back seat of my life. It is time you return to the driver's seat. You know where I am going. I do not. Never again let me place you as second in my life. No matter what vies for my attention, always be number one. Take the wheel; take control of my life. I need you, Father.

You are stripping me bare, and it is painful. Yet, I know it is a beneficial pain. I cannot comprehend it: How can I be stripped bare, and yet have hope? How can I have expended every ounce of my strength, only to find new reserves? Every athlete has his limit and yet this is not so with you. You grant joy and strength to the weak.

May this be an affirmation of past vows: that you, and you alone, will be my God. I will serve you all of my days. I ask for you to be my consuming passion; my one desire; my all in all. Fill me up with your love and have mercy upon me. Forgive me my weaknesses and give me strength for this next step.

As Lance continued to pray, his spirit was elevated with the certainty that God would be true to His promises: Healing. Renewal. A hope. A future. Yes, he would trust in these promises. They were humanly impossible but, with God, all things are possible.

Lost in heartfelt worship a hazy picture formed, and eventually materialised into an image of his condo. With it the decree returned:

"You cannot serve God and money."

Was God calling him to walk away from it all? Lance marvelled at the excitement he experienced in response to his question. Was it really that simple? Could he walk away from it? Just like that? Leave his job, sell his house, and go . . .?

But go where, God . . . ? If I leave my job, what will I do? If you would have me leave my house, where will I live?

Nothing came to mind. Surely this was happening to someone else? Was he crazy? His heart fluttered and began to race. Who did this? Who abandoned everything to walk towards a black void? He wasn't sure who else had done it, but he felt certain he would soon join their number.

Lance went indoors to prepare for bed, eager for the dawn when he would resign from his position and place his Manhattan Condo onto the real estate market. Snakes of excitement writhed in his stomach, making sleep difficult to find, until he finally dropped into an exhausted, heavy sleep in the early hours of the morning.

* * *

Lance awoke suddenly from a deep sleep to the sound of his alarm clock. It took only a moment until expectation caused him to jerk up in bed, remembering God's night-time call. Nervous anxiety caused a release of adrenalin into his blood stream making him come fully awake. He did not need coffee, or food; the Word of God was to be his breakfast!

He dressed quickly and then sat down on the soft rug beside his bed, resting his back against the mattress to wait upon God with the growing expectation of further revelation.

No directions came, yet still he waited.

For half an hour he waited for God to speak, before he decided that the cloud of God's presence must have dispersed from over him.

Doubts began to plague him. Surely God would reaffirm what he had heard the night before? Surely he would know, without doubt, that he knew, that he was definitely doing the right thing?

Lance tried to push the distracting questions aside in order to walk in obedience. He strengthened his will to plough on with his plans. God had promised him strength; He hadn't said anything about holding Lance's hand.

Nauseous with apprehension, Lance made his way down to the secondary conference room. It was empty.

Tiredness finally struck him. He made his way past the long, central table to the espresso machine sitting on top of the small serving cart in the back corner. Lance did not hear the beans buzz as they were ground, or register the rich aroma of the bitter coffee grinds. His attention was consumed by the draining of blood from his extremities and a growing weakness felt in his toned lower limbs.

Relieved to sit down at the table, he awaited his colleagues. Unable to pull himself into business mode, he leaned back in his chair, nursing his coffee and staring glassy-eyed ahead.

Finally, when ten minutes remained until the morning session was scheduled to commence, Lance pulled himself out of his lethargy. He went on to the company's system via remote access and retrieved the electronic resignation forms and made an immediate start, heedless of the limited time remaining before the first session.

Every pause in discussion during the meetings had him continuing the application, whilst casting furtive glances around to ensure his colleagues weren't able to see his computer screen. He knew the company would not take his resignation well on the best of occasions; he shied from considering their response when he sent it via e-mail during an overseas conference.

Lance swallowed and subconsciously rubbed his throat as he considered their response. They would question why he hadn't announced his intentions three weeks ago, thus allowing another representative to attend the conference in his place. They would ask him to stay on for a few weeks longer after he returned in order to complete a formal handover of the project.

Yet God had been clear: he must leave without looking back. Still, Lance found the idea unpleasant. He knew how he would react in their place and he did not want to wrong his employers as they had been decent enough to him over the years. Moreover, he was not thrilled by the thought of others coming to think badly of him. Yet Lance had chosen to walk in the fear of God, rather than in the fear of men; he would remain firm in his course, despite any pressure that would come from others and despite any taint made to his reputation.

By the time the lunch break was called, he had finished the forms and spent the first half hour of their break carefully composing and editing an e-mail to his direct manager.

Lance was interrupted in the process of attaching the forms by Tom's voice in the doorway, questioning whether he wanted food brought in.

"Thanks Tom. I'm coming now. Give me two minutes and I'll be with you."

Lance took a deep breath and pushed the "send" button.

CHAPTER 2

Tanya sat on her stripped mattress quietly surveying the ordered chaos of her dorm room. She had finished packing at two A.M. with the assistance of Sam and Becca.

All her belongings were now packed, sitting in there designated sections around the room. Her suitcase, containing the belongings she still needed, shared the bed with her; underneath the built-in desk along the side wall lay several boxes containing text books and university work to be shipped home to Australia; lastly, on the top of her desk sat some give-aways and presents.

Tanya was sad to leave this place, which she had called home for the past six months. It had felt like that to her; like a home. She could remember clearly when she flew into Cape Town. The plane had curved in its approach to afford her with a spectacular view of Table Mountain - and what a view it had been! It was a moment she would always remember for the words God had whispered to her:

"Rest in me, child, for I will be with you. Welcome to your new home."

And home it had been – the University of Cape Town. Nestled into the slopes of Devil's Peak, it sat beside the city. The university had provided Tanya with plenty of adventures. She had thoroughly enjoyed her classes, but, most of all, she was walking away with life-long friendships. As much as she loved the campus and wider city, it was the people she would miss.

The door of her room opened unceremoniously, admitting her two closest friends and fellow Nelson Hall residents.

Sam and Becca were talking jovially as they entered, excited for the holidays. Tanya smiled up at them. She would miss her friends. Becca, who was always on the move, asserting her indomitable will with a fiery confidence that matched her love of anything boldly red; and Sam, with her gentle ways, innocent brown eyes and sweet smile.

"Are you ready?" Sam asked.

"You betcha! Although, I'll admit I'm going to miss this place."

"Ha! No, you won't – you're going to come back to us next semester!"

Her friends had been nothing if not persistent in their attempts to convince Tanya to stay "just one more semester". She smiled, remembering how they would emphasize "just one more".

As much as she would have been pleased to have remained, Tanya knew that doing so would mean six more months away from her family and she had an unbearable longing to see them again, especially her sisters. Whether in Australia, or South Africa, she would be apart from someone close to her. Such was the cost of travel.

Thankfully for the three friends, they didn't have to think about farewells in the imminent future.

"Dad messaged me a couple of minutes ago to say he'll be here in fifteen," Becca advised.

Becca's parents owned a holiday house, on the coast between St James and Kalk Bay. Becca had convinced them to let the girls stay there for a month of relaxation at the beach as a way to celebrate the beginning of their summer holidays.

None of the girls owned a car and therefore, rather than catching a train loaded with Tanya's luggage, Becca's Dad had agreed to drive them down to the house; a fifty-minute trip.

"That soon? I wanted to duck down to Bonange quickly. Give me five?"

"Have ten," Becca replied with a wink.

"Thanks."

Tanya made to leave the room, whilst her friends took over her bed. Sam pushed the suitcase down to make room for two.

"Oh my gosh! I forgot Bryan!" Tanya blurted. She turned back to them, shocked at her own thoughtlessness at forgetting their small group leader.

"We'll say goodbye for you," Sam assured her.

"And apologise profusely for your forgetfulness," Becca quirked.

After smiling her gratitude, Tanya left to say goodbye to her young Swazi friend.

* * *

"Oh, thank you, Jesus!" Sam breathed out as Becca's father began to turn off the road.

Tanya was sitting beside Sam in the back and smiled upon hearing the remark, adding her silent agreement. When she thought "beach house" images of unkempt wooden shacks with chipping white paint and tacky décor came to mind. What was before her definitely did not fit such a description. The place was a coastal mansion!

The two storey house was situated back from the main road on the hill front and overlooked the sea. Partially hidden behind a large black gate and front hedges, a small corner of its red roof peeped out. Tanya could see a narrow strip of outer stone-work wall set slightly forward from the rest of the house, which was painted a deep yellow. The gate would have been imposing without the red roof and yellow wall endowing it with warmth. The resulting effect was one of a secluded hide-away, which only the privileged few could enter.

The large black gates swung inwards as Becca pressed the remote button and the car rolled up the pebble-set drive.

Becca's father helped carry their bags into the house and, after emphasizing that they weren't to hesitate to contact him for any reason, he wished them an enjoyable month and headed home.

The three friends spent the morning settling in before walking to the local grocery store in the neighbouring suburb of Muizenberg where they stocked up on food to last them a few days.

It was a warm and muggy day outside and they were sticky after the half hour walk home, making them grateful for the box of ice-creams nestled amongst the shopping.

The afternoon was whiled away in chatter and a discussion of the adventures to be had over the coming month, but as evening approached, Sam and Becca decided they had earned an afternoon nap. Not one to sleep during the day, Tanya took herself off towards Muizenberg.

White, fluffy clouds were gathering overhead as she wandered down the beach-side path. An occasional runner passed her by on their way to St. James and she smiled her greetings to each of them, sometimes clapping to encourage them on.

Coming around the last bend of the path, the mountains loomed up suddenly before her vision across the sparkling sea. She marvelled at the glorious setting and began glorifying God for His creation's majesty.

Her view once again turned her thoughts to South Africa. She could never grow accustomed to this country; culture after culture seemed to collide; wherever she looked there was a contrast staring back at her. Here, along the Cape Peninsula, the manifold mix of cultures rang with particular force.

In Muizenberg, nature's beauty dominated the landscape; ocean, sky and land rolled together in an imposing display. Small boys ran up to strangers to beg for money; impatient heads were shaken; curt words spoken. Then there were families buying ice-creams and young surfers gathered on the shore front as the shark-alert flags were raised; businessmen in work suits sat drinking coffee at the café as parking guards prowled between the vehicles outside, hoping to earn a small tip, worth twenty-five cents.

That was Muizenberg, but Tanya knew that just down the road sat a township and a little further on an even larger one. The sight still made

Tanya bereft of thought when she passed by: a sea of houses spanned a greater distance than the ocean before her – if you could call them houses, being only single rooms made of scrap metal. She could hardly credit how close such living quarters were to the grand beach-front houses like the one she where she was currently residing.

Tanya had spent four weeks working with the Xhosa people in the township as part of her major community development research project for her Master's degree. She winced at the thought of what a summer spent in those houses would be like. Pictures of suppressing heat radiating from the tin shelters haunted her mind. She shied from imagining a winter night in such a structure and she certainly didn't want to know how many died as a result of insufficient protection from the elements, let alone unemployment, HIV and AIDS, or poor sanitation.

What kind of world was this? Tanya shook her head negligibly.

God, sometimes I can't help thinking that I live in a messed up world. There is so much beauty, and yet so much suffering. I know the world is broken; it just hurts to see it so clearly.

It was in the midst of her heart-felt prayer that Tanya first saw Lance. She had been startled into smiling by the air of familiarity hanging over him. His broad, sun-tanned face responded in kind. Their eyes locked in a moment of unexpected intimacy. It was a brief moment of kinship with a stranger, but he had been sufficiently attractive to keep a partial smile on her lips after he had passed.

The interruption caused a lightening of her mood as she forgot the deep subject upon which she had been pondering. She turned right to take the stairs leading to the beach front all the while wondering if she had seen him before. She was almost certain that she hadn't, and yet his image stayed with her for the remainder of her walk.

* * *

Lance sat staring forward, recalling the beautiful woman he had passed on his evening stroll. He had left the hotel to clear his head only to return far more distracted.

It had only been meant as a short walk to give him a reprieve from the desk; a half-hour round trip to Muizenberg and back. When he had reached the end of the path in Muizenberg he had paused before turning back. Using the banister rail for support, he stretched his right quadriceps femoris muscle, pulling the foot up behind him. And then he saw her. He unconsciously lowered his leg and leaned back into the banister, watching her walk by.

Long curly locks, fiery red in colour, had been pulled back into a loose ponytail. Her face was round, almost plump, beguiling her slender figure. Lance hazarded a guess that she was in her early- to mid-twenties. A gust of the famous Muizenberg winds had swept a few strands of her hair loose and she had brushed them impatiently behind her ear.

She had smiled at Lance as she walked past. Brilliant green eyes, shining from the wind, had met his grey ones. He had been mesmerised. His head had turned to trace her retreating figure as she made her way down the steps to the beach front.

Lance frowned where he now sat at the suite's wide writing desk. Emotion was stirring within him. He sent up a question to the Lord. Hope had fluttered in his heart when her stunning eyes had made contact with his. It had been the longing of hope; an opening of the heart to the potential to heal, even from the sorest of wounds.

He had not noticed a woman in the ten months, which had passed since his divorce. Lance had purposefully clamped up his heart; partially from pain and brokenness, and partially as a form of self-inflicted punishment. He had determined to walk in singleness, without love, for the remainder of his life, serving God as a single man. It seemed as if he would need more determination than he had first realised to see that end accomplished.

The heart was too fickle for man to bridle and yet bridle it he must for his heart was shattered. Parting from his wife had left irreparable damage. He could not imagine a life of wholeness. Only a miracle of God could heal his wounds.

Lance prayed silently for healing and, not for the first time or for the last, he looked towards God for forgiveness.

Sighing, Lance struggled to focus on the work awaiting him, which had to be done before he could call it a night. He needed to finalise some of his hand-over notes if he wanted to be finished come Friday. Contemplation of the past, and dreams for a brighter future would have to be deferred. He must make an effort to conjure up his concentration if he wanted to sleep before the morning arrived.

* * *

An unpleasant meeting was unexpectedly waiting for Lance at the breakfast table the following morning.

He had awoken with an effort as the steady beeping of his alarm clock broke in on his awareness. A cold shower had cleared his head of the foggy mire, but this accentuated the sharp pain, which throbbed behind his eyes.

Entering the dining room, he had greeted each of his fellow contingents by name and proceeded to fill a bowl with muesli flakes at the buffet table, ignoring the tantalising aromas emanating from the various fried foods available.

He should have realised something was wrong when he sat down. The table had been oddly subdued. Lance had been unable to engage Tom in conversation. The party suddenly dispersed to prepare for the morning meetings, but Tom signalled for Lance to remain.

"Why?" Tom challenged in an oddly quiet voice when they were alone.

Only the one word: "Why?"

"Why?" Lance parroted, understandably perplexed.

"Why didn't you tell me you were leaving the company?"

"Oh," relieved, Lance responded that they had stipulated he remain quiet, allowing them a week to find a replacement before making his decision broadly known.

Lance swallowed the remaining dregs of his coffee.

"But the good news is, by replacement . . . they mean you!" he continued brightly. "Tom, you're the logical choice! We've been working together for eighteen months so they're bound to choose you. And, naturally, a promotion will mean a raise. Your new family . . ."

"Lance! They fired me."

"They *what?*" Lance demanded with consternation across his face.

"They said you were going to another company and they don't want me following you out the door in nine months' time to a competitor. Or forming our own company," he added. His voice was strained. It was clear Tom was close to breaking point.

"That's absurd! They really said that?"

"Essentially; that was the impression they gave me."

"But I told them I wanted time off to think! They knew I didn't have a job lined up!" Lance riled.

"Your words don't seem to have made a difference – I'm flying home today, to be out of the office come Friday."

"Before I have to leave?" Lance asked, still in shock. "Tom, I'm sorry. I am truly sorry! You must know: I am not leaving to go elsewhere . . . the whole Amanda thing . . . I just, I just need time out to gain some perspective."

Tom didn't make a reply. It wasn't necessary. He gave Lance a hurt look, before standing and walked slowly out of the dining room.

Dirty crockery sat unheeded before him. Lance was torn between exacerbation (that Tom felt he had dealt him a backhand trick), and guilt (that he hadn't informed Tom, his close colleague, of his resignation).

He was unable to comprehend his friend being unable to trust his story. It hurt. And he was angry, too. Angry at his soon-to-be ex-employers and Tom for blaming him. For the company to be back-handed enough, rude enough, low enough, to fire his friend because he was leaving offended his sensibilities. That they thought he was going to another firm and would somehow betray "big (nonexistent), company secrets" would have had him sniggering at its absurdity, if Tom hadn't been affected. They should know he was not some sleazy businessman prepared to jump ahead in the game by boarding a more luxurious boat sailing the same vast market!

How could this be happening?

God? God! It shouldn't be this way! I obeyed you. I trusted you. Now Tom is jobless.

Tom. Tom, Lord! He is about to start a family. No wonder he hates me! No wonder he only has bitter words for me.

Lance felt betrayed. He felt deserted. He had lost his wife, he had quit his job, and, from South Africa, he had put his home on the market. It seemed even more unfair that he looked set to lose a friend because his work had decided to take a petty stance against him.

The situation was unjust. Lance pushed his chair out in controlled anger.

God, help me. I have no idea how to solve this. I can't solve this. Will you? Look after Tom and his family.

Walking to the board room with his teeth not brushed and laptop absent, Lance was only physically present. Neither was he any more attentive on the following, final day of the conference. Tom's absence hung heavily in the air, creating an uneasy atmosphere.

It was a relief when the week came to an end and the luxurious hotel had emptied of conference participants. Lance had welcomed their departure. The week-long conference had tired him like a month-long one should have done.

He had decided after hearing of Tom's dismissal to stay on in South Africa for an extra three weeks. It was a long-awaited chance for a timeout. The extra days would allow him to relax and his mind to wander.

He was hungry to seek out the Presence of God. He missed it; craved it. He longed after the intimacy of standing before God. He was eager to enter His throne room. He had let his devotion slip during his marriage until the final months when a desperate yearning for God had been reawakened. Alas, too late to save his marriage, it had at least saved him from losing his self.

* * *

Saturday dawned with overcast skies threatening to release their burden, but Lance was not deterred. A physical longing had taken hold of him, which demanded he spend time with the Lord. This morning he would climb Muizenberg Mountain, whatever the weather.

He hoped an energetic hike would release the tension from his body and provide a time of prayer. It would be the ideal way to start his holiday.

A broad smile broke on his face. He was not on holidays, he amended – he was jobless. It was a freeing thought: not knowing where to next. No five year plan in place. No prospective job offers. Just - this - moment.

Making his way up a steep flight of stairs, Lance reached Boyes Drive, a scenic drive overlooking the towns below, and beyond them, the ocean.

Lance was sweating lightly as his muscles warmed with the exertion. The crescent road gently led him to Muizenberg. Mountain trails led from the road up the rugged hillside. Lance continued until the first houses appeared ahead and turned up onto the last trail.

The first part was the hardest with a steep incline, and high steps cut out of the mountain. Once he had cleared the initial hurdles, his lungs began to breathe more readily, and the ache in his leg muscles eased. He was invigorated. He felt alive!

Looking back, he froze. Two overlapping mountain faces formed a "v", which contained the ocean at its base. Overhead the sky was a brilliant blue, merging to one with the ocean beneath it.

It took Lance nearly an hour to reach the top. The mountain plateau afforded climbers a panoramic view of a snake-like river slithering across the plain, bordered on each side by a carpet of tiny houses; beyond the plains the sea grasped the horizon; and to its left stood Table Mountain, tall and proud despite the distance at which it sat.

The spectacular sight was lost on Lance. His gaze had been fixed by what he felt was a much prettier picture.

* * *

Tanya had spun around, startled. She had been lost in praise, awed by the outlook, until the sound of footsteps had broken her reverie.

Watching the bend of the path, the man from her walk came into view. She stared. He stopped short and returned her unblinking gaze. Finally, he broke into a delighted smile and moved forward.

He held out his hand and, out of reflex, she put hers gently into his. A gentle pressure was felt on her palm as he squeezed it, saying: "Hi, I'm Lance".

He released her hand and it dropped to her side.

"T-Tanya," she stuttered.

"It's beautiful here, isn't it?" Lance posed, looking around.

Tanya tried to attend as he continued with pleasantries. Close proximity to this particular man seemed to have an unnerving effect on her intellect. She prayed it didn't show upon her features, or in her speech. Why was she unsure with this stranger? She usually exuded confidence.

A wave of the familiar swept over her for the second time. It was as if they had met in the past only to have had all memory of the event wiped clear. Something akin to amnesia, she hypothesised.

Neither of them knew how they had broken from generic topics to the genuine and easy flow of friends; they didn't give it a thought, so easily did the transition occur.

Before long, Tanya found herself sitting beside him with their backs against two neighbouring boulders, staring out over the land below.

As they talked, she discovered that they were both staying by the coast on holiday, had come to the mountain for a quiet time of reflection with God, and were in no hurry for their holidays to end.

"And what brought you to South Africa?" Lance asked.

"I've been here on a semester exchange. I was studying at the University in Cape Town."

"You're at University? What are you studying?"

"I'm doing a Master's in international studies and community development. My Bachelor was in journalism."

"Right! Wow! You must be a bright cookie," Lance smiled.

"No, the studies aren't hugely difficult and my grades aren't brilliant. I chose the degree because I want to work in missions and supposed it would provide me with useful background skills," Tanya replied humbly.

Tanya went on to explain how she had been advised by her church to get a degree behind her before applying to join a full-time mission's team. From journalism she had "tumbled into the Master's program", a tumble she attributed to God who "always knows what He's doing, even when we don't".

Tanya was mindful of a slight pause when she asked Lance what he was doing in South Africa. She listened as he told her how he had initially come on business during which he had decided to stay on. When she commented that his work must understand to give him extra leave on short notice, he had let out a laugh and said it was "something along those lines". Tanya was left wondering about the details.

Lance shared with her that he was learning to put his trust in God and to believe in His faithfulness; he left out that he was struggling to accept God's grace and forgiveness. They spoke a long time about God and gave Him glory for what He was doing in their lives. Tanya told him that she was learning about the cost of following where He led her (wherever that might be).

Tanya wasn't sure what happened to the time, having become completely absorbed in their conversation and her immediate surrounds. She felt at peace with him and was aware of stillness in the atmosphere, which caught her up with it. It was as if time had paused for them, gifting them a moment in their own world atop the mountain, until pregnant pause in the flow of conversation checked her. Time hadn't stopped . . .

"It can't be midday already! I'm sorry, I really should head back down, or my friends will be worried."

Tanya had risen and was brushing loose dirt from her shorts. Lance followed her lead and stood to his feet.

"You said you didn't have a church to go to earlier?" she enquired abruptly.

"Yes, that's right."

"Well, the local community church is holding a worship evening tonight if you're interested," she suggested. "They also have a morning service, tomorrow. I'm not sure if we will be going – it will depend on what else we do, I guess – but I hear it's a good church. My friend Becca and her family go there whenever they are staying in St James."

Tanya gave Lance the details ahead of beginning a careful descent, navigating her way down the rocky path to the bottom of the mountain. From there she hastened back to St James, praying Becca and Sam wouldn't be too worried.

CHAPTER 3

Lance took up Tanya's invitation to attend the worship event at the local evangelical church. He was hesitant as he entered the building and proceeded up the internal staircase to the worship hall, situated on the second floor.

He was greeted at the top of the stairwell by a kindly Cape Coloured lady with her dark hair tightly pulled back to appear almost straight against her scalp, but only tamed as far as the hair tie, after which he burst into its curls again. She smiled brightly and offered him a flyer advertising their regular services and fellowship times.

Looking around the room he could not see Tanya so he took a seat near the back of the rows. Lance reached out to God as the lights dimmed, his head bowed in prayer:

Bring me close to you. Let my heart and mind be focused on you as we worship here tonight.

Remove all other thoughts from my mind. Let me come before you with adoration and praise.

The worship session was an informal affair run by a number of students attending the neighbouring seminary school, which had planted the church.

Lance added his voice softly to those surrounding him, never having been confident of his singing abilities. The voices of the congregation combined in joyous praise as they sang before the Lord, declaring their desire to bring the offering that He deserved.

Lance felt compelled to kneel before his God. He looked around, self-conscious. His fellow worshippers were engaged in the song and their own devotion. Thus assured of anonymity, he obediently sank to his knees.

Hunching over, Lance wished he was stronger. He longed to be consumed in worship to the extent that he ceased to be aware of those around him.

Father, bring it back to you. Just as the words of this song, make my life about worshipping you and magnifying your holy name.

I am sorry I do not give you what is your due.

I am sorry I have allowed life to take me from you.

Bring me back to a life devoted to worship. I long to give you more; I long to give you what you deserve. Become my all in all.

Lance looked back over the past twenty years. The events of his life felt surreal. Surely if he could only wake up, he would be eighteen years old again and full of plans to conquer the world for the Lord.

He had dreamed of living a life fully for the King. In retrospect, it seemed that all he had given his God was disappointment and disobedience.

The reality of the past twenty years haunted him as he drew to mind all the hurtful words he had spoken and the wounds he had caused.

A single tear fell from his eyes to land on the blue carpet.

Lance had met Amanda at college, having both attended an on-campus Christian group. They had fallen in love and six months later, after a wild romance, they were engaged to be married. Lance had been only too willing to give up his plans for Amanda.

He had dreamed of adventuring into Africa as a missionary after the likeness of Nate Saint, a Missionary Aviation Fellowship (MAF) pilot, who willingly laid down his own life trying to evangelise the Indians in Ecuador; or David Livingstone, who mapped much of Southern Africa. The dream faded when he had married. He had listened to the voices around him, telling him of his obligation to earn money in order to support his family.

Family.

He grasped his head and pulled it down to bury his face in the crook of his elbows.

Lance grieved having no children. He grieved not having anything to show from his years of marriage. His adult years resembled an empty shell.

A second tear rolled down his face as God's Spirit gently touched his heart. The touch was as delicate as the tip of a finger caressing the skin of a peach; enough to be felt, whilst not enough to bruise the flesh.

Oh God, what has my life been? What do I have to show for it? I have not served you. I have no children to raise in your ways.

I am living a selfish life. I blamed Amanda for being selfish, for not giving me what I demanded; however, I was the one who was selfish. I did not try hard enough. I did not fight for our marriage. I thought I had, but I hadn't. I was so consumed about what I was owed, what she wasn't giving to me, and what I felt I required.

Have mercy on me. Forgive me.

Can I ever be free from this guilt? You bound us together in marriage and we did not honour the sacred union. You say your Son died for our sins, for all sins, but I cannot seem to accept forgiveness for this one – they call it holy matrimony and I have left it profaned.

Oh, God, have mercy on me!

The carpet was beginning to itch as it sunk into his flesh. The physical discomfort brought the raw pain in his heart to the surface. It seemed God would not leave him to clean and care for his wound in his own time.

Since the divorce, it had been all he could do to make it through a day. Waves of depression had threatened to drown him and hence he had tried to suffocate his emotions. It had seemed the only way to be saved from the crushing weight of water. Until now.

God was declaring it time to expose his heart to air and light. The pain was intensifying now the bandage had been removed, but the wound needed to breathe. God had not been content to leave his son's wound to fester and, thereafter, spread disease through his entire body.

Lance clung desperately to the knowledge that God was there with him. God was about to lance the wound. He could only hope that the pain would be drained alongside the puss of infection.

* * *

Downward pressure to his shoulder caused Lance to glance up. A broad-shouldered Xhosa man stood above him, eyes closed in prayer. Lance found it tricky to gauge the years of the Xhosa people, not knowing how to assess their dark skin for signs of aging. He took a guess that the man was somewhere in his fifties.

Lance bowed his head, accepting the prayer of the older man. Unable to catch the soft words, Lance was nevertheless comforted by his presence and thankful for his prayers.

The Xhosa man opened his eyes and, giving a gentle squeeze to Lance's shoulder, wandered forward to retake his place on an aisle seat, midway down the rows.

* * *

The prayerful African man came over to Lance to introduce himself after the service with a large smile and outstretched hand. He was known as Pastor David.

"It is nice to have you here tonight, brother. Do you live around this area?" he asked.

"I was here on business; staying in St James . . ."

"Welcome!" Pastor David cut in jovially. "Where are you from? The States?"

"Yes: from New York. It isn't as peaceful as it is here in your little part of the world."

A short burst of laughter escaped from the pastor, his large gut quivering. "In some ways, I suppose not, but not in all of them. Will you stay around to fellowship for a time? Come get a cup of tea with me and I will introduce you to my Marlee."

Leading the way over to the drinks' area, Pastor David made his way up to a robust lady, who looked to be a few years his junior.

"This is my wife, Marlee. Marlee, this is Lance; he is over on business from the States."

Marlee greeted Lance, welcoming him to the church and trusting for him to fellowship with them whilst in the country. The volume of her voice rivalled that of her husband's and her disposition was equally buoyant.

Turning to Lance, the pastor asked him how he would have his tea. David maintained his position when Lance replied white with two sugars, which momentarily puzzled Lance. He tried to catch up with what the Pastor was saying:

". . . did a good job. It was their first time running a session by themselves. As much as possible, we encourage the students to become involved in the church - of course, it helps them to engage when we include participating in services as part of their assignments!"

The pastor chuckled at his own humour and continued to explain more about the running of the college and its subsequent involvement with the church.

Marlee came up to Lance holding out a mug of white tea out to him in offering. Lance realised the Pastor had been asking about his preferences on his wife's behalf.

Thanking her, Lance took the cup and readjusted his thinking, trying not to judge the cultural custom dictating a wife must wait upon her husband. Lance considered what Amanda would have done if he had tried placing the same expectations upon her. It wouldn't have ended well, he thought grimly.

The pastor proceeded to introduce Lance to several members of the congregation, invited him to attend their Sunday church service on the following morning, and then left Lance engaged in a lively discussion of the Soccer World Cup currently being played in the nation as he moved off to greet others in the hall.

The time of fellowship lasted about half an hour. As people began to disperse, Lance made his way from the hall with three of the men to whom Pastor David had introduced him.

Wally, a sprightly young Cape Coloured man who looked as if he could out run a cheetah in a race, asked Lance where he was staying. When he replied "in St James", the three of them offered to accompany him back to the hotel.

"It's best not to walk alone at night if you can help it, Bru," Wally explained. "I imagine you'd be okay, but it's better to be safe – especially as you flash "tourist"," he added with a cheeky grin.

* * *

With no plans for the day, Lance returned to the community church for their Sunday morning service. On only his second visit, the place had a warm, homely air. People smiled and nodded greetings to him as he entered.

Lance chose the same seat at the back as he had occupied the previous evening. As he sat, he saw Tanya walk in with two other women who looked about her age. One was tall and slim with an air of confidence; the other was petite, with a sweet face.

They rose for the first song. Lance noticed Tanya was one of those people whose attention became wholly absorbed in God during worship. Watching her avidly praising God made joy rise within his own heart.

He sent up prayers of thanks to the Lord:

You are good. Regardless of what happens in my own life, I will give you praise. I can empathise with old Job at the moment – and not at the end of his story. Just as Job praised you when all was stripped from him, I pray you will strengthen me to sing your praises regardless of my physical circumstances.

I know you are giving me hope for restoration. I will trust you to bring it in season. And I will trust you through any pain that comes upon the road to restoration.

As the rest of the congregation continued to sing around him, Lance sat and opened his Bible to the book of Psalms. He read:

". . .Cast me not away from your presence, and take not your Holy Spirit from me. Restore to me the joy of your salvation, and uphold me with a willing spirit.

"Then I will teach transgressors your ways, and sinners will return to you.

"Deliver me from bloodguiltiness, O God, O God of my salvation, and my tongue will sing aloud of your righteousness. O Lord, open my lips, and my mouth will declare your praise.

"For you will not delight in sacrifice, or I would give it; you will not be pleased with a burnt offering. The sacrifices of God are a broken spirit; a broken and contrite heart, O God, you will not despise . . ." [1]

Through all weather the psalmists trusted you. They clung to your mercy and grace; trusted in the steadfastness of your love; and hoped in your faithfulness.

I pray that I, too, will place such hope in you. I ask you to make my heart unwavering in its devotion and reliance upon you.

Worship concluding, Pastor David made his way to the microphone as the congregation resumed their seats. Lance listened to the pastor as he shared on the rejuvenating love of the Lord, which came as the changing of winter to spring and gave new warmth to man's heart.

Lance felt as if the sermon had been solely written to him. The Pastor's illustration caught his attention and burned itself into his mind:

"God takes us through seasons in our lives. Some here this morning will be in a winter season; numb from cold. You may be unaware when the winds changed and the snow began to drift in. You may have even rejoiced in the cooler weather as it gave you a reprieve from God's refining fire.

Awaken and see how it has left you numb to the convicting voice of the Holy Spirit.

"In this place, you are vulnerable. The cold has prevented your roots from sucking up the nutrients of Christ. The leaves fall from your branches and no fruit is produced. You become bare and barren. To those in this season, I want to say: God desires to bring you back into the joys of spring; into the joy of your salvation!" the pastor's voice rose in crescendo.

"You feel ice-cold. It reaches down into your bones. Cry out to Him! Ask for Him to bring the sun down upon your face. Ask Him to wrap you in the blanket of His love. There is no winter season too long for Him to restore to life."

Lance became caught up in private meditation as the pastor continued. The barrenness of winter was an apt illustration for his heart. He was cold; frozen inside. Could God bring spring sunshine? Would he enter into a Thaw? He was afraid at what his heart would like if not for the icicles around it. He feared that it had been badly injured by many tiny cuts and now would be beyond repair from frostbite.

Lance broke from his contemplation as the service closed on a benediction. He was aware that he would have to seek time alone during the afternoon to pray and process the message and what God was speaking through it.

Pastor David greeted Lance warmly with a hand shake and half-hug. He soon bundled Lance off to meet a few more of the church regulars. Lance tracked Tanya with his gaze as he was led away and noted how she looked around the crowd, as if looking for someone. He hoped that someone was him; however, he couldn't be certain.

Lance excused himself after ten minutes of making small talk and made his way through the crowd looking for Tanya.

Spotting her by the urn, he walked up behind her, standing a clear head above her in height.

"Were your friends worried when you made it home yesterday?"

Tanya spun around.

"Hi! How are you?" she replied in delight. "They were a little bit upset with me for not having messaged them . . . I said there hadn't been any reception on the mountain and that I was hurrying too much to think of it by the time I reached the road."

Lance gave a short laugh. "Well, so long as I didn't place you in any trouble . . . I came last night as you suggested. It was definitely worth it. I think you would have liked it. The sermon was short and to the point as they gave most of the time to songs and reflection. A few people shared testimonies, which were encouraging."

"Oh, I'm sorry I missed it, then! We decided to be rather ungodly, I'm afraid, and stayed home, ate pizza and watched a movie."

"I'm sure He didn't mind . . . too much. But I think I was the one who earned the brownie points," Lance responded in jest.

Going on nervously, and willing his voice to a calm, casual tone, Lance asked if Tanya had any plans for the day and, if not, whether she cared to join him for an ice cream at the Muizenberg beach front.

One of Tanya's friends came up hastily and broke in on them before she could give her reply. It was the petite, mouse-like one.

"Tanya – Hi, sorry to interrupt – Tanya, are you nearly ready?" she appealed.

"Yes, give me one minute and I'll be right with you."

"Okay, well Beck is out front. You know how she is – bull at a gate when she decides it is time to make a move!"

"That was Sam," Tanya commented as her friend moved off through the crowd towards the stairs.

She looked at Lance in apology, saying: "Sorry, we already had plans for today."

"No, no that's okay. It was just a suggestion – "

Tanya saw a boyish embarrassment in his response much like one who had taken a risk and come off second best. She thought he was making light of it and, as she was also disappointed, impulsively volunteered the information that she was free the following day.

". . . Perhaps we could go for a walk?" she ended.

Arranging to meet him at ten the next morning, Tanya ran to catch up with her friends who were waiting outside. Only after she left did she realise how recklessly she had responded. What were his motives?

Tanya put concerns aside; she'd find out soon enough.

* * *

"What's this?" Tanya piped up.

The friends had made their way to the beach, which sat across the main road from the church. Removing their shoes, they walked barefoot in the sand.

"Becca has a boy interest – one of the seminary students!" Sam replied with glee.

"I do not! He's a friend from way back," she defended. "His family lives close by and I spent a lot of summers playing with him as our parents nattered on."

"That's your story is it?" Tanya pressed.

"Yeah, not even a little interested?" Sam quipped.

Becca blushed. She gave off an outward confidence and was ever forward in her opinions, yet inwardly she hid a hunger for acceptance and, when it came to matters of the heart, she tended towards a more private disposition.

"Well, maybe a little – But I hardly ever see him! And he has a girlfriend.

He was telling me about her this morning," Becca added in disgust.

"How rude! I mean honestly! – the nerve of the fellow when he knew you would be returning this summer!"

"Oh hush, Sam! I'm not going into mourning over him!"

They paused at the edge of the markets to slip their shoes on.

Most of the stalls contained items for daily living such as beauty products, clothes and storage items, although there were a few souvenir stalls scattered here and there amidst the rest, and that is why they had come. It was much smaller than Greenmarket Square, a vibrant flea market, which swarmed with tourists in the heart of the city. The girls were not currently energetic enough to make the long trek into Cape Town on a crowded train, and so the local market place it had been when Tanya requested they make time for her to buy a few last-minute gifts for people back home in Australia.

Sam turned her attention to Tanya as they meandered through the stalls.

"What about you Tanya? See any guys of interest?"

"Please, I'm only in the country for another three weeks. What would be the point?"

"Good answer; hardly convincing."

"Okay Sam – what about you? All these questions . . ." Tanya fired back.

"There were a couple of cuties, but sadly, no." She blushed as she joked, revealing her embarrassment at being addressed on the topic.

"Yes, well, you always were the picky one, weren't you," Becca snipped.

"That's me," she declared proudly, although in truth it was natural shyness which prevented her from pursuing an interest. "And what about the guy you were talking to at the end, Tanya?"

"What? Lance? No!"

"Lance! So he has a name," Becca teased. "Who was he, Sam? I didn't see."

"Serves you right for hurrying us all out the door," Tanya replied, hoping to move matters on. She succeeded. They began to tease Becca about her impatience before moving on to general comments about the goods on display.

Tanya found a few gifts; a brightly beaded fruit bowl, a pair of hand-crafted wooded giraffes with intertwining necks, and a South African soccer jersey proudly embellished with the team nickname "Bafana Bafana" (meaning "Go Boys, Go Boys"). She doubted whether her father would ever don the bright yellow jersey, but had bought it anyway, knowing he would appreciate it.

Shopping completed, the trio bought curry beef samousas for lunch, which they ate hot on their walk back to their beach house.

* * *

Later in the afternoon, Sam reintroduced the topic of boys. In the lounge room, Tanya was lying on her stomach on top of a Persian silk rug with her legs pumping back and forth, whilst Sam sat up, resting her back against the maroon, leather sofa.

Sam had been gently plying Tanya with questions and when Tanya went quiet, immediately knew she had hit the spot.

"Tanya! Do you like him? I don't believe it, do you really?" Sam cried in delighted discovery.

Tanya began to trace the maroon patterning of the rug.

"May – be," was her sheepish reply.

"But isn't he – older – than you?" Sam hadn't meant to sound blunt; the question had popped out before she could prevent it.

"I think about ten years . . ."

"*Only*," she said. Being the youngest in her family, she struggled not to think of any guy beyond a couple of years her senior as old.

Once Sam had digested the age gap, however, she was able to join her friend's excitement, asking her all the right questions: How did they meet (and how had she managed to keep it from them this long!)? What did he do? Why was he in South Africa? What was his most attractive feature? Had he asked her out? And: Did she think they would stay in touch when she went home?

Tanya laughed.

"I hardly know him! And he hasn't said anything to me to suggest he is looking for a relationship, or is even interested in me in that way. We've literally only talked a couple of times!"

"But clearly, he likes you!" she declared. "You spent three hours talking together on the mountain top! He wouldn't have stayed if he wasn't interested."

Tanya smiled at what she perceived as naive innocence from her friend.

"Yeah, except he is here on his own and might just be grateful for some company. And besides, could you imagine if he was married or something?"

"You don't know if he is married!" Sam exclaimed, incredulous.

"You don't know if who is married?" Becca enquired, coming in from the kitchen. She carried a bowl of reheated koeksisters, which they'd bought at the markets. The plaited Afrikaans donuts were dripping with syrup and the smell made all three mouths salivate. Yet Sam's focus was not distracted from what she perceived as the more interesting object.

"Tanya's man; Lance. She doesn't know if he's married! How could that not have made its way into the conversation?"

"What, the guy from church you didn't introduce us to?"

"Hey, you left, remember! And I don't think he's married. At least, I am pretty sure he isn't," she amended. "I just can't see why he isn't."

"Have you asked him?" responded Becca, with irritating practicality.

"No. I know I should – only, it's kind of awkward: "Hey Lance, I'm interested in you, but are you, like, married?""'"

"Funny," was the dry reply. "I don't know how you should go about it, but you need to."

Becca was always black and white.

"Seriously guys! We've talked on two occasions!"

"But you'll see him again?" Sam prompted.

There was a pause. A slow smile crept on to Tanya's face.

"Tomorrow," she replied.

"Tanya!" Becca reproved.

"Okay, okay! I *promise* I will ask him tomorrow."

Tanya laughed at the look of doubt on the two faces looking back at her.

"So, interrogation over . . .?" she queried hopefully.

"Hasn't even begun! . . ."

Becca and Sam continued to ply Tanya with questions. When they were satisfied Tanya had told them everything, the girls mustered only enough energy as required to make hot chocolates, grab three fleece blankets and turn on the television. They snuggled up to watch "How to Lose a Guy in 10 days", Tanya's boy interest temporarily forgotten.

CHAPTER 4

Tanya was running late, which wasn't unusual in itself, except this time she was intentionally dawdling. She was unsure of what to expect. A giddy excitement bubbled within her as she headed away from her friends.

She made it to the beach front. Lance was sitting in front of a bright blue and yellow changing shed with red roof, gazing at the ground with the appearance of one perfectly content and not at all flustered at her untimely arrival. He looked up at her and smiled a greeting, rising to meet her.

Tanya was made easy by his stature. Maybe she had been over thinking it and he was simply looking for company and some one to talk to during his holiday.

The pair decided on a walk to Kalk Bay for coffee, requiring them to back track from the beach up onto the path beside the road. Turning left they made their way towards the neighbouring town.

"I think it is amazing how they make those. It must take loads of patience to simply sit and work their beads," Lance commented, walking past a grey-haired Xhosa man who was sitting in front of an Italian restaurant, working bright-coloured beads and wire into ornaments.

"Have you been to the pier in Cape Town? What do they call it? The Waterfront?"

"No, I don't think so."

"Oh, you should! I mean, if you have time before you go. I think it's about half an hour walk from the train station, although you could always grab a taxi. We used to go there on Fridays during the semester to relax before beginning our weekend work on assignments – it was a change of scenery.

"Anyway, the reason I bring it up is because they have this massive beaded elephant worked with incredible attention to detail. It'd be taller than you. Huge!"

"Perfect for children to try and climb!"

"Do you have any kids?"

Tanya waited nervously for his response. She wished she could have unspoken the words the moment she heard them tumble out of her mouth. He had alluded several times to having been married, but had never expanded upon the subject. She waited silently, wondering how he would reply.

After a slight pause, Lance replied that he didn't have children.

Tanya was relieved and chided herself: You're only here for three more weeks! Whilst to him, she uttered: "Oh, I'm sorry. I shouldn't have brought it up."

"No, it's okay. My wife – my ex-wife, I should say – well, we never had children. I think we both sort of knew our marriage was too fractious to raise children; it wouldn't have been fair on them."

And there it was, Tanya thought, out in the open without a pause, without even an intake of breath.

Tanya wasn't sure how she ought to reply and stumbled over her next words: "Maybe it was for the best? Not bringing children in, I mean."

"Yes. Though I'd still like to have children, someday. I have a niece and nephew, though. They give me plenty of laughs."

Tanya smiled as he went on to share a few of his six year old nephew's antics, such as the time he had become fully caught up in the world of make-believe, playing "firemen", and took the garden hose full blast to the inside walls of the house.

His little niece, on the other hand, was a princess who loved parading around in frilly dresses and a plastic tiara. When he went to visit he was expected to bring his four year old niece a new piece of jewellery. Her room gave testament to this, filled as it was with plastic bangles, hair clips, ribbons and beads all from her "Uncle Wan-nie", a nickname he had received when she was a toddler learning to speak.

Hearing him talk fondly of his niece and nephew, Tanya found herself wishing he was not divorced. He seemed astonishingly perfect. She couldn't help wondering why his marriage ended. What brought them to that place?

Having broached the subject of children, she felt it better not to take up the ex-wife topic, too. She therefore proceeded to ask more questions about his family; his parents, the number of his sister and brothers, and whether he missed them.

Houses turned to shop fronts as they walked into town. Tanya hadn't explored in the direction of Kalk Bay before and was fascinated by the array of shops.

"It's definitely different to Muizenberg and St James," she commented as they passed a shop full of Indian skirts, hippie dresses and candles. The smell of incense wafted out of the store onto the footpath.

They continued past bric-a-brac stores, antiques, artsy cafés, boutiques and second hand bookstores. Tanya noticed the price tags bore much higher figures here in Kalk Bay.

They entered into a glamorous café with black and white décor. Electric chandeliers hung from the ceiling over chic tables and straight-backed chairs. They chose a table near the back wall near the drinks counter. A plastic palm branch brushed against Tanya's arm as she sat down.

"This place is awesome!"

"I agree," Lance said. "I found it yesterday and chose it for my quiet time."

"It would make a great place to journal," Tanya commented.

It was another thing they found in common. Lance was surprised as, having tagged Tanya as an extrovert, he had assumed she would rather talk than write. She explained that whilst she was generally outgoing, she required time alone to refuel.

". . . and I doddle and draw in it as much as I write," she added.

Tanya ordered a honey-crunch frappe; Lance the peanut-choc-chip frappe.

Tanya laughed as Lance nearly snorted some out of his nose overhearing a stray comment from a neighbouring table labelling Americans as "rude and overbearing".

"I certainly hope we aren't?" he queried in slight dismay.

"Maybe not all of you . . ." she answered mischievously.

"I'm going to put myself in that number!" he replied with dignity.

They sat together for a long while only occasionally sipping their drinks; sometimes in discussion and sometimes in companionable silence.

That he loved her Lord was evident from the genuine passion in his voice when the conversation turned to God and he began to speak of faith. His voice seemed to quiver and, watching his expression, Tanya wondered if he was even aware she remained beside him.

Tanya had to keep her thoughts from jumping forward. She wanted to pepper him with all kinds of personal questions: to explore his past and how he had come to be where he was; to learn what his interests were and how he spent his time; to discover more about his family. She had to hold back such probing questions as the pull she felt for the man before her continued to grow.

They were all questions she would not have hesitated to ask one of her many girlfriends, or even most of her male acquaintances, but this time she chose to remain on safe ground, following his lead in the topic choices. She also had to fight back the knowing smile, which threatened to come to her lips.

They ordered a second round of drinks, this time choosing coffees, and talked for a further hour before heading back towards St James.

* * *

Tanya didn't see Lance for nearly a week after their walk to Kalk Bay. When it came time to part she had made a hasty exit, rushing off without giving him time to formalise a future plan.

She tried to avoid thinking about Lance. Yet, in spite of such grand intensions, she often ended up day-dreaming about him. She talked a little about her feelings with her friends and was relieved when they were understanding and supportive. When she first reported to them after the walk on Monday she had expected Becca to say something along the lines of: "Well, you thought he was probably divorced, or widowed, didn't you?". Instead, Becca had rounded them up, shuffling them out the door to the shops, where they loaded a basket with chocolate, ice cream and lollies, ahead of marching them home for a night watching "Anne of Green Gables".

Tanya enjoyed spending time with Becca and Sam over the week. They mainly stayed indoors watching movies, giving back rubs, painting nails and eating an unhealthy quantity of junk food.

Outside of their hang out sessions she sought time with God, bringing her heart before Him. On one such occasion, Tanya had walked down to Kalk Bay and discovered a small park a few streets up from the main road.

A children's playground sat in the centre of the grass-covered lot. Next to it stood a grand old yellowwood tree. Lying on her towel beneath the shade of its limbs, she relaxed in company with God, seeking His guidance. She had been unable to shake the sudden affection she had developed for Lance, and yet – she hesitated, unable to shake the sorrow that stirred within her soul whenever she thought of his divorce. Looking up at a great white cloud in the otherwise blue sky, she prayed:

God, I give this into your hands. I cannot change his past. And you have dictated the time I have remaining in South Africa. I know it is foolishness to entertain this crush. Give me great time with the girls and help me to put thoughts of Lance aside.

I pray for his healing after a divorce and ask you to ever keep him in your care. Thank you for having blessed me with his company.

Rolling on to her stomach, she pulled her journal out of her canvas rucksack and began to write out her hopes for a husband, praying she would wait patiently for God's timing.

* * *

Tanya's path did not cross again with Lance until the Sunday church service.

The congregation began to dance energetically to an African song as the service commenced. Rather than joining in the lively worship, Lance sat quietly in prayer.

In contrast, Tanya was at the front of the church with Sam and Becca in the center of the merriment. The girls joyfully joined in the dancing; jumping up and down, waving arms and shouting loudly, in true African style. For Tanya, it was an outlet. She was anxious about having to face Lance and tried to muster the determination to maintain only a detached friendliness towards him.

Her mind was in opposition to her deceitful heart, which pictured a whirl wind romance with a near stranger. Her fortifying stance was an unwillingness to cheat two of her closest friends of the quality time they deserved with her. It was how it had to be with the limited time she had left in Africa.

They began to talk after the service, which proved so effortless that Tanya gave up trying to distance herself, choosing to enjoy his company and friendship.

Lance invited her a second time for ice-cream and on this occasion, she accepted. There was a small gelato shop on the corner opposite to the church. They made their way over and Lance proceeded to buy two cups of the largest take-away size. Tanya chose Ferrero Rocher; Lance, the fudge-brownie.

Tanya had to keep brushing back straying stands of her hair as she licked the small spoon, even after which a few red locks managed to enjoy some of her ice-cream.

They went to sit on the beach close to the beach where the swirling wind whipped sand against their legs.

"This isn't the best spot to enjoy ice-cream," Tanya laughed.

"No. It was a poor choice by me."

They eventually found themselves on the pedestrian bridge, which spanned the Muizenberg River. Sitting on a bench overlooking the ocean, the wind continued to blow with gusto, yet was without the sand to bite them.

"This was a failed expedition," Tanya commented with amusement.

"Yeah . . . sorry about that!"

"No – it's turned it into an adventure: a 101 of how not to eat ice-cream at the beach."

Tanya smiled up at him. He looked into her eyes and saw youth, innocence and beauty. A wrenching force took hold of his stomach and he clasped his jaw shut against the emotional pain.

Silence took over as they each turned their focus to eating their ice-cream.

Lance was not alone in downbeat thoughts. Tanya found little enjoyment in her ice-cream as she tried to fathom his mind and repel her guilt at having deserted her friends in favour of Lance's company.

It was an awkward goodbye when the time came. They walked down the bridge and back to the road. It forked in three directions: the right wound up into the suburbs, straight ahead lead to the shops, and to the left, the beachside path snaked its way to St James.

Lance made pretense of having to buy something at the shop, enabling their paths to naturally diverge when Tanya excused herself in order to return to her friends. They both walked hastily away and neither looked back.

Tanya decided as she hurried home, tears falling down her cheeks, that she'd come to the beach for Becca and Sam and she wasn't going to ditch them for some guy. She had two weeks left and she was determined to spend them with her friends. Whilst she liked Lance, it would only be a moment of foolish infatuation – better to spend the remaining time building on friendships, which would last, she reasoned.

* * *

Lance didn't go into the shops. Instead, he continued ahead and climbed the steep cement steps leading up to Boyes Drive in order to take an alternative route home. He passed by St James to obtain more time to clear his mind.

Lance paused as he neared Kalk Bay to look out on the setting sun, colouring the sky shades of purple and pink above the darkening sea. The outlines of harboured yachts could still be made out by the water's edge. It was a majestic vista.

He longed to see God's majesty in his own life. He had never before felt this alone and directionless. Here he was, near the tip of Africa, with no family, no home and no job, and he'd just turned his only friend away. He felt empty.

God, I see evidence of you all around me; I just don't see you in my own life. I am barren – frozen by winter's cruelty, as the pastor said.

If you are all I need, why were we created for relationship? Nevertheless, you are the One we are called to rely upon. I am sorry that I have been seeking a friend to unload my burden upon rather than coming to you. Although, I did enjoy talking to Tanya – that is, before Amanda came into it.

Same with the Pastor . . . When my divorce came up over dinner last night all he wanted to talk about was forgiveness and healing, and overcoming the divorce. I appreciate that I need these things, except I don't think I can face them at the moment. The world looks bleak when I look at it through eyes taunted by divorce.

Can you comfort and guide me? I can't rely on Tanya. It's not fair on her. I was heading that way and I thank you for stopping me. I wish to see her, and talk with her, and hang out with her; except I understand that by doing so, I would burden her.

What was I thinking keeping company with a young, intelligent and beautiful girl like her? She deserves newness; things untarred, unbroken, unstained.

Lance sighed and turned from the beautiful vista to continue his walk along the darkening roadside.

In other words: not me, he added.

A dark cloud of depression came over him. He had to be humble and realise he was in no state to befriend women, let alone beautiful ones who bore the joy and energy of youth. He wasn't too old for love; rather, he was too damaged. He was broken. He was bruised.

Lance came to a flight of stairs leading down the mountain side from Boyes Drive through the suburban houses of Kalk Bay. Unfamiliar with the back streets, Lance decided to explore and see if he could find his way back to the hotel. He left the stairs at a side street and began his mission.

The evening was losing heat quickly with the sun no longer radiating its heat upon the road. Lance was too caught up in his adventure to notice. Twisting and winding, he gently made his way north east, in the rough direction of the hotel.

Imitating an adventurous young boy, he strode through the streets and around bends expecting some hidden mishap or surprise to meet him at every turn.

Delighting in the freedom of the moment, Lance gave out a laugh as he jumped around a corner in expectation to pounce on a mystery offender.

He leaped forward . . . to be met by another evening pedestrian. His combined momentum and weight sent his much smaller victim stumbling backwards and the pair landed in an undignified tangle of limbs.

The guiltless party was a young man who, whilst startled, was up on his feet quickly. Lance was forced to apologise, caught between laughter and embarrassment.

"Lance?" a youthful Cape-coloured man exclaimed.

Lance leant forward slightly to inspect the face before him.

"I've seen you at church, haven't I?" the younger man queried.

"Yes; I was there the last couple of Sundays."

The man put out a slender hand.

"I'm Sergio. I go to Full Frontier Church and study at the college next door."

"Nice to meet you, *Sargio*?"

"Sergio," he repeated with a smile.

"Sergio. Sorry. And sorry I didn't recognise you – a lot of new faces to take in."

Lance went on to apologise profusely for knocking his young acquaintance over. He was suitably abashed and his earnest apology prevented Sergio from taking offense.

Lance soon uncovered that Sergio had come over to St James in an unsuccessful attempt to find a friend with whom he could find entertainment. Sergio asked hopefully whether Lance would join him, if he didn't have plans.

Lance was interested except he had little idea as to what one could do in the area of a night time. It had seemed to him that most places in the area closed early. He asked Sergio what entertainment was available.

"To be honest, not much. Unless you have a car?" Sergio added hopefully.

"Sorry."

"Well, that certainly limits us. Saturday night, or not, there isn't much to do around here. There's the White Monkey," he suggested, referring to a restaurant-come-bar in Kalk Bay. "Although, I don't think it'd be your thing. My friends and I sometimes go there dancing."

Lance was amused at how easily he was written off for such entertainment. The eighteen year old pup had summarily appraised Lance and determined him to be "too old" for that type of crowd.

Lance came up with the winning idea.

"You could always come and hang out with me at Richmond House? There's a pool table and general entertainment area. Mind you, there won't be any dancing, or loud music . . ."

Sergio, who had never stayed in a hotel, and especially not one rivalling the elegance of Richmond House, hastily took up what he thought to be an excellent suggestion.

* * *

Lance found his longing for company answered in Sergio, whose life quickly put Lance's perspective into proper alignment.

Lance didn't do much talking. He certainly wasn't offered a chance to express any of his burdens. He had always been well-equipped for youth ministry and his gifting showed itself with Sergio.

Sergio found in Lance an easy companion, willing to listen without rushing in to give superior advice.

Lance was content to play pool for three hours as his young friend talked about his childhood, his hopes and his current struggles.

Lance attended as Sergio recounted caring for his six younger siblings (two brothers and four sisters), whilst avoiding the drunken swings of his father's arm. His testimony was the more powerful for the matter-of-fact tone in which it was conveyed.

"I became involved in a gang . . . to provide for me family, you see? Fed them from ill-gotten gain. But gangs own you. You live for them; breathe for them; die for them. I nearly died in a fight between rival gangs . . . God's hand saved me.

"I still don't know how I survived. I guess the cops came, which is strange – they usually stay out of it. Put me in hospital for three months – knife to the kidney and a couple o' other internal injuries."

Sergio's eyes watered when he recalled the days in the hospital when God began to call.

"A young nurse gave me a Bybel. It was English and I struggled a bit; we only spoke Afrikaans growing up. Eventually boredom had me read it.

When the pain woke me up there was not even nurses to talk to so I lay and read. I never got the chance to thank the nurse. She saved my life by giving me that Bybel."

Sergio's story of faith in the face of hardship touched Lance, as did his humility. Sergio had hit rock bottom and, from there, grace appeared all the more wondrous. It made Lance appreciate how little he had actually had gone through when compared to Sergio and others like him.

During the hospitalisation, Pastor David had come for a pastoral visit and took Sergio under his wing. The pastor helped Sergio finish his schooling, whilst supporting his siblings, and later offered him a scholarship into the seminary college.

Sergio was trying to obtain his theology degree so that he could bring the church into his home town and hopefully make a difference in the lives of boys facing the same trials he had undergone.

Lance had to acknowledge that, whilst South Africa might have its share of national problems, it had an abundance of unsung heroes, too.

They talked about faith long into the night and Sergio ended up crashing on a trundle bed, pulled out of the closet in Lance's room. He paid for an extra person at the buffet the next morning to allow Sergio to join him for breakfast.

The younger man was delighted. He heaped his plate up high, and returned for multiple helpings. "Better than college food," was his comment.

After breakfast Lance and Sergio prayed for one another before Sergio headed off into the fresh morning air.

His time with Sergio had revitalised his mood and from then on he formed the habit of hiking Muizenberg Mountain in the morning where he prayed and sought the Lord, finally open to analysing the bitterness and pain in his heart. The afternoons saw him running along the beachfront, reflecting on the glory of God's created world. In between these times, he sought out local coffee shops where he sat journaling, reading, and people-watching.

Before he knew it, his final week of holidays was drawing to a close and it was time to board the plane, which would bear him home to the States.

He felt peace for the return leg. He knew it was time to head home to face the demons of his past. Whilst the next season might appear black and full of the unknown, Lance would follow in David's footsteps, declaring: **"He makes me lie down in green pastures. He leads me beside still waters. He restores my soul. He leads me in paths of righteousness for his name's sake. Even though I walk through the valley of the shadow of death, I will fear no evil, for you are with me . . ."** [2]

CHAPTER 5

"Sweet-heart, tell me everything! Right from the start – and don't leave a single thing out!" Gwen commanded. At sixty-three years old, she was as sprightly as ever, even if her hair had whitened and her face was now lined.

Lance arrived home expecting a mix of responses from his family to his recent life changes, but off his mother's support he was certain from past experience. His divorce had been almost as painful for her as for him, yet she had supported him throughout its lengthy process.

Lance and Amanda had managed to hide their marital problems for a long time; yet in the end, the hidden structural cracks proved as detrimental as any visible damage. Their issues had finally surfaced amongst family and friends about six months prior to the separation and by then, the damage seemed irreparable.

Gwen had prayed every night for the couple from the moment she heard of their troubles. Faithfully, she set aside time specifically to lift up her son and daughter-in-law before the Lord. She prayed for His intervention, for His love to conqueror, and for His forgiveness and mercy to heal. She had clung to her hope in God's saving grace to restore the rocky marriage.

When the announcement of the divorce came, she had watched with open grief as her son bought Amanda out of the condo, and the daughter-of-her-heart moved interstate to be with her parents.

Gwen's distress had lasted a long time and she took much of the blame upon herself. She wondered if she and her late husband had been good role models. Her heart had sought the Lord to understand how only one of her three boys had come to love and serve Him, and how this same son could break the sanctity of marriage.

Gwen had hoped for reconciliation; she had hoped for a miracle. Her hopes were dashed when Lance received the finalised paperwork.

And therefore as she looked upon her son's renewed intimacy with her Lord, Gwen felt some solace of heart. As a woman of God she was pleased to see that his new direction was centred on the Lord.

She sat with Lance over hot cocoa on his first evening home, listening to him tell of all God was doing in his life. The pair had taken up positions on the white leather couches of his Manhattan condo, allowing the hot drinks to warm their hands.

Lance, who was jet-lagged from his three-legged journey home, was enjoying the relaxed atmosphere, being in his own place, and having a supportive audience. He willing took up her request to share of his time abroad:

"The whole time I was over there I felt His Presence. It was like carrying something around with me; like wearing a shirt: even though you are aware it's there, your attention does not fixate on it."

Lance gave a quick tug to his shirt sleeve in demonstration.

"So . . . I don't know . . . the time away seems so far removed from life here . . . and yet, I have no doubt it was God who led me to do the things I did. Who would have thought when I boarded the plane to South Africa that my life was about to change this drastically!"

Gwen listened thoughtfully as he spoke of his decision to resign and place his house on the market. When she enquired about his next step she was told truthfully that he didn't have one.

"I'm still waiting for direction. It just seems blank - the future. I can't even make a guess at what it may hold."

Lance threw up his hands in frustration.

"Don't fret over not having all the answers right at this moment. Give it time; it will come," Gwen tried to reassure her son, unaware that his thoughts had shifted from his future to rest upon that of another.

"Do you remember Tom?" Lance questioned suddenly. "From my office."

"Vaguely, I think. Pleasant fellow who came to your birthday party with a sweet, little Asian wife?"

Lance nodded. "He was fired."

"Fired? But . . . why?"

"He was fired because of me."

"Oh, darling . . ."

"Well, not because of me – not exactly – when I resigned (to go to the "competition"), they decided to be rid of my "apprentice", too. Just to be safe, you know, because naturally that would be my next career move after telling them I wanted some time away from the industry," Lance finished acerbically.

After a pause in speech, which Gwen met with expectant silence, Lance continued to share about the circumstances around Tom's forced departure. Lance was concerned for his friend's well-being.

"I feel bad for him, Mom. I know it wasn't my fault, but I wish I could *do* something for him. I keep going over my associates and connections, wondering if there would be a way of getting him a job."

"It isn't your role to be his provider. That role belongs to God alone," his mother gently reminded him. "All you can do is keep him in your prayers. Be comforted by the knowledge God will take care of him."

"Yes, I know – and still I feel rotten. Except . . . when I remember how he treated me (and whilst I partly understand), it makes me want to slap the fellow!"

"Maybe you should try to call him. He may have calmed down."

"Perhaps. I think I might give it a bit of time, first."

"Have you seen your sister yet?" Gwen asked to change subjects.

"No. She's asked me over to dinner tomorrow night. I thought you would be coming, too?"

"Oh, she did say something about dinner Friday . . . Unfortunately I already had plans!"

"Oh, okay. Are Rob and Dave coming here for Christmas?"

"I think so. I suppose it depends on what their partners will be doing."

Rob and Dave were Lance's older brothers. Dave had been married once before and was living with a new partner, following a messy divorce. Rob had never been married, being the perpetual bachelor, and could be relied upon to bring a new girl to each family gathering. Their father had died four years previously.

Gwen began to tell Lance the family gossip before shuffling him off to bed when he became unable to hold back his yawns. Staying the night in the guest room, Gwen knelt upon the plush carpet to beg the Lord to continue His restoring work in Lance's life.

* * *

The next evening Lance drove up to Fiona's home, situated in the hills. She greeted him at the front door with a kiss on the cheek, looking as fit as ever in a pink halter-neck top revealing her toned arms and falling softly over a trim waistline.

Fiona was Lance's little sister and the closest to him in age of his siblings. She had taken on the role of his protector since the divorce and felt this gave her the right to know his business. Not that Lance minded; he felt touched by her care.

"You look good, Lance! More relaxed than when we last saw you."

"Thanks, Fi. You look stunning, as always."

"Uncle Wannie!" Johnnie interrupted.

Lance bent down to greet the six-year old terror.

"Hey, big man! Give me five! How've you been, hey?"

"Johnnie, go wash your hands for dinner and let Uncle Lance settle in."

"He's okay, Fi."

"Now, please," she commanded John.

John looked surly as he wandered off towards the bathroom. His mother proceeded towards the kitchen, Lance in tow.

"You can spoil him all you want later; I want a chat with you first, before dinner."

Fiona began shuffling jars of tea and coffee, paper work and keys to create space for five plates.

"The place is such a mad house; once dinner begins there will be no time for quiet talk until the little munchkins head off to bed!"

Lance gave a short laugh. He could picture the dinner antics, which were sure to come. His last visit had ended with Johnnie crying hysterically, having pushed a pea into his left nostril. Fiona had had to drive him to the emergency department to have it removed.

"I had a chat with Mom a few days back. Have you really quit your job and sold the condo?" Fiona asked, setting out the plates.

"News travels quickly in this family."

"Did you expect differently?" she laughed.

"No – I guess not. I've certainly resigned, and the house is on the market; although, it hasn't been sold yet. The agent reckons it could sit there for any length of time between three and eighteen months."

Resigned, Lance asked: "So, what's your opinion on the matter?"

"Don't use that tone!" she said, hurt. "I simply wanted to make sure you have thought this through properly. After all, they are rather large decisions to be making on the spur of the moment . . ."

"I thought them through. I am convinced they are the right decisions for me. Now that's cleared up: what's for dinner and how can I help?"

Fiona pulled out the cutlery draw in frustration at her brother's cheek.

Lance went off to set the table. The dining room came off of the kitchen, its oval table able to seat six people. It was a small room, which opened out on to the main lounge room, thus preventing diners from becoming claustrophobic.

As Lance was setting the last place he heard footsteps on the stairwell and sure enough, down came his brother-in-law. Jo was smaller in build than Lance and his brothers whilst still of an athletic appearance. The boys in Fiona's family (or more correctly, Rob), had affectionately dubbed him the "Runt of the Litter".

"Lance! Welcome home, buddy," he greeted, shaking Lance's hand and giving him a clap on the back.

"Thanks, Jo. How's life treating you?"

"Same old, same old. Want a beer?"

"Yeah, that'd be great. Thanks."

Jo grabbed a couple of beers from the fridge and the brothers-in-law went to sit in the lounge room, remaining out from under foot until dinner was cooked.

"Has Fi cornered you yet?" Jo asked, eyes twinkling with mischief and understanding.

"She tried to," Lance smiled. "I made a ready escape and yet, somehow, I don't think my manoeuvres are good enough to avoid her all evening, especially with you being kind enough to have me over for the night!"

"Well, regardless of what she says – I'm proud of you, bro; it takes a lot of guts to do what you did. We only live once, right? Might as well make the most of it!"

"Thanks, Jo. Truly, that is an encouragement."

Jo shrugged the comment off, self-deprecatingly.

They were soon joined by Jo's children, John and Ann, who vied for their uncle's attention as well as his lap.

Half an hour later they sat down to a dinner of macaroni and cheese, a favourite for Lance. Johnnie took centre stage telling his uncle all about his bug collection and soccer team. He had joined a junior football league mid-year and believed he was a world champion.

Lance won his instant awe by telling him that he had visited the stadium where the Soccer World Cup had been held in South Africa. Johnnie was not at all sure what the World Cup entailed, but as his father had watched it enthusiastically, it had to be cool.

Bellies full and table cleared, it was time for gift giving. The family moved into the lounge room and Lance further delighted his young nephew by giving him a South African World Cup soccer jersey as well as a small soccer ball patterned with the flags of the participating countries.

Lance tried to explain who the teams were, until he realised Johnnie was not interested in such minor details. Instead, Johnnie began to work on his uncle for a game of soccer.

"Not right now, Johnnie."

Ann was softer in spirit than her boisterous big brother. Nonetheless, Lance could see the anticipation in her large eyes as she looked expectantly at the gift in his hands. He gave the parcel to her. A smile broke forth on his face when she squealed in delight.

"Pretty!" Ann declared and hugged the doll closely. It was clothed in the traditional tribal dress of the Zulus.

Ann sat down on the floor and began to stroke the curly, black locks of the doll, which were greatly different to her own straight, flaxen hair.

"Come on, Uncle Wannie, come play ball," Johnnie began to whine.

"Just a minute, buddy. I have something for your parents, too. It wouldn't be fair to leave them out, would it?"

"No," was the submissive, yet unrepentant, answer.

"I wanted to get you something. It's nothing big, mind you," Lance said, turning to Fiona and Jo. He handed a small, wrapped present to each of them.

"Oh, Lance! Really, you shouldn't have. But, thank you! It is beautiful. I love it! Thank you." Fiona held a silken scarf of mixed gold and peach thread.

"I thought it would suit you."

"Sweet! This is fantastic!" was the declaration from Jo.

He had a boyish streak in him, which was why Lance had bought him a small wooden drum with a skin cover and African paintings on the side.

"I was a little worried about quarantine on that one, but they didn't seem to care less about the skin, or the wood!"

As Jo began to play on the drum, his son crawled up beside him on the couch, waiting eagerly for a turn.

"Be careful, Johnnie," his mother warned.

"He's fine, Fi," Jo assured her. "I don't think it would be easy to break. Seems pretty sturdy."

Johnnie had to forgo a time of outdoor play. Jo herded him upstairs after the gift-giving with Ann in toe, to complete their night time routine.

"Thanks, honey," Fiona called out to her husband.

"Yes: I am sure this is the right thing for me. No: this is not a premature midlife crisis (that was the divorce). And no: I have no idea what I will be doing next. Have I covered everything?" Lance cut in before his sister could ask the questions he knew were coming.

"But the job, the house . . .? What do you plan on doing?"

"It isn't like that, Fi. I don't intend to become a drunkard, a lay-about, or a bum. I'm trusting God in this. I truly believe this is what He wants me to do. He'll give me direction for the next step in His time."

"You don't have anything else lined up, then?"

"Not at this stage. I'm not worried though – God will reveal it in the right time."

Lance picked up Ann's doll as he contemplated his next words.

"Do you remember when you went down to Mexico for a month-long mission trip?" he asked. "I think it was when you were in high school, or perhaps your freshman year at college. You were utterly convinced it was from God; you knew it was Him calling you to go on the camp."

"Yes, but that was when I was a teen. You grow older and life throws different things your way."

"Fi, life may throw whatever it likes at me; however, when God asks me to jump, I'm going to."

"I'm not doubting God has something for you, I'm merely making sure – "

Fiona found herself cut off by a shriek omitted from upstairs. She was preparing to go and investigate what the fuss was about when Jo peeped his head down the stairwell. Just visible from where the pair sat in the lounge, he stated Johnnie was "requesting" his uncle come to say goodnight.

"Honestly!" his mother exclaimed. "I try not to indulge his fits, but seeing you aren't here all that often . . . would you mind saying goodnight to him, and maybe read him a story?"

"Love to."

When Lance returned, he found his sister cuddled up beside her husband, the pair talking softly. He stood frozen at the base of the stairwell. They were a well paired match who worked seamlessly together. Lance couldn't see how they managed it as a couple, or how his sister ran her family as admirably as she did. He was proud of his little sister and her family. A loving home was an accomplishment too rarely acknowledged.

Reluctant to break their moment of stolen serenity he nevertheless made his way over to the second two-seater couch.

Nothing more was said about his future. The evening wound down talking quietly over a bottle of wine until Fiona began to yawn, at which point the party broke up for the evening.

* * *

Lance trundled up to the spare bedroom, wishing he had someone to share it with. It was a tranquil room. The double-bed was covered in a rose-patterned doona, and an antique dressing table with accompanying stool sat to the right of a lace-curtained window.

In the quiet of his room, Lance released his fears to the Lord:

Father, please help me to trust in you. I meant what I said to Fi earlier: I will follow wherever you lead. I ask that you give me the courage to wait and to trust.

I know you have me on a journey and you know the destination. I only wish you'd let me in on it!

What is it you have for me? Where is it you are leading? Where will I go and what will I do? Teach me be patient. I wait on you.

Lance opened his Bible to the book of Psalms. He sought the strength of those who had gone before him, walking with God.

Lance didn't proceed past the first two verses of the very first psalm. In them he found his answer; he discovered what God was directing Him to do:

"Blessed is the man who walks not in the counsel of the wicked, nor stands in the way of sinners, nor sits in the seat of scoffers; but his delight is in the law of the LORD, and on his law he meditates day and night." [3]

Changing into blue flannelette pyjamas, Lance prayed his delight would be found in God. He asked that his would be a life lived in devotion to the King.

Whilst no clearer picture of the future had emerged, Lance was able to crawl under the mass of blankets comforted that the present had a purpose;

God wanted him to dig into His Word and meditate upon the Truth.

* * *

Little known to Lance, his sister was also in fervent prayer. He would have been surprised to hear words:

God, I'm struggling with life. I'm in a rut and there's no way out. I can't escape from my responsibilities and I won't be freed from them for a long time to come.

My mind is preoccupied with the cares of the world. I'm Martha wanting to work when I should be sitting at your feet. Maybe Lance has it right. Lance is Mary — drinking in your presence. I want to believe it is you calling him to quit his job, sell his house, and entrust his future to you.

Except — it is different for him! she added defensively. *He doesn't have a family to support, to care for, or to consider.*

Oh God, help him and help me . . .

Fiona climbed into bed with anxiety in her breast and no peace in her heart. She was wrestling against growing dissatisfaction. She had no one to confide in as she didn't want to upset Jo with her burdened mind. The strain was beginning to leave her tired and overwhelmed. There were too many things to juggle.

She could now add anxiety for her brother to her other worries. She feared losing control. If she dropped just one of her concerns, the rest of them would fall and her life would tumble down. She was caught in a juggling act and her arms were growing weary.

CHAPTER 6

Greeting his mother with a hug, Lance removed his coat and added it to those dangling from the hallway rack.

"How was your time up at Fi's last night?" his mother asked.

"Really great! I really missed those kids! Johnnie is as much the rascal as ever – although I concede that he is an adorable rascal."

Inside the alien entryway with coats hanging neatly on the side wall, Lance found himself wishing for the old family home with all its smells and fond childhood memories. It was the first time he had stepped inside his mother's new home as his business trip have fallen right when she was to move, though he had seen plenty of pictures on email sent by his sister.

Lance knew that the move was advantageous for his mother. It took her away from a house rich in the memories of her late husband. Her new Brooklyn home was also much smaller - a mere cottage - which would lower the maintenance she stubbornly completed without assistance. In spite of this, for Lance the new house signalled more change right at the time when he longed to find security and that which was familiar.

They moved into the quaint kitchen. The familiar objects that met his eyes, such as her china coffee pot and old spice rack, appeared strangely out of place in their new surroundings.

Lance took a seat on a counter stool whilst Gwen stirred a pot of rich tomato soup. His stomach gave a grumble of appreciation.

"Something smells divine! Are you baking bread?"

"Sorry, no home-made loaves today. Merely heating some up in the oven."

"It's making my mouth water wherever it was made! How was your dinner last night? You were meeting with friends, weren't you?" he asked.

"You have actually hit on the very thing I wanted to discuss with you. Let me serve up our lunch first and we'll talk about it as we eat."

"Oooh, mystery! Okay, how can I help?"

"Umm – the glasses need to be brought out. They're in the top cupboard," she said, gesturing behind her.

Lance took the glasses and a bottle of refrigerated mineral water to the small kitchen table, which would (tightly) seat four people. A broad window allowed a view across the front lawn onto the street.

Steaming bowls of soup and crusty bread before them at the table, Lance said grace.

As he broke off a piece of bread he asked a second time about the previous evening.

"You were saying there was something you wanted to talk to me about?" Lance probed, assuming it related to his house, or job.

"Yes, that's right. Okay, here it goes . . . It's been four years since your father's death, Lance."

Gwen paused, waiting for a reply.

"Already? Yes, I guess it has been."

"And I was never one to "go it alone", so to speak."

Lance's heart skipped a beat as he sensed where she was leading.

"No. No, you weren't. You always did things as a pair; you and Dad."

A grin slowly crept upon his face.

"Yes, well, I'm not cut out to live alone and, well . . . lately I have been, well, I might as well say it: I've been courted. He is a wonderful man and I am sure you will get along with him splendidly," she ended in a rush.

She looked up at him, trying to gage his reaction.

"Who is he?" Lance asked. He hadn't meant to say it quite as bluntly as it came out, and he certainly hadn't planned on letting a short laugh escape; yet, to be fair, he had been taken by surprise. Of all the announcements his mother could have made, this was not one he would have anticipated.

"You may have met him once, or twice. I imagine you would have, at any rate. His name is Markus. He used to work with your father. That's how we met; he sent me condolence flowers after Grant's death and was one of the ones who has faithfully continued to check in on me.

"At first it was out of consideration – for your father, I suppose – making sure I was okay, offering to mow the lawn, and all the rest of those "manly tasks", which clearly I "couldn't manage on my own"."

Lance chuckled. His mother proved weekly that she was more than capable of completing such tasks.

"Anyway, I never accepted help for those tasks, though I was always willing to chat and grateful for company. Over phone calls, and later coffees, a friendship grew and . . . now here we are"

"Markus," Lance considered the name. "He wasn't the one involved in the bungled merger, was he?"

"Well, yes, he was . . . although I suspect it did not go down quite as your father let on," Gwen rallied in defence. "Of course Markus considerately blames himself for the fall out. However, I think the truth is that they both made some wrong business moves, another company outbid them and, when the deal went south, their egos were too big to accept personal responsibility."

"I can see Dad not wanting to admit being wrong!"

Lance shook some pepper into his soup.

"How long have you been seeing him for?" Lance asked.

"A couple of months; in a serious way, I mean. Before that . . .? As I mentioned, we've kept in touch on and off ever since your father's death."

"And it's going well?"

"I'd say so – last night he asked me to move in with him."

"Mom!"

Lance sat holding his spoon mid-way to mouth with a shocked expression on his face.

"I didn't say "yes"!" Gwen replied with dignity. "I told him I would not move in with a man I was not married to. However, I did tell him that if he asked me to marry him, and committed to come to church with me on Sundays – well, I said I would consider such a proposal."

Lance returned his spoon to the bowl.

"*And?*" he prompted.

Gwen shrugged. "*And*, that was the end of the matter. It's up to him to go away and decide whether I am worth marrying!"

"You are the most amazing woman I know!" Lance laughed. "You absurd woman! To take it all as-casual-as-you-please! The poor fellow. I only hope you didn't reprimand him too severely."

"You aren't upset? I was afraid you would be . . ."

"No, I'm not upset. Surprised? Yes. However, it's as you said: Dad has been gone for four years and you deserve to be happy. If this man brings a glow to your cheeks, then he's okay by me."

Whilst they ate, Lance continued to ask his mother questions about Markus and his family. Lance could see their friendship had been of long standing and was glad on her behalf. Lance drew forth a promise from his mother to be introduced to Markus at the earliest opportunity and she agreed.

After lunch they moved out into the back garden, glasses of sherry in hand.

Lance noticed his mother was beginning to add her touch to the small backyard. A vegetable garden had been prepared along one wall; barren except for a few small lettuces. An assortment of pots stood under her pergola, containing seedlings. A couple of half-used bags of potting mix sat neatly next to the pots. Leaf litter and twigs were strewn across the small area of lawn near to recently-pruned bushes.

"It's still a bit of a mess. You should have seen the weeds when I moved in!" she exclaimed.

"Looks as if you're bringing it around quickly enough!"

They took opposing seats at the small patio table. Lance took a sip of sherry and put his drink down on the glass table-top.

Conversation turned to Lance's evening with the McCarthy's.

Gwen could tell there was something on her son's mind and soon had it out of him.

"I can't believe it came from Fi!" he exclaimed. "I expect Rob and Dave to give me grief about the decisions, but I hadn't expected it from Fi, too. Of all the people in the family, I thought I would find her to be an ally."

Lance had left his sister's home convinced she disapproved of his choice and thought him a fool. Whether accurate or not, he could not rid himself of the suspicion.

"She's concerned about you, darling."

"Yes, only, she was always the one who was going to "save the world". It was hard to see that she's let her passion grow cold."

"People grow up; they have families; other things take over. God values families and expects us to care for them ever so greatly."

"You mean we let them take over. Family is important, don't get me wrong, but I believe if God calls us to do something, then we can be confident He has included our family in the plan. And as I don't have a family, why can't she support me in this?" He was beginning to sound akin to a petulant child.

"Maybe she envies you. Maybe she fears for you. Who knows? All any of us can do is walk in faithful obedience and trust Him to be our Defender."

"True enough."

Silence reigned as they studied the back garden.

"She looks happy," Lance commented. "Maybe because she's content she wonders why I'm not, too. But I'll tell you what: it was good to see the kids again! I missed them the most when I was away, wondering what they were learning. And with them growing up a mile a minute . . . every day that I was gone I felt like I was missing seeing them achieve new milestones!"

Gwen could talk for hours about her two delightful grandchildren and they proceeded to amuse each other with various anecdotes of Johnnie's misadventures and Ann's quaint phrases.

It wasn't until Lance was kissing his mother goodbye at the front door that his attention returned to the stressful changes taking place in his life.

"I'll be praying for you, dear. And try not to worry: you are in God's hands."

"Thanks, Mom."

He gave her a second kiss, squeezed her hand, and walked out to his car wondering where God would take him next.

CHAPTER 7

Two weeks later, Lance was staring aimlessly out of his large kitchen window across the tops of apartment buildings and the green treetops of Central Park to the city beyond, when his mobile phone began to vibrate on the counter top. It broke into the "Mission Impossible" theme song as he crossed the kitchen floor to answer its summons.

Turning from the view, he moved to the counter to answer.

"Hi Lance! It's Jane here – from Real Estate Active. How are you?" he heard in his ear.

Lance drew breath to answer, but she went straight on:

"The reason why I'm calling is to see if I can bring a couple around for a house inspection this afternoon. They are quite eager to see the condo and I'm confident they'll put in a tentative offer."

"Oh . . . Umm . . . I haven't had a chance to get the place thoroughly scrubbed yet. I mean, it's clean, it's only that you asked for personal affects to be removed and the walls scrubbed, cupboards cleaned . . ."

"It'll be fine. Just make sure all the dishes are put away and give it a quick tidy up," Jane instructed.

"Okay," Lance responded numbly.

"I have arranged to bring them around at four o'clock. Could you be out of the house by three-thirty, just in case? The inspection shouldn't take more than an hour."

"Alright . . ."

"Great! I'll ring you tomorrow to let you know how it goes. Bye!"

The receiver went dead.

Lance glanced at the house around him: across at the bare kitchen table, the pristine lounge suit, and the spiraling staircase leading up to the bedrooms. There wouldn't be much to do in order to make it ready for the inspection.

Lance spent an hour giving his condo a superfluous tidy before making a call to see if his mother would be up for a coffee. Gwen, however, had already made plans with her beau. She suggested he try his sister who would, no doubt, welcome an extra hand looking after the children.

Calling up Fiona, he was met with a negative. She was with her in-laws who wanted to spend some time with their grandchildren. Lance remembered her mentioning they were going for a weekend visit. Fiona had decided to drive up early with the children, with Jo to follow at the end of the business week.

Lance hadn't seen many of his friends since his return and was at a loss to know who else to try. Most of them were couples and he had found it hard to maintain these friendships without Amanda by his side.

In the end, Lance decided that Central Park was as good a place as any to while away the time. He walked down Fifth Avenue and entered via Terrace Drive.

The paths were clear of snow with white lawns on each side. He buttoned the front of his coat and readjusted his scarf.

The air was refreshingly crisp on his face as he set off on a walk around the looping path. He had avoided being alone the last couple of weeks in an attempt to hide from God's disquieting touch, but alone in the afternoon's freshness, he found his spirits lifted enough to open his heart before God:

Who am I to feel as though life is spiralling away from me? You are the God of all creation and your plans never fail to bear fruit.

I have my family; I have food and clothes, and a roof over my head; I am provided for. Yet in spite of this I am restless and the uncertainty of the future has left my nerves in a state of perpetual alertness. My heart is anxious.

How is this meant to teach me to trust in you? Does being forced to wait teach one patience? If I enter into a similar situation again, will I not be the same as I am now? What are you trying to teach me in this time?

The tranquil white wilderness gave no reply to his questions and neither did God.

Lance wiped a light layer of snow off a park bench, which sat beneath a laden tree, and pulled a small Gideon's Bible out from his pocket.

Surely if I have to wait for the next step, you must be teaching me something. At least I hope that is the case. I don't believe you do anything without reason and I guess I have to trust to that truth.

He returned to the first psalm.

How many times had he read those first two verses during these past weeks? They had become his source of light in an otherwise black night.

"Blessed is the man who walks not in the counsel of the wicked, nor stands in the way of sinners, nor sits in the seat of scoffers; but his delight is in the law of the LORD, and on his law he meditates day and night." [3]

Pursue God; that was what mattered. Pursue God, His Word, and His will.

Lance read to the end of the psalm. He was always uncertain as to how to apply the verses on battling against adversaries. What had he experienced of war, or persecution? Perhaps it was enough that the words of the psalmists motivated him to press into God and seek His counsel.

He stared down the tree-lined path. There were a few orange leaves holding valiantly to their branches. Lance considered how the vantage from one bench could dramatically change with each new season through the course of one year as the words of Pastor David's sermon came back to him.

Whilst it was a winter season for the park, there was always something happening within the trees. A few held off shedding their last leaves; some were bowed down with snow; others had shaken off their load. They went through a continual cycle, inwardly alive whilst outwardly in a phase of bareness.

That is how I feel, Lord: I am weighed down by snow and whilst the park looks to the thaw, I cannot see an ending to the burden on my heart. There is no promise for new buds of life.

Will these scars remain forever? Will the loneliness fade, or will I continue as this empty park? What change am I undergoing? What do you have waiting for me?

Please renew my hope. Please transform my life. Bring me into spring.

Lance was restless to receive guidance for the next step. When God told him the next destination on life's map, he'd go that same day. However, it was not impatience, or inactivity, at the root of Lance's turbulent emotions; rather, the stilling of life's momentum had forced him to give due examination to his heart. It had given his mind the freedom to wander into previously padlocked domains.

Lance stood to continue the route leading him down to the glass-like lake.

God had decided it was time to give Lance's heart a spring clean in preparation for the changing of seasons. Lance had allowed the insults and injuries of thirty plus years of his life to accumulate in his heart; from friends, from family, and especially from Amanda over the eight short-lived years of their marriage.

The divorce papers had not caused the wound – for a paper cut is easily mended. No, Lance's injury was of the chronic kind and had been allowed to fester; its poison leaching into his veins, infecting his blood stream, and flowing freely through his body.

God, I don't think I'm up to your healing process. My heart aches with even the briefest glimpse at my marriage and I have to quickly suppress memories of Amanda.

Lance was beginning to question whether there were any moments of joy in his marriage. All that came to mind were arguments, fights, and conflict. His mind rebelled at what God might require from him. He wanted to be healed without having to go through its long and painful process.

Glancing at his watch, Lance decided it would be safe to return home. The air was no longer refreshing. It bit into his face and chaffed at his skin.

* * *

Jane called the following morning as promised and advised Lance that the young couple had placed an offer on the condo.

"It's a good offer and I have another gentleman who wants to see the place this afternoon. Any chance you'd be able to head out around noon for an hour?"

The second prospective buyer was a gentleman about Lance's age who was searching for a home for his young family. Lance gave Jane permission to conduct the inspection even though he was satisfied with the first couple's offer, and agreed to be out of his house between noon and one o'clock.

* * *

Aware Christmas was sneaking up, Lance went off to do some Christmas shopping and did not arrive home until nearly two P.M. He was surprised to see the agent's car still parked out front.

Calling Jane he discovered that the couple had wanted a second look and therefore she had made a last minute arrangement for them to come past.

"We're nearly done," she informed, talking softly. "Can you give me another ten minutes?"

Pushing open the heavy front door some fifteen minutes later, Lance was met by Jane's excited persona. She was radiating pride in how quickly she had been able to provide him with not merely one but two offers for his condo.

"It normally isn't this quick, I can tell you! We are lucky to have two buyers on the market for this place."

"I thought Manhattan would be sought-after real estate given its location?"

"It was until increased living costs made people hesitant to make a final offer."

"Final offer . . .?"

"Yes! Not the family (they did put in a tentative offer at the lower range of your price scale). The first couple are keen for the paper work to be drawn up A.S.A.P., assuming you accept the offer. And I must say (in my opinion), you would be foolish to let it go! It is a respectable offer, plus you would remove the cost of keeping your house on the market."

Events were moving too quickly for Lance. He asked Jane to have the weekend to think over the offer and she agreed, saying she'd expect his call on Monday. Lance sank down on to his sofa as the door closed behind her.

* * *

The weekend afforded him less opportunity to think over the offer than he'd anticipated. His brothers had arrived for the festive season and the weekend rapidly filled with family engagements.

Rob had flown in the previous night, for once without a lady friend, and was followed by Dave on the Friday morning. Dave's partner of eighteen months joined him, the three squeezing into his mother's Brooklyn home.

Lance was invited to join them for Friday night dinner in order to meet Markus. Pulling into his mother's cobbled drive, he stepped out of his car to be greeted by Rob's crushing arms, followed by a friendly thump on the arm.

Dave met him in the entrance hall in a more sedate manner. One arm around Amy, he stretched the other out to Lance.

"Good to see you, Lance," Dave greeted as the brothers gripped hands. "Mom's been telling us about your interesting career move . . . and other changes."

"Yeah, you must be crazy!" Rob chipped in with emphasis. "You were on an awesome wage – why'd you go giving it up?"

"Hi Amy. It's nice to see you again!" Lance spoke pointedly before continuing, "Things change. I don't need the money, so why stay in a job I find draining?"

Dave shrugged.

They made their way into the kitchen. Rob still looked gob smacked.

"Darling, help yourself to a drink; you can see your brothers have," Gwen instructed as Lance gave her a hug.

Lance poured himself a glass of his mother's famous hot apple cider and took up a seat on a kitchen stool next to Rob. Dave, Amy, and Gwen sat around the kitchen table.

"No Markus?" he enquired.

Lance wasn't sure how his brothers would respond to Gwen having a man in her life and was curious to find out. He was also anxious to meet Markus for himself.

"No. I told him not to come until six. I thought you boys might want to catch up a bit before we head out to the restaurant."

The brothers proceeded to do just that. Rob and Dave did most of the talking. Both lawyers, they fell to discussing different projects their firms had taken on as well as some of their more upmarket clients. There was a healthy dose of brotherly rivalry weaved into their dialogue.

Lance enjoyed being back in their company, although their material focus saddened him, especially when he recalled how he had been tied up in similar concerns for much of his marriage. He was also realistic enough to anticipate a negative response to his career change, even whilst he longed to bring God into the equation and to share with them that money, in light of eternity, means nothing.

He loved his brothers even though he had as little in common with them as day and night. Rob and Dave were money-driven; he was seeking to be Kingdom-focused. They wanted the acclaim of men; he wanted to glorify God.

Lord, help me to relate to them, to love them, and not to judge them. I don't know how to witness to them. Give me the words to speak. Let my life bear testimony to your goodness.

Markus arrived five minutes ahead of time.

Lance was surprised by his mother's other half. He had mistaken him for another of his late father's work colleagues (a rather short, dumpy fellow with a good-humoured personality). In contrast, Markus was tall and slender with the appearance of fitness, despite his sixty-seven years. His hair had begun to turn from grey to white, but his arms displayed stringy cords of muscle.

Lance could not be pleased with the knowledge his father had fallen out with Markus, yet was determined to be generous for his mother's sake.

Markus greeted each of Gwen's sons with a sturdy handshake and warm smile as they were introduced. Amy was greeted with a gentle hug and a kiss on the cheek.

After the introductions had been made the party split; Rob, Dave and Amy went with Lance, and Gwen joined Markus, to drive to Park Slope. They found car parks on opposite sides of the street and the two parties merged to wander down to their chosen restaurant.

Gwen had voted for her favourite haunt; a little Italian restaurant on a corner block, which was immensely popular with the locals and, as a result, no reservations could be made. As it was earlier they were not obliged to wait in a line for a table. A pleasant waitress introduced herself and seated them in the centre of the dining floor.

Lance had to commend his mother's taste, even if it wasn't quite his favourite spot, too. It was a quaint restaurant. Candles lit the room whilst large glass windows looked out on to the street. A chandelier above their table added its dull glow to the gentle light of the candles. It was intimate and cosy. A shelf along one wall held old bottles of Italian wine and rich red drapes pulled back beside the door contrasted with the bright aqua tiled floor.

Lance spent little time studying the menu choosing rather to study how Markus interacted with his mother. They seemed to be comfortable in their relationship and with each other; discussing the menu in regards to one another's taste preferences.

Lance ordered the homemade ravioli filled with squash and a butter-sage sauce. He hoped it wouldn't take too long to come out as his stomach began to tighten in hunger.

The meals took twenty minutes and they were supplied with a basket of fresh bread and a balsamic dip to satisfy them during the wait.

Rob leaned forward to address Markus as the meals were delivered.

"Mom says you used to work with Dad before the Danby Incident?"

"Yes, that's right. I worked closely with your father on several projects, but that was one of them," Markus answered.

"The last one?"

Lance noted his assumption to be correct that Rob would be less than pleased to have to share his mother's affections with an outsider, although he would be loath to admit it.

"Yes; after that, we unfortunately never had another chance to work together," Markus replied.

There was a moment's awkward silence.

"Gwen tells me you're a lawyer? What type of practice are you in?" Markus tactfully changed the subject.

After Rob's unthoughtful words the family settled into their usual flow. Markus was shifted from primary focus to a background character, becoming a spectator to the family's interactions.

Lance was sitting next to Markus on one side of the table, Amy and Dave on the other. Gwen and Rob were seated at opposing ends.

Lance initiated a quiet discourse with Markus as his brothers talked over their latest motor bike purchases like enthusiastic school boys.

"Have you retired from the business world?"

"Yes, thankfully. And I've never looked back! It was only ever a job for me; never becoming my passion as it seems to become for some."

"What do you do now with all your spare time?"

"My current property is rather large and the maintenance of that alone takes up the majority of my time. Nothing strenuous, mind you, and I enjoy pottering around the yard doing this and that. I'm currently working on adding a water feature to the backyard – although I have been thinking about selling up and moving into a smaller place. I might ask for the name of your agent if you're happy with them."

"I have been so far. In fact, Jane has already found me two prospective buyers. I have an offer to consider this weekend so that she can give them an answer on Monday."

"You've sold?" Dave interrupted.

"Not yet. Ask me again on Monday and the answer might have changed," he answered with a smile.

"Do you have somewhere else to go?"

"No, although I don't expect them to kick me out straight away!" Lance laughed.

"Thanks," he added to the waiter, who was collecting their empty plates.

"You're really going through with this?" Rob asked in astonishment.

Lance was amused.

"I wouldn't have put it on the market if I wasn't planning to go through with it . . ."

"Yes, but what do you plan to *do*?"

"I'm still waiting on the next step though I'm sure something will turn up." Shifting the focus, Lance asked: "What about you, Markus – what do you have planned when you move house?"

"Your mother's recent move highlighted the advantages of a smaller place. With the reduced home maintenance, I'd have more time with the grandkids, amongst my other pursuits."

"I wouldn't mind some more grandchildren of my own to waste time on, boys . . ." Gwen hinted.

"Well, you can adopt Markus' as your own!" Rob suggested helpfully.

"That's an idea since you three don't seem to be in a hurry to fulfil my wish. Although, I haven't lost hope . . ."

Gwen winked at Amy, who turned slightly pink and looked towards Dave sheepishly.

All eyes turned to Dave. Ignoring their fellow diners he'd pushed his chair out and stood up.

For a crazy moment Lance thought that Dave had been irrationally provoked by their Mom's words until Amy stood to join him. Dave put his arm around her.

"We had planned on leaving this announcement until Fiona could join us, but since it's come up: Mum, and others, Amy's pregnant!" he announced.

"We're having a baby," Amy added rather needlessly.

"Oh, my darlings, how fabulous!" Gwen crooned.

She stood and embraced Amy before repeating the gesture with Dave. Her movements were echoed by the rest of the table. Handshakes ensued. On-lookers smiled at the family's happy moment and a few people clapped in shared delight.

"I'm an ape for having had a go at you earlier for not drinking!" Rob said to Amy, uncharacteristically abashed. "Sorry about that. Guess we'll have to start calling you sis' now; won't we, Lance? No ring, but a little one ties you to us. There is no escaping now – welcome to the family."

Rob startled Amy by giving her a second hug.

"Hear, hear," Lance concurred. "Not that we didn't consider you family already, Amy . . ."

Amy thanked them genuinely and they resumed their places. Coffees and desserts were ordered to celebrate the occasion. The manager brought over a pear tart with earl grey ice cream for Amy, free of charge. Rob was piqued that they hadn't given Dave a free desert, too; however, his brother didn't notice as he was too busy staring adoringly at Amy.

The party headed back to Gwen's house after the last coffee was finished. Markus took his leave almost immediately whilst Lance stayed talking with his family until midnight, at which time everyone headed to bed and Lance was given the sofa and a pile of blankets.

* * *

Lance awoke early from habit and read a passage of Scripture before dressing for a run, his gym bag living permanently in his car trunk.

The morning air cleared his head of its wispy fog. He took a jumbled route through the streets enjoying a new environment. The sky was brilliant blue with not a cloud in sight. The naked trees stood against it, offering a bleak contrast.

Lance smiled. Winter had its beauty no matter how he longed for it to end.

You have turned my focus back on to you, my God and my King. That makes this season worth its pain. Be my sustenance in this season of lack. The only offering I have to bring is my sorrow, and yet you take even that as a fragrant offering.

He was back at the house before his brothers had stirred. Taking his running shoes off at the front door he entered the house, sweater plastered to his back with perspiration.

He was breathing heavily as he passed the kitchen on his way to the bathroom.

"Morning Mom," he greeted.

"Towels are in the linen closet to the right of the bathroom," she called out after him.

When Lance re-emerged fifteen minutes later, Gwen had a pot of coffee ready, some breakfast muffins in the toaster and eggs sizzling in the frying pan. Lance couldn't believe the rest of the household hadn't been woken by the delicious aroma.

"You were saying last night you have some offers? That is exciting news."

"Rob didn't seem to think so," he answered, giving her a slight smile.

"That's your brother for you. Surely you know not to take his words too seriously?"

"I do."

He poured them out full mugs of the freshly brewed coffee.

"But I was thinking on it again when reading Ezekiel this morning. The prophets were called by God to do some incredibly wacky things. Like when Ezekiel had to lie on his side for a total of four hundred and thirty days to prophesy the years of God's coming punishment upon Israel and Judah for their continued disobedience.

"The prophets acted on the commands of God and the people laughed. Their messages went unheeded. They were mocked and ridiculed and beaten. We have it easy nowadays. We face such little suffering."

Gwen held her mug between both hands, smiling that her son was seeking after the Lord even before he exercised of a morning.

"This had me thinking," Lance continued, "whether I would be prepared to do something crazy for God, today. If he asked me to stand on my head, would I obey?"

Lance beamed at her.

"Then I felt God show me that what I am doing - by resigning and selling up with no clear guideline to the future - is crazy in the eyes of the world! I only have to look at Rob's response to see that! They don't understand."

"My son: the prophet. I am proud of you. If you need a place to stay, let me know. You're always welcome."

"A thirty-five year old living at home with his mother – what will people think of me?"

"A handsome man such as yourself? They'll think you are being kind to an old lady."

Lance laughed.

Lance and Gwen had finished their tête-à-tête by the time the others made their way down stairs. Rob wanted to continue the baby celebrations with morning drinks, of which suggestion Gwen firmly vetoed, in honour of Amy's request for them to wait until Fiona could join them. Lance kissed his mother goodbye, heading home to think. She followed him out the door not long afterwards to meet Markus, leaving Amy, Dave and Rob to arrange for their own entertainment.

CHAPTER 8

In contrast to Markus' belief, Gwen was not upset at the slight friction displayed by her middle son the previous evening. In fact, she had anticipated some degree of unpleasantness to be felt by her boys and was only thankful that David and Lance appeared to be accepting the match.

Gwen drove to Markus' home in Madison to provide them with some time alone, which would not be found at her house. She was grateful that he did most of the commuting in their relationship. However, on the occasions that she did drive out to him, she would usually continue on to Montville for a visit to Fiona.

Gwen loved Markus' house. It was far too large for one person and he could not have kept his garden and lawns in their immaculate condition without outside help, and yet in spite of its impracticability for a single man, it was a grand house.

The two storey home was panelled with grey slats made dashing by white panelled windows. A brick chimney rose from the roof and gentle puffs of smoke signalled the lounge room fireplace was earning its keep.

Three lattice-work chairs with matching table sat in the front court yard overlooking a soft white wonderland. They were covered by the overhanging branches of a magnificent two hundred year old oak, providing the perfect spot for a summer interlude. They wouldn't be sitting out there today.

The pair sat cosily in two red-leather lounge chairs close to the fire. Markus sipped his brandy. Gwen was nursing a steaming mug of coffee, watching as the last white blob of cream was absorbed into the brown liquid.

"How do you gauge last night to have gone, sweetheart?" he enquired, smiling over at her with affection.

"It certainly wasn't short of events! I am glad you were there for the off-the-cuff announcement. They will remember that and I think it will help to subtly bring you into the family."

"I'd like to be part of your family."

Gwen glanced up quickly at his tone. Her ears had not deceived her; his eyes were telling the same unspoken words.

"I am sorry about Rob's little go at you," she apologised, a jitter in her voice as she glided away from alarming territory. "I'm sure you must have anticipated some show of unpleasantness. Did it make you uncomfortable?"

"No, not in the least. Like you said, my dear – it was to be expected."

"Yes . . . I'm sure he will warm up to you. He is protective of me – that's all. And I think he views himself somewhat as my favourite, so is probably a little put off that there is one more man competing for my attention."

"You certainly aren't short of them! I am only glad I manage to hold a small place amongst your large audience of admirers."

"Charmer!"

Markus smiled captivatingly.

"I've been wondering, though, whether it would be helpful for me to talk to your boys?" he asked, more seriously. "One at a time, of course . . . give them a chance to get to know me a bit."

"What a wonderful idea!"

Gwen reached out with one hand and grasped his in gratitude.

Soon afterwards, the couple moved into the kitchen where Markus began dishing out their lunch of baked salmon with roast vegetables. They began to discuss their Christmas plans, Markus having decided to remain in New Jersey to celebrate with Gwen. It would be their first Christmas spent together as a couple.

* * *

Meanwhile, Lance's thoughts were far from his mother's budding romance and his brother's pending fatherhood. He was trying to come to a decision about his home.

Rob's response the previous evening had left Lance with a desire to recklessly sell his condo without further contemplation. It took considerable restraint to curb the impulse. If he sold now, he might be unable to assure himself in the future that it had been the Lord's will and so He continued to seek God's guidance.

After a morning spent assessing the decision from every conceivable angle, he was no closer to a decision. All he had gained was a headache.

Lance flicked the switch to grind beans for another coffee. It would be his fifth for the day.

Lance surveyed his home as the machine hummed and rattled beside him. He liked living here. He would miss its familiarity. His gaze swept across the open floor plan; at his white couches standing square and symmetrical, the small black coffee table, and the black cast-iron stair case. It was more sterile than a hospital ward. It was comfortable enough, but it wasn't how a home should feel; it was nothing more than a cold bachelor pad.

Lance envied the atmosphere within the grubby walls of his sister's home. It was chaotic. It was untidy and crowded. There were always dirty dishes in the sink. Yet there was also life, anticipation and excitement. The children became animated at new discoveries. Their delightful phrases brought laughter. There was love, fellowship and adventure.

Loneliness swept over Lance as he took his coffee over to the lounge. He longed for what his sister had and the companionship of a cherished marriage partner.

As if knowing his thoughts, the telephone began to ring. Fiona's voice sounded through the ear piece.

"I just heard the family news! And Amy has asked to meet up to talk about the pregnancy and what she should look into first. I positively feel like an old hand!"

"You know then?"

"Amy and Dave came for a drive to see us this morning and broke the news over morning tea." Fiona continued: "Dave also mentioned that you've had an offer. Do you have a place to stay? I've talked it over with Jo and we would love to host you!"

"I wouldn't want to encroach on you guys. Your life is hectic enough as it is."

"You wouldn't be! The children adore you and it would be nice for them to have (let's face it), their favourite uncle around!"

Lance was truly humbled by the offer and had a twinge of guilt for having anticipated a lecture from her, rather than support.

"Thanks Fi, truly. However, you know I can't accept. Not with Rob, Dave and Amy set to shift in there over Christmas. You won't have room."

"That's just it! Mom has told Dave and Amy they have to stay with her. I think she is going to ask Rob, too, so he doesn't feel left out. And even if Rob is here, I imagine he will be speedily bored entertaining little ones and would appreciate your company."

"Alright, then, thank you. I won't be too proud to accept. Although I still need to agree to the offer."

"Well, you know there is a bed here for you if you need it! I better get going, sorry – I promised I'd take the children down to the park for a play."

Lance was struck by a sense of peace as he put the phone back into its holder. Moving in with his sister was his next step.

He sipped his coffee as exhilaration churned within him.

I take it this means that I am to accept the couple's offer and move out?

Talk about humility: I never thought I'd be accepting charity from Fiona! Although I must admit it will be a delightful blessing to spend time with her rug-rats!

Thank you, Lord!

The decision made, he went into a time of Bible study, at last being able to focus on the words before him.

Settling his heart, he sought the Lord and what He had in store.

Words of rest and restoration filtered into his mind.

He tucked his feet up underneath him on the couch as he opened to the Gospel of Matthew and began skimming the pages until he found the paragraph he was seeking:

"Come to Me all you who labour and are heavy laden, and I will give you rest." [4]

That would be nice, Lord. I am in need of rest.

A reply echoed across his mind:

"This will be a season of rest. You are entering into a time of My refreshment.

"Seek Me and My ways. Allow Me to bring the restoration."

An image of a dry, withered tree by a river bank appeared before his open eyes, shutting out his physical view of the lounge room . . . Lance watched as the tree began to soak up water from the stream. Nutrients began to flow within its limbs; internal repairs were made; buds began to form and new leaves sprouted . . . yet, there was no fruit. Lance was concerned about the lack of fruit.

Aren't we meant to be spreading the Good News? Shouldn't I be serving the church, the body, the community? Surely I ought to be producing fruit?

The Lord's gentle whisper floated across his awareness:

"Not in this season. That time will come but you cannot give out until you are strengthened. If a drought comes upon the land as the fruit tree buds, will not the stress cause it to drop its fruit? Will the tree not reserve its strength to remain alive? It has seasons ahead in which to bear fruit.

"You need to rest and allow Me to heal you. The fruit will come with time. The fruit tree, by power of will, does not bring forth a crop. The burden of fruit will come naturally. You do not need it added to your load in this season."

Lance put down his empty cup, trying to digest God's promise. It contradicted what he believed to be foundational to discipleship. Surely he should be doing something to build God's Kingdom?

Again, the words of Jesus came to him:

"Take My yoke on you and learn from Me, for I am meek and lowly in heart, and you shall find rest to your souls. For My yoke is easy, and My burden is light." [5]

I can't see what this rest will look like and, at the moment, I'm not certain if I even want you to heal me. I'm unworthy of your healing grace. Who am I to deserve your mercy? I have broken your Laws. I have walked in disobedience.

And yet here you are, in your great mercy, promising me new life. How I long for a sip of that refreshing water. Fill me to overflowing with your water of life.

I bow before you with a humble spirit. I offer you my thanks and praise.

Thank you, Lord Jesus. Thank you.

Lance felt a comforting weight pressing down on his shoulders although there was no one behind him. His head dropped into his lap. His fingers interlaced themselves between tufts of hair. Lance gave way to grief.

* * *

The following week passed as a blur, leaving Lance questioning God's idea of rest. Despite knowing it wasn't a physical rest God had promised, by the end of the week he was praying for that, too.

He called his agent on the Monday morning and she had the paper work finished by the same afternoon. The couple were eager to move into their new home as soon as possible.

As a result, Lance found himself packing up house and shifting over to his sister's home between family gatherings and Christmas get-togethers.

Thankfully the couple agreed to his offer and bought most of his home furnishings, most of which had been specifically designed for the condo, and for which he no longer had a need. The left over items were able to fit into a small storage facility on the outskirts of the city he had rented on an initial six month lease.

Lance was slightly disappointed when neither of his brothers offered to help with the move. Whilst he could understand they had friends they wanted to catch up with during their brief visit home, he was nevertheless forced to see the distance spreading between them. No longer were they the "Three Amigos" of his childhood. Even Rob and Dave didn't seem particularly close anymore. Yet in Jo, Lance was discovering an unexpected friend and confidant.

Jo had come by after work on both the Tuesday and Wednesday to help with the shift. On the Wednesday evening, with most of his remaining possessions contained in boxes loaded onto the back of Jo's pick-up, the pair ordered take-away for what Fiona fondly declared was, "much long over due man-to-man bonding time."

"Ah – the bachelor life," Jo commented as he opened the fridge door to pull out a beer. "Gone are the days in my life when I could open a fridge door and find little else but beer."

This was an exaggeration as the pair had emptied Lance's fridge earlier that day and it had been Jo who had brought the six-pack of beer over with him to refresh them as they worked.

"You'll find your memory is hazy – it certainly isn't all it is cracked up to be," Lance replied, accepting the proffered beer.

"Lucky you feel that way because in less than twenty-four hours you will be experiencing how the other half of us live."

"I already know – I can hardly find anything in your over-crowded fridge. Surely half the stuff at the back has gone mouldy!"

"I can't comment about that: the kitchen is not my domain and I am quite happy to leave it that way."

"What – no hidden cooking talents?" Lance joked.

"Believe me: you take your health into your own hands with my cooking!"

"Speaking of which . . ." Lance remarked, rising to answer a knock on the door.

"Thanks," Lance said as he collected their burgers and fries, and paid the delivery man.

He closed the door.

Jo had already removed from the couch, picking up their half-drunken beers, and was sitting at the table.

"Oh yeah! Boy, am I hungry!" Jo said and he eagerly unwrapped his burger, leant forward, and took a large bite. Juice dripped down on to its discarded paper, sitting on the table.

Around the mass in his mouth, he commenced: "I'm sorry: I know you are getting this question from everyone at the moment and I've tried to hold my tongue, but: why? I mean, I understand your reasons and all. I just can't grasp why it has to be now? What happened in South Africa to tip the scale?"

Lance looked at Jo, studying his friend's face as he weighed how to answer.

It wasn't the same with Jo as it was with his brothers. In Jo he saw someone genuinely interested in him. Jo was not asking in rhetorical astonishment; he wanted to hear the answer.

Jo's features were attentive. He wasn't asking merely because it was expected. In fact, his words had conveyed the opposite; he had tried to give Lance some breathing space out of courtesy, waiting, even whilst others had demanded an answer.

"Why in Africa?" Lance parroted. "Honestly, I can't say. I would have wished it to have happened at any other time . . . You see . . . God gave me no say."

"Sorry?"

"I heard God calling me to do it. His initial request remained as a suffocating cloud until I gave in, being the weaker willed."

"Not that that's a bad thing – having a weaker will than God," Jo responded.

"No indeed!"

"And that was it? God told you to jump and you did?" Jo sounded impressed.

"More, or less. It was hard because it wasn't how I would have liked to leave the company. I certainly can't blame them for being angry at my timing."

Lance began picking at his fries.

"The worst of it is: I lost a friend," Lance spoke down at his burger.

"Fiona said something about that. One of your colleagues was fired?" Jo prompted.

Lance smiled. "She must have heard from Mom. It was my friend, Tom. I haven't heard from him since. I hope he found another job."

"I'm sure he has."

Jo took another bite. "Any closer to knowing what's next?" he queried with a half-full mouth.

"No. Look, I'm really sorry about barging in on you, too – especially at Christmas. It was really kind of Fi to offer, but if it is any hassle –"

"Are you kidding? Fiona considers it an early Christmas present! And (to be truthful), I'm looking forward to another male presence in the house! Plus, the kids adore you – it'll be good for Fi to have someone else to help de-energise Johnnie whilst I'm at work."

"Is that possible?"

"I hope so, Lance. I hope so!"

* * *

Lance moved in as planned the next day, bringing with him a backpack containing the last of his personal affects.

The house was in a greater state of chaos than usual due to the Christmas preparations being undertaken within its walls and a sense of excitement was in the air, fuelled by two little ones who were all eagerness for a visit from Santa Claus and his reindeer.

Lance tried to slot himself into their routine as seamlessly as he was able. He had no time to consider the finality of his move, or the uncertainty of his future. These were swept aside by the contagious joy of the Christmas season spread by his niece and nephew.

The Christmas tree was already up in the lounge and not a room was bare of bright golden tinsel, or cheery decorations. Lance was touched to see that a stocking with his name on it had appeared in the line hanging from the mantel over the fire place. The only thing missing to make the seasonal picture complete was a pile of loot under the tree and thus, on his first evening with the McCarthy's he was recruited to aid in the gift-wrapping ritual.

The children were tucked soundly into their beds upstairs and Jo opened a bottle of wine as Fiona came down the stairs heavily laden with shopping bags of presents and a few rolls of wrapping paper. Lance was handed a roll printed with Disney characters wearing festive Christmas dress.

They fell into a pattern: Fiona began on the larger presents, Lance wrapped the small gifts for the Santa stockings, and Jo cut tape, handing it to the wrappers as needed.

Fiona reminisced with Lance about their childhood Christmases as they worked.

"Do you know when it was I stopped believing in Santa?" she asked.

"No? I stopped when Dave found out from a kid at school and, naturally, just had to share!"

"Ha! Well I found out when I overheard you talking to Ben about it." She spoke of their cousin, the same age as Lance. She paused in her cutting. "The three of us had been sitting on the floor in your room – playing, I suppose – when Ben announced Santa wasn't true. I naturally looked to you and you firmly stated that he was real, even going as far as to say you had caught a glimpse of him the previous year."

"Very grand of me!"

"Yes. My faith in you, at that stage, was unshakable, and thus I was reassured – until Ben began to tease you. You kicked me promptly out of the room. Hard done by, I listened by the door and heard you say that of course you no longer believed in Saint Nick, but that didn't mean they should ruin it for me. Whilst naturally shattered at the discovery Santa was make-believe, it struck me how incredibly special I was to have a big brother who wanted to keep my childhood dreams alive."

"And in years to come we will hear from John that he discovered Santa wasn't real because he heard us speaking about it as he listened from upstairs, being unable to sleep in anticipation . . ." Jo inserted.

At his words, three heads turned to look up the stairs. No little face was seen peeping around the stair banister in the grief of disillusionment. They laughed it off and continued their activities.

"Can I ask why you and Amanda never had children?"

Luckily Lance didn't see the reproving look Fiona shot at her husband, or else a chuckle may have inadvertently broken forth from his lips. He was looking at his scissors, considering the question.

Why didn't we ever have children? Maybe they would have become a tie that kept us together. In truth, probably not . . .

Lance was saddened by his reflections.

"Many reasons, I suppose," he said, starting to fidget with the scissors. "Initially, it was because Amanda wanted to secure a name in her career before having to take maternity leave. Later, by the time she was established, and we'd made head-way paying off the mortgage, the marriage had disintegrated and it didn't seem reasonable to bring children in."

"I'm sorry, Lance," Fiona uttered.

"Yeah, I should have thought that one through a bit more," Jo added, lightly hitting his head in mock daftness.

"It's okay. You don't have to walk on egg shells when it comes to things between Amanda and me. I actually prefer you don't. Sure it hurts at times, but I'm getting through and speaking with people who care can help the healing process."

As he began folding the paper up over the sides of a red, match-box Ferrari, Lance added: "And, yes, I would have liked to have had children. Luckily for me, I have a delightful niece and nephew to spoil rotten!"

"Not to that point, please," Fiona requested with a slight smile.

They continued with the wrapping in silence for a time. Fiona left to turn on the kettle and proceeded to make three mugs of hot apple cider. Whilst Fiona followed after her mother and specialised in brewing the drink, tonight she opted for the more convenient powdered-form.

They had an interlude from their work, removing from the floor to the couches as they sipped the hot amber liquid. Lance thanked God for His goodness, glad to be in the company of family.

CHAPTER 9

Saturday saw Lance heading out with Markus to a local diner, leaving Gwen and Fiona to plan the Christmas meal in peace. Jo had taken Johnnie and Ann to visit his parents for the day.

Hurrying from the car bare of overcoats, they gratefully pushed open the swinging glass door and stepped into the restaurant's shelter. A friendly waitress in her adolescence escorted them to a side booth and handed them two menus to study.

"Can I get you guys some drinks?" she invited.

They ordered two large cokes and she wandered off, collecting a tray load of glasses from a nearby table on her way to the counter.

"The move went okay, did it?" Markus asked.

"Yeah, thanks. Jo was a great help. He even found the place where I'm storing a lot of the bigger articles, or unnecessary belongings — such as swimming clothes at this time. Burr!"

Markus grinned. "Only too true! I must admit: I am a warmer-weather man. Or at least I am since I've gotten old. Enjoy your robust health whilst you can."

"Health! You are as fit as any of us! What is your sport of interest, by the way?"

"I was always partial to basketball until I gave it up at, oh — forty, forty-five. I can't remember precisely. These days I mostly walk and swim."

"I see common interests with Mom in those. Have you been on many walks up around Mount Tammany and Worthington Forest?"

"Yeah, we quite often end up there on weekends. Stunning area. Gwen worries a little about bears, though. It was how Fiona found out — being convenient for your Mom to stop by Montville on the way home. Fiona's been great! I'm sorry you only found out now . . . We didn't want to say anything until it became more established, if you can understand?"

"Sure. And I appreciate it, too. No point getting families involved only to have it end in friendship before it began."

"You boys ready to order?" The waitress had come back over, writing pad and pen in hand.

"Oh, no – we haven't looked yet," Lance answered apologetically. "Give us five?"

Lance and Markus proceeded to order shortly afterwards and kept up a steady flow of generic conversation until their orders arrived. For Lance, it was a Wangu beef burger with tex-mex potato wedges; for Markus, the Big Breakfast.

Over lunch, Markus shared more about his family. He had three daughters. Two of his girls were married, lived interstate, and between them had given him five grandchildren. His middle child had remained single (although currently had a boyfriend who looked promising), and lived in the United Kingdom.

After the meal, the waitress offered to take drink orders and handed them a dessert menu.

"Flat white, please," Lance requested.

"Make it two, thank you."

"Any desserts?"

"No thanks."

"Not for me, either."

"Did you want to ask my thoughts on the subject of you and Mom?" Lance took a gamble as the waitress left them. "I'm sorry if I'm on the wrong track . . . just thought I'd ask," he concluded hastily.

"Perceptive of you! You're close, though I also just wanted to make time to get to know you. Your mother told me how she had mentioned my initial request for us to move in together and her subsequent proposal back to me?"

Lance nodded in affirmation.

"I've considered it and I want to ask your mother to marry me." Lance's spontaneous smile emboldened Markus to continue: "But before I "pop the question", I was hoping to obtain your permission."

Lance stared at Markus with a blank-face.

"You're asking my permission – to propose to my Mom?"

Markus shrugged a shoulder. "I'm old fashioned."

"But why me?"

"I can hardly ask her father . . ."

"Yeah, but . . ."

"From the sound of it, you are the closest to Gwen - at least in beliefs and confidences - and I know she respects your opinion," Markus explained.

"You're asking for my opinion?"

"Yes."

"About proposing – to my mother?"

"Yes, I thought we'd established that."

"My honest opinion?"

"Of course! Lance, I want you to be open with me. What do you think of it?"

Lance began working his lower lip between his teeth, contemplating the question. He was grateful for the interlude afforded by the delivery of their flat whites. He took a sip of the luke-warm coffee before answering.

"My Mom's faith is very important to her."

"I know."

"She will always love Jesus – another man – more than you."

"Yes."

"And you are okay with that?"

"Yes," Markus replied earnestly, making eye contact.

"She said she asked you if you were willing to accompany her to church . . . ?"

"Yes. I won't pretend to be religious, or anything; however, I do have a general belief in a god and I can commit to attending church with her each week. I know her faith is important to her."

"Family is also important to her."

"As it is to me."

Lance took another sip of coffee and absently studied the restaurant, trying to think of questions he never thought he'd have to ask.

"How do you plan to divide the time between the two families?"

"We have to think further about that. Our initial plan is to spend nine months here at her home. I'd sell and buy a small place in Arizona for the remaining three months, being where two of my girls are and, of course, David and Amy."

"I really can't think of anything else . . ."

"Meaning . . . you are okay with me asking?" Markus put forth cautiously.

"Yes, I suppose I am!" Lance returned cheerfully, before adding: "Good luck to you!"

"Thanks. Next question: do you think it is okay to ask her whilst Amy and Dave's announcement remains recent news? I believe it would be her wish to have her family here to celebrate – assuming she says yes, of course."

"Yes! I think that would be marvellous."

Lance could not wipe the jubilant smile from his face as they paid their bill and braved the chilly wind once more. It took considerable self-control for Lance to keep mum on the subject. Instead, with only a few days remaining until Christmas, he tried to focus his mind on the joyful event of

Christ's birth.

* * *

The rest of the family arrived at the McCarthy's home late-morning the day before Christmas. Amy and the boys came ahead of Gwen, who was delayed on the claim she had a few remaining errands to complete.

Lance was in the kitchen preparing some platters when Gwen let herself in. The others had moved out to the enclosed back patio. Lance looked up expectantly at his mother and his gaze became a question when he noticed that Markus wasn't with her.

"He flew to Arizona to be with his family," Gwen replied to the unspoken enquiry.

"Are they okay? – I mean, has something happened?"

"I said "no"," Gwen's voice broke on the words.

"Oh, Mom! I'm sorry."

Lance meant it. He wanted his mother to be happy. She deserved to be loved and cherished and adored. His father had left her too soon.

"It's okay. I'm okay."

Lance left the platters to embrace her, being careful not to let dirty hands touch her red satin blouse.

"First, the house proposal and finally last night . . . when he asked for my hand . . . it made me really consider my relationship with him. When I looked closely, I saw in my heart that he has always been a friend, a close and a dear one, but a friend nonetheless," Gwen muttered disjointedly into her son's chest.

"That doesn't mean it doesn't hurt," Lance soothed.

"No, you are right. It hurts. It hurts a lot; like I've lost one of my best friends. Yet I simply couldn't go through with it. I told him my God was too important to me."

"I must admit I was also concerned about his lack of faith, but I didn't realise it was affecting you and certainly not that much. I thought it was because you are stronger of faith than me."

They had pulled apart and Gwen moved to the bench where she began fiddling with the platters.

"It didn't affect me until recently. Since he asked me to move in with him my spirit has not possessed peace. As my heart was fluttering in excitement, my spirit wiggled in anxiety. I can't ignore that."

"No. And I admire you for it. I would have been tempted to push my spirit-man aside."

"Thank you. I am lucky to have such a caring, loving son. But," she continued with forced determination, "it is the day before Christmas and I am with my family! I can't ask for more. Let's get these trays out to the others."

They finished placing the last few hot fruit mince pies on to the final dishes and carried them out to those gathered under the patio.

* * *

Fiona was next to hear her mother's news and it astounded her.

The party broke up soon after lunch. David took a weary Amy back to Gwen's home for a quiet evening of rest. Rob followed the couple out the door to seek a "little Christmas entertainment". He was convinced no excitement would be had with his family, especially with his niece and nephew present.

Gwen and Fiona were in the kitchen cleaning up; Gwen washing the dishes for Fiona to dry and put away what wouldn't be used for Christmas lunch. The growing collection on the kitchen bench far out weighed what was returned to its usual location.

"Are you sure you're going to be okay with your decision?" she asked.

"Yes. God has called us who believe to look to things above, not on the earth. My faith would be hampered with Markus, no matter how well intentioned he is to be supportive."

Fiona could not believe the strength of her mother's faith to turn away from a man she had come to love. She wished to possess such steadfast resolve. Hadn't she given up going to church because of life's "busyness"? – And that with a Christian husband!

What happened to my faith, Jesus? When did I become too busy for you? How will my children grow to know of your love if I do not introduce them to it?

"I'll be okay," her mother continued. "I had an amazing time in Christ's presence last night; worshipping Him, our God, Emmanuel."

Emmanuel, God with us. Fiona considered her mother's words and they lead her to pray:

Here we are on Christmas Eve and I can't remember once stopping to think of what it is we are celebrating! What brought me to this place? I want to be radical for you as I once was. I want to live for you. Help me to change my life! Bring it back to you.

"I think you are amazing, Mom!" Fiona exclaimed, looking at her with something approaching awe.

Gwen smiled.

"You are pretty amazing yourself, sweetheart. Come, let's join the men."

Hanging the tea-towel on the oven door, Fiona followed her mother back out to where Lance and Jo remained in camping chairs on the back patio. The children sat building a Lego castle on a play mat beside them, lost in a world of fantasy where dragons lived and maidens needed saving.

* * *

The evening was enjoyable for Lance as the family sat in the lounge room. The wood fireplace sent forth its warmth and the television was tuned to the broadcast of Central Park's Christmas Eve carol service. John and Ann sat on the shaggy, cream carpet whilst the adults talked quietly behind them between songs.

It was a peaceful atmosphere and Lance, hot buttered rum in hand, found the tension easing from him as his barriers came down. It was freeing to be in a safe place where he could drop his guard.

Whilst Jo shared Lance's contentment that evening, the women did not. Sitting beside Lance on the three-seater couch, Gwen silently grieved the choice she had been forced to make. On the neighbouring couch Fiona sat within her husband's arms, yet their strong support could not chase away her growing unrest.

Fiona's heart raced as she considered asking the room a question about faith. She was rarely the one to introduce God in to family discussions; even alone with her husband she struggled to voice concerns, or fears.

Overcome with an incredible vulnerability, she struggled to muster her voice. Courage deserted her. For half an hour she tried to talk herself into sharing.

The children had dozed off in front of the television following a sickening amount of toasted marshmallows and a couple of S'mores Bars. Jo rose and carried each upstairs in turn.

Taking the chance of a lessened audience, Fiona wrung her hands as she tentatively put forth her question: "This might be . . . well, the question might seem a little silly . . . but I've been wondering: how do you know when God is directing you towards something? Both of you have recently made such big decisions in your life and credited Him for it. What made you so confident that it was from Him?"

Embarrassment came upon her when silence met her question. She was looking at her hands and could not see the contemplation upon both faces.

"You certainly don't choose easy questions, Fiona!" Lance smiled.

His words encouraged her and she looked up at him as he continued.

"I guess, for me, it isn't an audible voice; rather an impression, or a thought that won't leave me. Sometimes a verse, or theme continuously pops up in different places. For example: first at church, followed by my quiet time, and finally in a book."

"I agree with Lance. It's slightly different for everyone, of course. For me, I sometimes see an image and an interpretation comes to me with it."

Lance nodded in agreement.

"Sometimes it is in the words of a song," Gwen continued. "With Markus it was weeks of restlessness between two decisions before a deep peace came over my heart and a certainty about the choice I must make."

Fiona looked down, weighing their words with a crestfallen heart. Surely if God spoke to them in such ways, He would also speak to her. So why didn't He?

"It takes time, too," Gwen added. "It took me years of listening to become attuned to His voice and I still fail to get it right at times – or fail to listen, as is more often the case!"

"Can emotions be part of it?" Fiona wondered aloud. "I mean, I have a restlessness, which, quite frankly, scares me. I don't know what to do to make it go away."

Her eyes were opened wide and pleading, giving a glimpse within her troubled mind. Lance was put forcibly in mind of a little girl lost all alone in a large wood.

"Do you have an idea of what is causing it?" her mother prompted.

"I'm sorry, I didn't want to move into this with you," she apologised hastily, closing herself off. "Especially as its Christmas time . . . and I probably should speak to Jo about it first."

"Yes dear. By all means talk to Jo. That is probably best."

"Are you sure you're okay, though?" Lance asked in concern.

"Yes, yes. It's nothing. Just wondering."

"Okay, well you know I'm always willing to talk about God and faith, at any time! And not only God; anything at all, even cooking – night or day."

Fiona laughed.

"Thank you, Lance. Really, thank you."

They talked no more about hearing God's voice. In fact, they did not speak much more about anything. Gwen gave her farewells as Jo returned, declining an offer from him to sleep the night under their roof.

As Gwen's car reversed down the drive, the remaining three trundled up to bed on Fiona's warning to expect an early wake up call.

CHAPTER 10

"Mommy! Mommy! Mommy! Mommy!"

Fiona awoke on Christmas morning to Johnnie's voice, trembling with excitement.

"Mommy, get up. Quick, Mommy, quick!"

"Johnnie, it's," reaching over Fiona looked at the clock on her bedside table, "it's five-thirty. Go back to bed."

"But Santa's come, Mommy! You've got to come look."

"Morning, Fi!" Lance chirped as he stuck his head in through the doorway. "You're lucky he only woke you up now. I had a little face appear over me an hour ago!"

Fiona shook her head at Lance and, sitting up in bed, sighed in resignation.

"Alright you two – out! I will join you shortly. Leave your father in peace," she directed, waving them away.

Jo had pulled the doona up over his head and was moaning softly.

Joining the pair downstairs, Fiona questioned whether Ann had stirred.

"Hasn't mouthed a peep."

"Well, that's something. She'll be terrible come lunch if she can't sleep a little while longer."

"Mom!" Johnnie whined.

He tugged at her hand in an attempt to obtain her attention.

"Come see what Santa got me."

"Yes, darling, what has Santa brought for you?"

Fiona spent the next fifteen minutes trying to add enthusiasm to her voice in order to satisfactorily "oooh" and "ahhh" over toys she had wrapped not a week earlier.

"Okay, Johnnie, Mommy needs to start getting breakfast ready and preparing for our big special lunch with Gran and your Uncles. Why don't you come in with me?"

"Okay."

Johnnie marched to the kitchen behind Fiona. He began driving two match-box cars around the kitchen floor; he had received a blue Jeep in addition to his Ferrari. Fiona nearly tripped over him on several occasions.

"You are going to church with Mom this morning, aren't you? Did she say what time it will finish?" Fiona asked Lance. "I'll try and plan lunch accordingly."

"I imagine most people will head straight off after church - being Christmas and having their families to go home to. However, as there's no rush for our meal, why don't you come with us? Cooking can wait until we get home."

"I don't know . . . What if the others arrive before us?"

"There is plenty of snack food for them to nibble on if they chance to arrive before we're back."

"I guess . . . Although, I don't know that Jo will be up to looking after the children. He isn't a morning person . . ."

"Bring them with us! It'll be a short service and I'm sure there will be activities for them, or a children's talk, or something."

"Oh dear. I suppose I probably should go, being Christmas and all. What time does it start?"

"Eight. It will finish by about nine, I'd say."

"Alright – if you help me keep the kids in check!"

"I think I'm up to that! And now on to other important matters – how can I help with breakfast? And we need to put some Christmas mood-music on!"

The pair spent the next hour listening to Christmas carols whilst working away in the kitchen. Lance did according to Fiona's instructions, impressed as she managed, in addition to the lunch preparations, to brew coffee, put croissants in the oven, and fry bacon and eggs for their breakfast.

The kitchen was a mix of delightful aromas by the time Jo joined them. He was at last enticed to leave his warm bed by Ann, who trotted in to the main bedroom carrying her favoured African doll.

"Smells delicious!" he praised, stretching. "Is there coffee?"

"In the pot."

"You are wonderful!" He gave his wife a kiss on the cheek before pouring a cup of coffee and topping up Lance and Fiona's cups.

Jo looked mildly surprised when his wife informed him she'd be attending church – it was out of character for Fiona to give up last-minute preparation time. Moreover, Jo felt obligated to tag along so, as a result, Lance drove his car into the city and collected Gwen, whilst Jo drove his family direct to the church.

The small church was a hive of excited activity as people moved in greeting one another, called across pews to wish friends "Merry Christmas!" and shook hands with strangers as they introduced themselves. Seats were soon filled with the regular attendees as well as those making a special effort to come at Christmas.

The service commenced right on time with a few carols. Johnnie stood on his seat to see like one of the adults whilst his father held Ann up in his arms.

During the time of greeting, some friendly folk in front of them turned and greeted the family, engaging them in light pleasantries. Gwen smiled and nodded to a few of her acquaintances.

"What if I were to ask you to share with me some of your most significant Christmas memories?" the minister put forth to the mass as a few stragglers returned to their seats and he commenced his sermon. "I consider myself safe in suggesting most, if not all, of those memories will have something to do with your childhood. Would I be correct?"

Fiona thought about the question. The image that came to mind caused her to give a silent, yet emphatic, "no". The treasured memory that had come to her mind was not from her childhood. It had been formed only six years ago, but she had not thought on it for some time.

It was a memory of the first Christmas with her little Johnnie, then only three months old. She had been nursing him in her arms during the carol "Joy to the World" when God gave her a promise; the promise He would grow Johnnie into a man after His own heart.

Fiona glanced down at her son with warmth. Unconsciously she sat up slightly in the pew.

She listened as the pastor disclosed three of his own Christmas memories. The first was of the air of anticipation each Christmas Eve:

"Our family always went to the midnight service to await "the coming of the King". I would sit next to my younger brother, the pair of us enthralled by the dramatic telling of Christ's coming birth, until, at midnight, we joined the animals, shepherds and wise men as they bowed down to the baby boy-child King."

Next he spoke of disappointment when, instead of receiving an eagerly desired guitar, he was given a banjo from his father:

"My spirit fell in boyhood anguish at the sight of the banjo. How cool it was to own a guitar; how uncool a banjo!"

Lastly, he told of how, on the Christmas immediately following his banjo disappointment, he had received exactly what he wanted:

"I was given a David Crockett hat, bow and arrows set . . . and I learned the lesson of pain. Trying out my new "toy", I aimed an arrow at our back door. The arrow had a splinter, which went undetected as I pulled it back, making the string taunt. The splinter caused the arrow to rebound. It shot straight through my hand. . ."

The pastor had been taken to the emergency department where he underwent a general anaesthetic and finished Christmas in a hospital bed, spewing into a bucket. Better the banjo than the bow and arrow!

Fiona remembered some of the disappointments and pain she had suffered on Christmases gone by. She was sinking into sympathetic self-pity when the minister moved on. He brought to mind those for whom Christmas meant loneliness, the grieving of lost loved ones, emptiness, or arguments.

She realised none of her stories could compare to facing such sorrows. Hers were selfish disappointments, relating to presents, or failed expectations.

As the sermon continued, Fiona remained thinking of the homeless and the poor who would only be wishing for a warm corner out of the snow-filled breeze, and perhaps, if they were lucky, a warm bowl of soup.

Fiona was overcome by sadness. How could Christmases with her children, which had started with such a beautiful promise, have spiralled rapidly into her current habit of stressing over what gifts to buy, fighting long lines at the shops with hardly-contained impatience, and trying to catch up with as many of the people she had neglected through the year as she could in as short a time span as possible?

Fiona realised she had forgotten to focus on who had been given. She had forgotten to include Christ in her Christmases.

Picking up the message, she heard the pastor say: ". . . people return their unwanted gifts to stores, or they forget the day, as one in a sea of many. When the sun goes down today, signalling the end of another Christmas, only emptiness will remain in many hearts. There is a hole in man's heart only God can fit.

"Life is like a jigsaw puzzle. We can fit it all together except for one part. There is always a piece missing without Christ. People all over the globe are celebrating Christmas – getting presents and eating roast dinners – yet they are unable to shake an incomprehensible emptiness because the puzzle of their lives is left incomplete.

"We need the God-shaped piece to give our life meaning. When it comes to giving at Christmas, God knew what we needed; or rather, He knew who we needed. Jesus Christ is the perfect gift for everyone. We will never grow out of Him nor will we ever out grow of our need for him. And we will never have to replace Him with someone, or something, else."

He is right, Lord. You are the perfect gift and I have neglected to give you to my children. Not daily, not weekly, and not even at Christmas, or Easter, have I brought them to you, or taught them your ways.

Despite my neglect, bring them close to you. Show me how to introduce them to their Saviour.

The pastor talked on.

"He really is the perfect gift. He can't be lost and He can't be broken by little fingers before today is at an end. He promises He will never leave us. He challenges us to reorder our priorities."

Yes, I see I need to reorder my priorities – I just can't grasp how.

I am so frustrated. You are showing me how I have neglected my children and their faith walk. How can this be possible when they have been my world? How can I have tried to give them everything and still failed to give them anything of worth?

* * *

Up until this point, Lance, sitting on the other side of Johnnie to his sister, had been agreeing with the minister's words and had not felt any uncomfortable tugging at his heart. No application was revealed to him. He felt truly blessed to have found the "God-shaped piece" of his puzzle, which had sat seamlessly within the whole.

Nevertheless, Christ was not the only gift the pastor was set to speak on:

"Not only is He the perfect gift, He brings us the truly wonderful gifts of grace, forgiveness and mercy, and kindness and love. These are the gifts of real value. We can give them not only to our friends and family, but to our enemies, as well. And when we do, the peace of Christ will be real.

"Jesus invites us into a life-changing relationship with God. He gives us a sense of purpose, not possible without Him."

I have been lacking your peace, Lord. What must I do to bring the purpose of my life back to you? What enemy must I love?

I do not believe I am up to loving Amanda . . . I have chosen to forgive her with my intellect, but I can't even dwell on her yet without my heart wrenching back. And how am I to show kindness to her since we have gone our separate ways?

Show me what your grace and mercy looks like in this situation. What would you have me do? Who are you calling me to love?

I desire above all else to gain your peace again.

As he stilled his heart, it was not Amanda who filled his mind. It was Tom.

Lance immediately repelled the thought. Tom wasn't his enemy; he was a friend – albeit a friend who had rejected him.

He didn't want to be at odds with Tom. It was what Tom had chosen as his response (which Lance understood, given the circumstance). No – the rift between them was of Tom's desire, not his.

Despite his reasoning, the broken relationship with Tom continued to eat away at his mind, robbing his heart of peace.

"May you discover at Christmas that God has given you everything you need. Let this be true for you this Christmas. Amen."

The sermon concluded, but Lance's thoughts were not interrupted, focused as they were on his lost friend. He excused himself from his family group as they stepped out into the frosty air.

Soft white puffs of snow were falling gently down upon the earth as he huddled underneath the eve of the red-brick church.

Drawing his phone out from an inside jacket pocket, Lance flicked down through his list of contacts.

"Tom."

Lance pressed the dial button.

He stood watching his mother beside the McCarthy's car as they prepared to depart. In his ear the pattern of ring tone and silence, ring tone and silence, repeated itself.

Lance ended the call, his attempt at contact unsuccessful.

God! This makes me angry! Why can't he take responsibility for his nonsensical actions? As much as I want to be on friendly terms with him again, surely it should be up to him to take the first step towards narrowing the divide between us?

I don't know why I have to be the one to revive the friendship – I know you desire for damaged relationships to be healed and bitterness cut short – I just believe, since I'm not the one in the wrong, that Tom should be first to seek amends.

Gwen was talking to a few elderly ladies, who were wrapped from head to toe in woollen garments. One of whom was wearing a home-knitted pullover with a giant reindeer worked into the pattern, complete with a red pom pom as its nose. Lance made eye contact and his mother took leave of her friends.

Driving from the quaint Harrison church, Lance consciously pushed aside his conviction to breach the rift with Tom. He tried to focus on his mother's words. The church organist had chosen her favourite Christmas carol, "What Child Is This?", which she had not heard in many years and was delightedly reflecting on her days carolling in the streets as a child.

* * *

In the McCarthy car, another member of the family was caught up in their own thoughts.

Fiona's silence caused Jo to ask what was wrong.

"Oh, nothing," she lied, not ready to reveal the guilt turning over and over within her stomach. The sermon had left her convicted and she sat dwelling on her family's lack of devotion towards the Lord.

Her words left Jo unconvinced.

"Are you sure?"

"Yes. I was simply thinking: we really should go to church more often."

She reached over and placed a hand behind her husband's head.

"What did you think of the church? Would you mind going back sometime?" she asked, playing with his hair.

Jo stole a glance at his wife.

"No, I wouldn't mind – they seemed friendly enough. If it's what you want, I'm willing to give it another shot," he answered.

"Thank you."

Fiona's mood improved. At a request from the backseat duo, she turned on the radio and began singing along to "Jingle Bells" with the children. Even Jo's deep voice joined in, adding a baritone element to their quartet.

Turning into their drive, Fiona was relieved to see no blue-lipped relatives standing forlorn on their front porch.

Jo took over care of the children as Fiona busied herself getting the roast turkey back in the oven.

Half an hour later, three additional voices, belonging to Amy, Dave and Rob, brought new gusto to the Christmas gathering.

Fiona was distracted with a sensation akin to knowing there was something important to do and yet being unable to recall what it was. She declined offers of assistance from both Gwen and Amy, chasing them out of the kitchen to relax with the men in the sunroom.

In truth, Fiona was glad to find a space of alone time to allow her thoughts to settle before lunch.

As she made the preparations and served the meal, the sermon began once more to niggle away at her peace. Images of lonely people on street corners and cold, dilapidated buildings filtered through her mind in imitation of an old, still-picture film.

"Fiona, come back and sit down," her husband chided as she stepped up from the sunroom to the main house.

"I'm just going to collect some more ice."

"I'll do it. You relax."

Jo placed his half-finished plate of food down on the serving table and steered Fiona to his seat. She sat fidgeting through the meal as Jo talked cars with Dave and Rob, and a clucky Amy gained experience entertaining young children.

Lance and Gwen tried to include her in a discussion of the latest version of "A Christmas Carol", which had been released late that November.

"I haven't seen it," she said. "What was it like?"

"I enjoyed it. Although (since I was half-asleep on a plane when I watched it), it might not be as good as my memory makes it out to have been," Lance warned.

"I saw it in the cinema, fully awake, and enjoyed it. Very dramatic, though – I was tense from start to finish. The ending is especially well done – the way they contrast time with family, the spirit of Christmas, and today's focus on presents and the mentality of getting, rather than giving."

"Presents! Is it present time?" Johnnie was beside his mother's chair, having knocked over another of the plastic chairs in his enthusiasm to reach her.

"Talking of which . . ." Fiona murmured over her son's head to her laughing mother.

Opening presents did not help ease Fiona's swelling heart. She sat silently at the back of the circle in the living room as eager hands worked away at wrapping paper, and excited voices exclaimed at their gifts.

She smiled encouragingly whenever her children looked her way and worked her face into the appropriate expression of excitement or joy.

Her own pile of loot was by no means shabby yet she would have struggled if requested to recount what it contained. She did recall opening an electric grill press from Jo. She had commented several months previously that one would be handy, except now she couldn't remember why she thought they would benefit from owning one.

Her eyes lit with sudden revelation as she watched Ann opening her new tea set. Hadn't she just been trying to pile the left over food into her already fit-to-burst fridge? Surely there was someone out there in the city she could give it to! She didn't know where to go; however, she was certain it would not be difficult to find someone.

Delighted to have an outlet for her desire to give, she was able to honestly enjoy the remaining time of gift-giving with her family and offered hot drinks as the follow on event.

Back in the kitchen waiting for the kettle to boil, Fiona began to visually inspect the food in the fridge and determine what could go. She mentally assessed what amounts she would send home with her mother for the troop staying there and what her own family would eat in the next couple of days.

Lance came in to help her deliver the various coffees, hot chocolates and cocoas. He glanced questioningly at Fiona, who had begun pulling items out from the fridge.

"I'm going to take them down to a shelter," she mouthed.

He nodded back at her and moved to the window whilst he waited for the drinks to be made. Lance had tried unsuccessfully throughout lunch to push aside the nagging compulsion within him to call Tom, justifying the delay by claiming that Tom could always respond to his missed calls. Nonetheless, the words continued to echo in his mind: "**love your enemies, and do good, . . . Judge not, and you will not be judged; condemn not, and you will not be condemned; forgive, and you will be forgiven.**" [6]

Lance stood watching the persistent fall of light snow; the softness of the scene eased his heart and resentment slid from his chest as a silk garment's graceful fall to the floor.

Lance turned away from the scene as a familiar voice filtered through the phone.

"Yes. Hi. Tom? It's Lance here."

"Hi."

"Look, sorry to bother you on Christmas and all. I just . . . I was thinking about you in church this morning and . . . I wanted to apologise. No, more than that: I want to ask for your forgiveness."

There was silence at the other end of the line. Lance continued: "I didn't take the time to think through the implications my actions would have on others, on you. And I know I should have told you of my intentions – even before I sent off my resignation. If I had, you may, at least, have had some warning. I should have told you, and I am sorry. Will you forgive me?"

There was another pause.

"Lance . . . you don't have to . . . I mean, like you said at the time, it wasn't your fault. I was angry. I wanted to lash out. That's all."

"Yes, but, all the same, I would like to hear that it has been forgiven".

"It's in the past. I look set to receive a better job offer this week. Really, there isn't a need for all of this."

Lance wasn't sure why he had such a strong desire to hear Tom say he was forgiven and, since his friend was clearly uncomfortable with the gesture, he allowed the subject to be dropped.

"That is great news about the job!" he responded. "I'm in town for at least a little while longer; if you have time in the next few weeks maybe we could grab a drink? You can tell me about this new job of yours."

"Yeah, we'll do that. Merry Christmas, Lance," Tom ended the call.

"Merry Christmas! Give Angie my love. I'll get in touch about the drink."

Lance praised God as he placed his phone down on the window sill. His load felt lighter. Words came to him:

". . . if you are presenting your gift at the altar and remember there that your brother has something against you, leave your gift there before the altar and first go and be reconciled to your brother. Then come and offer your gift." [7]

Thank you, Father! You truly do know what is best for us.

I did not realise how much release I would gain from making one simple call. I do not understand how all this spiritual stuff works, but I do know my heart is at peace and a joy has returned because my relationship with Tom is mended.

Thank you, Father. Thank you!

His gaze once more moved to alight upon his sister.

"And now, Miss Fiona, tell me what you are up to in this kitchen of yours?"

"Oh, nothing much. Only, we have way too much left over food so I thought I'd duck out for half an hour and drop some off at one of the soup kitchens, or something . . ."

Smiling up at her brother, she added: "You'll let the others know I've popped out for a minute if they ask, won't you? Thanks Lance."

Moving to the inter-connecting archway, Fiona stuck her head into the lounge room and asked Johnnie to come and help her with a special job.

Jo lifted his head at this request and followed Johnnie out in order to offer an extra hand. Lance let them be and went to rejoin the others, carrying the tray of drinks with him.

Fiona reluctantly brought her husband into her confidence and he was less than happy to hear of her plans.

"Fiona, really, this is very good of you – and very charitable, I'm sure – but . . . do you even know where to find the homeless in our city?"

"No, I don't. However, I am sure I will find someone who will be grateful for the food. Central Park – yes, that's it – that will be where I start. There are bound to be people there."

"I would be far more comfortable if you let me come with you."

"I know, dear," Fiona replied with understanding. "Try not to worry; we will be fine. Please, Jo, I really think I should do this with only Johnnie for company."

Johnnie was uncertain of what was passing between his parents. At the mention of his name he silently lifted his small hand and grasped hold of Fiona's one. He wanted to be with his mother.

Fiona glanced down at her son. "Okay, my Big Man, let us be gone! Do you want to carry this bag out to the car for Mommy?"

Johnnie nodded his head, a slight smile of determination upon his lips. Fiona squeezed her husband's hand before lifting the remaining box.

CHAPTER 11

Fiona planned to drive straight down Route 46 to the city and from there to head into Central Park, but without realising she passed the turn off. Her foot punched down on the break pedal in alarm and a squeak sounded from the back, the sudden jolt having startled Johnnie.

Fiona was shaken by her absentmindedness; nevertheless, she did not turn around. A new sensation of serenity had descended upon her, stilling her mind. She threw off the last lurking hint of anxiety and took a chance on the outrageous side of life, choosing to be guided by the strange quietness.

Feeling ridiculous, Fiona made a right turn into an unfamiliar suburb. She continued to be directed on her unknown route by seemingly random, yet decisive, decisions.

"Mommy, where are we going?" Johnnie asked with a slight tremor in his voice as he watched the unfamiliar landscape whiz past his window. His father's tone of concern had not been lost on him.

Glancing at her son in the rear-view mirror, Fiona tried to instil him with confidence.

"We are going on a Grand Adventure with God! I don't know where we will end up because He is showing me the way."

"Does God like adventures?" Johnnie was curious.

"Yes, He does – very much – and more so when we go with Him."

"Like we are!" was the bright response.

"Yes, like we are."

Fiona was surprised she had been able to answer her son in a normal voice. Even greater was her wonder at his simple faith; what she wouldn't give to be able to trust as a child again.

"You will . . ."

Fiona felt slightly rattled and, at the same time, thrilled at the soft whisper.

Glancing once more at her now-smiling son, she responsively warmed to their adventure. A rising excitement entered into her body, quickening her heart rate.

Smiling as she took another turn, she slowed, and finally stopped outside of a small, single story house with a neatly kept yard.

She turned off the ignition and undid her seatbelt. Before her hand reached the doorhandle she had thought better of it and re-buckled the strap. Her fingers began to play with the keys. She promptly brought them together, resting them in her lap.

Help me to be brave, Jesus.

Oh please, Jesus. Oh God, let this be you! I am so vulnerable . . . and with Johnnie . . . Please, oh please, oh please, Jesus, keep us safe.

Taking in a deep breath, Fiona committed herself: "Okay Johnnie, this is it. Do you want to help me take the food in?"

"Yes!"

Johnnie undid his seat belt and waited for his mother to open the door before eagerly clambering out on to the lawn.

"Let me take that one!" he exclaimed, grabbing the bag.

Fiona propped the box onto one hip, took her son's hand, and made her way up the pebbled path, full of anxiety.

Her first knock was barely audible and she tentatively made a second, louder one.

She heard footsteps within, sounding as if shoes were tapping on wooden floorboards. The door opened . . .

Fiona was taken by surprise. It was the minister from her mother's church!

Her amazement was furthered by his words.

"Oh, thank the Good Lord!"

The pastor turned to say more loudly over his shoulder: "It's here! The first of the food has arrived."

Fiona murmured that if he was waiting for a food delivery, she wasn't it: explaining that her decision to donate had been sudden.

"It's kind of hard to explain, actually," she stammered. "You see, I didn't know where to go and sort of ended up here."

The minister smiled at her.

"Yes, and I did not know who to expect! God lead you to our door because He knows our needs."

Seeing Fiona's evident confusion, he continued: "We are doing a food run in half an hour, except thus far we have received very little to give. A small group of us have been praying for more donations and now – here you are! Truly, your offering is more than a start! Hopefully, the first of several . . ."

"God brought us on an adventure! I've never been here before," Johnnie confided, not content to stand forgotten by his mother's side

The minister smiled down at him.

"Did you enjoy your adventure?"

"Oh yes, very much!"

"I am sure God will take you down many more exciting paths as you grow!"

Johnnie beamed at the grey-haired minister, delighted at the thought of more adventures.

"Can I invite you in?" he invited, gesturing down the hall. "You are welcome to join us as we make the donation run."

"Oh, I should head back home . . ." Fiona said looking down at her watch, suddenly conscious of the time.

"Of course; it is Christmas and you want to be with your family."

The minister found himself drawn in spirit to the young woman before him.

"My name is Father George; I minister at the Harrison Community Parish," he was prompted to add. "Please feel welcome to come visit us here again. In fact, you should come to dinner this week with my wife and I. Bring your family with you."

"Umm, well, I wouldn't want to be any trouble . . ."

"Not at all! We love to entertain and our own children live interstate giving us little time with our own grandchildren," he gestured down at Johnnie. "You would bless us if you came. Let me go and grab a notebook so I can write down your number."

Fiona waited whilst he gathered paper and a pen from his hallway desk before relaying her contact details. She hoped Jo wouldn't mind, but perhaps Lance would come with her if needs be. Fiona only knew that the connection was too strange to be a coincidence and thus she wouldn't let it pass her by. If God had something special for her son and had chosen him, then she would be faithful to make sure he was united to a church body.

"Thank you for being faithful to God's call," Pastor George said after they had exchanged phone numbers. "Today you have been used by God.

When you leave here, do not doubt that He used you today."

* * *

"You're home!"

Fiona was greeted in the carport by a relieved husband.

"Yes, we're home."

"Did you go down to Central Park?"

"No – to the pastor of Mom's church."

"We went on an adventure with God, Daddy!"

"Is that right, son? – Well, I am just glad you are both home safely!"

He lifted his son into an embrace and shepherded Fiona inside.

"You are just in time to have a last drink with the others. Gwen's put the kettle on for apple cider before Amy and Dave head off."

* * *

Jo was right. Amy and Dave left after warming their insides, Rob in tow. The sound of the car engine faded as Dave took a left turn at the end of the street.

"I worry about that boy," Gwen said, referring to Rob as she seated herself comfortably in the lounge with Fiona.

Rob had mentioned to Dave over lunch that he planned to meet up with a few old college buddies for a drinking session after the compulsory family activities were finished. Unfortunately for his mother's peace, she had been within hearing range of the passing comment.

Fiona leaned across the divide between couches and grasped her mother's hand.

"He'll be alright, Mom. I've always believed God has a hand on him – no matter how he fights against it."

"I pray so, dear."

"Is it silly that that is already a concern I have for John? And I suppose Ann ought to be considered, too! I don't want them to end up with the wrong crowd."

"Johnnie seemed pretty excited about the trip you took him on this afternoon. I think he is another we can say God has His hand on."

"Yes, isn't it incredible? I simply cannot find the words to express the joy I have knowing God has chosen my boy for something special."

"Jo mentioned you ended up at the pastor's house. I wasn't aware you knew George and Mary?"

"I didn't. It was incredible. He led me there, Mom! Pastor – George, did you say? He did tell me – anyway, he was there waiting for me. He told me I was an answer to their prayers! I never thought God would use me in such a way!"

"Fiona, it isn't only Johnnie He has chosen; He has picked you, too. Only consider what you have just shared," Lance said, coming in with Jo from washing the dishes.

The excitement left Fiona's face as she turned and nodded.

"I'm beginning to see that and it scares me. I don't know what He will ask of me and I fear it will be more than I can handle."

"Do you know what I have come back to over and over again since . . . Over the last couple of years?" Lance asked.

"No?"

Fiona waited in hope for a piece of information, which would bring revelation.

"The words of Mr E.M. Forster. I think they might relate to your sense of restlessness. He said: "We must be willing to let go of the life we have planned, so as to have the life that is waiting for us". The split from Amanda has me made me wrestle with disappointed hopes and my own shortcomings. And it's been hard! Hard to let it all go and yet I know I must. My question to you is what plans have you made? Once you're aware of them, you can release them into God's care."

As much as Fiona felt privileged to be given her brother's confidence, his words left her unsettled. Apprehension grew within her as night descended upon them. It was the strangest, most fearfully wonderful Christmas she had lived through.

* * *

Once in bed, Fiona rolled over to face her husband.

"Jo?" she asked tentatively.

"Mmm?"

"Do you think Lance is right? Do you think I must let go of my plans; that God has something else in store for me?"

Jo propped himself up on his elbows and looked directly at her. "I think it might be a case of waiting to see. You can't change anything, or gain any clues, by worrying about it."

"Yes, I know, it's only – it scares me."

It had been a long time since she had allowed Jo to glimpse what she perceived as weakness.

"I wasn't sure where the events of the past few weeks were leading us and it has given me no little anxiety myself," Jo admitted. "That is: until I saw you venture bravely out today. My heart swelled! I was as nervous as a beetle standing beside an elephant for you – but ever so proud."

She gave a half smile at his use of their long-standing elephant joke before asking: "It doesn't bother you?"

"No."

He pulled her close.

"I only had to look at your face this afternoon as you recounted the story to Gwen and Lance to see the joy you have found in God," he whispered into her ear. "I have no idea where it might take us, but you can be assured I won't allow you to face it alone."

He shifted her slightly to fit the curve of his body.

Fiona wrapped his arms around her more tightly and held them close.

Thank you, Father, for giving me such a wonderful and loving husband. Please let him continue as he has professed. Let him join this high speed ride with me. Keep us together through all you have in store.

She felt safe in Jo's arms and confident that, by his side, she could face (almost) anything.

* * *

In the room at the opposing end of the top floor, Lance lacked the comfort his sister had found. He was pleased Fiona was exploring her faith, being drawn closer to God; he was just frustrated the same didn't hold true for his life.

He had experienced a deep closeness to God for the complete length of his stay in South Africa. In that season he had heard God's quiet voice constantly whispering in his ear. In contrast, his time in Fiona's house seemed void of time with God. It was as if the Almighty had forsaken him in favour of his sister; leaving Lance alone, abandoned.

Lance listened in the stillness of his room for a whisper, a hint, a sign of God's presence.

The oppressive silence held.

God seemed to be a tantalisingly hand's span out of reach. Lance would sense a call to stop and listen, only to be met by silence when he obeyed. As a result, his prayer life was suffering. It was hard to be motivated to pray when there was no guiding voice. Prayer had become a matter of listing the names of his friends and family, ticking a mental checklist, and moving on with his day. His mind had become blocked to intercessory prayer.

In contrast, he entreated God almost constantly for his own emotional wellbeing, resembling a song placed on "repeat". This only added a sense of guilt to his burden.

Bring me close to you again. I cry out with the psalmists to be heard and not left here in my distress.

I am helpless without you. I need you beside me. I need to hear your voice; I need your guidance; I need to see your presence beside me. I miss being close to you.

It is hard to wait on you when I cannot see you, or feel you, or hear you. How can I have such confidence that you have a promise to give me and yet hear no words?

Lance's plea was met by further silence.

CHAPTER 12

"I've been thinking about what you said a few weeks back."

"Oh? What did I say?" Lance responded, closing his book.

The Christmas tree and stockings had been packed away for another year and the sky outside was darkening, although it was only early in the afternoon. Fiona was sitting on the floor sorting a load of washing whilst Lance kept her company from the couch.

"It was after I went to the pastor's house that first time with Johnnie. You said it wasn't only John He is calling; that He has a purpose for me, too."

"Of course He does! I stand by my original words."

Fiona smiled.

"That's what I wanted to say: I think you are right."

"Go on. Tell me what has brought on this conviction; although, I can't pretend I doubted it," Lance smiled cheekily.

"Have you ever had a time where everything you listen to seems to be directed specifically at you? God seems to be using every medium at His disposal; lyrics in songs, a chat with a friend, the words in a book, a whole sermon . . . All of which seem solely meant for me. It is an utter thrill to be hearing Him again!"

Jo came quietly into the room and knelt beside his wife.

"Is there anything you can share about what He has been speaking?" Lance asked. "If you want more time to mull it over alone, I understand. Please don't feel compelled to share."

"Oh, I would love to! Only . . . there isn't much to share. It's hardly ground-breaking stuff. More small encouragements, such as: I am wanted, I am loved, I am valuable, I am worth it . . ."

"Not ground breaking, but definitely necessary!"

"Yes. Although – never mind."

"No, what?"

"I feel guilty because I can't help wishing (as beautiful as His encouragement is), that He would give me a direction to move in. If He is calling me to a life other than the one I have planned . . . doesn't He need to let me in on it at some point?"

Jo gave her shoulder a gentle squeeze.

Lance breathed in deeply. His sister's words reverberated with his own desires:

Direction. Guidance. Action.

Wasn't that what he wanted? He was struggling to be content with simply resting and refreshing himself in the Lord. The words echoed across his mind once more:

"Blessed is the man who walks not in the counsel of the wicked, nor stands in the way of sinners, nor sits in the seat of scoffers; but his delight is in the law of the LORD, and on his law he meditates day and night. He is like a tree planted by streams of water that yields its fruit in its season, and its leaf does not wither. In all that he does, he prospers." [8]

"It's okay to wait," Jo spoke into the silence. "Remember we are only a few weeks out from Christmas and already you have requested to become a member of the church, agreed to help out with the weekly food distribution project, and have signed us up for morning tea roster! Not to mention that we've had two dinners with George and Mary, with a third planned, and each has provided us with more food for thought than food to eat!"

"I suppose you are right," she replied, even though her heart did not agree with the concession.

Perhaps Jo was right, she thought as she mulled on his words. Perhaps God didn't want her to be involved in more activities. Perhaps. Nevertheless, she knew He was calling her name and she was itching to see where the call would lead her.

PART 2 – SPRING'S THAW

"Heal me, O LORD, and I shall be healed; save me, and I shall be saved, for you are my praise". (Jeremiah 17:14)

CHAPTER 1

As January shifted into February and February into March, neither Fiona nor Lance received further instructions from the Lord. Lance became so much a part of the McCarthy family that both Fiona and Jo could not remember a time without Lance's presence at meal times, or being greeted cheerfully by him of a morning with a welcome offering of fresh, hot coffee.

Lance tried to be faithful to his conviction that he needed to rest in God. He tried to be patient when he could detect little sign of restoration, longing to see the fruit of God's healing in his life.

With the passing of months his silent discontent grew into an urgent desire for action and, with continued inactivity, came frustration.

How could one rest in God's presence if one did not sense it?

He fluctuated between discontentment, impassioned pursuit of God, and apathy. He could read the Bible for hours one day, only to leave it untouched for the whole of the following week. The pages of his journal remained blank and he began to suspect he had missed his boat. Surely God would have called to him by now?

Lance spent little time alone. He threw himself into the role of doting uncle. For his sister, he assumed the role of house cleaner extraordinaire. He continued his early morning runs, enjoying lighter skies as the days slowly began to lengthen.

And at length, with the leisurely shift of seasons, Lance noticed that a shift in his perspective had also occurred. He did not understand how God had brought it about and yet the change was evident.

Lance first noticed the shift when in the company of Ann and Johnnie in Central Park. He had taken charge of the young ones to give Fiona a well deserved break.

"Bye, Mommy!" Ann called out the car window as Lance delivered

Fiona outside the coffee shop where she was to meet Gwen.

"Bye, my darlings. Make sure you behave yourself for Uncle Lance."

They nodded their assent and Lance waved as he pulled the car out from the curb and continued on to find a car park.

Walking the short distance from the parking garage to the park involved all his concentration with Johnnie eagerly tugging his left arm forward, and Ann's small steps struggling to keep pace on his right.

Stepping up onto the pavement bordering the park, Johnnie's attention was immediately seized by the hot dog vendor wearing a gimmicky costume. Meanwhile, Ann wandered over to the trees, trying to catch, or pat, the pigeons – Lance wasn't sure which one.

"How does Fi do this?" Lance wondered aloud to no one in particular.

He promised Johnnie that hot dogs would be considered when it was time for lunch. After which, taking hold of Ann's hand, he led the trio down onto a patch of the Park Green.

The park still bore winter's toll. The landscape glared back at them, bleak brown. The trees, presently barren of leaves and snow alike, stood out in stark contrast against a radiant blue sky. Standing proudly above them, the sun valiantly emitted gentle rays as it fought back against winter's lingering chill.

"Uncle Wannie, will you play dolls with me?"

"No – you said we could play soccer! You are always playing with her silly dolls!"

"Stop squabbling, or I will plonk myself down and not budge!" Lance imitated Johnnie's whining and sat down on the grass with arms folded and lip pouting to demonstrate his point.

Ann started giggling; Johnnie tugged on his arm.

"Come on, Uncle Lance! Come. You can play dolls in a little bit."

"Are you okay if I play with John for a bit first, Ann?"

Ann, who had began making motions with her two dolls, nodded absently, and Lance engaged in a game of soccer with John, regularly glancing over at Ann.

Half an hour later, Lance disengaged himself from the kicking practise. He had developed a light sweat from chasing after the straying ball.

Johnnie went to take his comic book out of their Elmo bag.

Lance, who had been moving towards Ann, stopped like a statue. He stood transfixed as she began to hum the "Bridal March".

Watching the delight on Ann's face as the dolls partook of a wedding ceremony, Lance realised his heart was full of gladness. No painful constrictions seized his chest. No bitter memories reared in his mind.

Restoration.

God had promised it, and here he saw it happening.

I don't know when you set to work on my heart, God, but I see you have been busy.

You are a mystery to me. I thank you.

He remained in his trance, giving contemplation to his heart.

How could this be? He could not understand how the anger, resentment and sorrow had become detached from marriage. Whilst he continued to harbour pain from his own failed relationship, he could finally look upon a marriage ceremony as a beautiful event, separate to his own pain.

Ann became aware of his gaze. The busy dolls stopped their activities.

"You can play the husband if you like, Uncle Wannie."

Ann stretched out the doll to him.

"Thank you."

Please, merciful Father, do not let Ann ever experience the sorrow and pain of a broken marriage. Protect her heart and spirit from the brokenness I have experienced and have in turn caused. May she only know joy and love in marriage.

Lance saw anew the joy of marriage as he joined in Ann's imaginary play and saw the hope she envisioned for it.

A further game of soccer was squeezed in before lunch and this time Ann joined in with the boys. Johnnie, out of brotherly consideration, became less energetic with his kicking foot.

Lance smiled as Johnnie became head coach and started teaching Ann how to kick.

After the children wearied of the game, Lance spoiled them to hot dogs for lunch (he had to finish half of Ann's), and, an hour later, after a horse and carriage ride, he bought them both a rainbow ice-cream. Sugary goodness in hand, they walked, tired and content, through the tree-lined path, as they headed back to the car park and from there to collect Fiona.

* * *

Gwen greeted her children warmly with a kiss as they entered her home the following day. They took seats on the kitchen stools whilst she finished slicing a red onion for the salad.

"The place looks good! You've outdone yourself," Fiona told her brother, looking at the recently painted walls.

"Yes, thank you, Lance! Although, I think we will eat on the back porch today . . ." she said in reference to the lingering smell of fresh paint.

Fiona carried the salad; Lance, the utensils and plates; and Gwen, her famous honey-glazed chicken wings.

"This lunch is all about you," Gwen told her son as they seated themselves around the circular table.

"Me? Why – what did I do?"

"Don't be silly! We had a thorough catch up over coffee yesterday – thanks to you – and now we want to hear how you have been going."

"What can I say, other than: Fiona is a regular taskmaster and keeps me on my toes," Lance winked at his sister.

"What about emotionally? Even if you men aren't partial to talking about it, you need to. Keeping it contained inside is not healthy," Gwen said.

A pale shade of pink broke forth on Fiona's cheeks. Notwithstanding the fact that Lance had been one of a dozen topics discussed over their chai lattes, she had hoped her mother would raise the subject with a faint show of delicacy.

"Amanda?" Lance questioned.

He dished two scoops of salad on to his plate.

"To be honest, I hadn't been thinking much on the subject for the past couple of months. Not since the trip – it hurt too much; all the bitterness, regret and anger – until yesterday when I saw that God has already visited where I dared not go. He's workmanship is incredible!"

Lance proceeded to share the journey of restoration he had been travelling.

"He gave me a promise . . . I saw a picture of a tree soaking up nutrients from the stream of life. There is healing in His words. That is what I have been doing for three months: pressing into His Word. I clung to the verse He gave me, telling me to delight in his Law, meditate on it, and He will make me a tree by the stream of life."

"I've heard that before. Where is it from?" Fiona interrupted.

"Psalm one: verses one to three."

"Right, sorry, go on."

"That's it – in short. I didn't realise that during all the time I spent reading His Word, He was also letting the poison seep out of old wounds. I am not saying the healing is finished; just that God has cleaned the wound and laid it bare to fresh air."

"Praise God, my darling, I have been praying for that!"

"My Mom – the Prayer Warrior. Thank you."

Lance truly was thankful to have two such faithful women in his life. He needed their prayers.

However, the strength of his gratitude towards mother and sister alike was to be tested three nights later.

* * *

Fiona invited her mother out for dinner on the Friday night so that she could spend time with her grandchildren. Gwen had requested to bring a woman from the church as Genevieve was new in town and Gwen wanted to help welcome her into the church family.

Introductions were made when Genevieve arrived; after which, Gwen asked her son to take their guest into the lounge room, whilst she remained the kitchen on the narrow pretence of helping Fiona with the dishes whilst they waited for Jo to arrive home from work.

"So . . . What brings you to the Big City?" Lance asked, outwardly polite. Inwardly he was praying for God's patience. It had been a long time since he was the focus of his mother's match-making and yet the years had not increased her subtlety.

"Work – essentially. I work in design and retail. The past six years I have been stationed in London . . ."

Lance detachedly surveyed Genevieve as she talked. She was well-dressed in a black skirt and cream, silk blouse, with each strand of her short blonde hair sitting neatly in place. The shabby couches and toy-strewn floor contrasted vividly with her manicured person, making her appear out of place in her surroundings.

" . . . when my boss opened a boutique in New York City I took the opportunity to come back home," she ended.

"Had enough of London?"

Lance, sitting on the opposing couch, was wearing jeans and a plain, black polo shirt. He fought a slight smile at an imagined picture of how Genevieve would look when entering the local family restaurant "A County Pig" later on in the evening.

"No, I don't think so," she replied thoughtfully. "I have committed a year to the New York boutique as it establishes itself, after which . . . who knows?"

"And what will that involve – establishing a store?"

"America has a different taste to London, and indeed Europe; therefore, we have the tricky task of trying to keep our British flavour whilst tailoring it to the American perception of what British design should look like. Our clientele group is high-end; business women, wives of influential men, the wealthy . . ."

"Do you design clothes, too?"

"A little. I'm mainly involved in marketing and research. At least half of my time is spent in meetings with potential clients, organisers of industry events, and our design team. It's essential to keep abreast of market trends so we know where to direct our energy."

"Sounds full-on!"

"It can be. What about you? Your mother mentioned a trip to South Africa, recently?"

"Yes; about two, nearly three, months ago."

"Oh, right. Personally, I think I would be a bit hesitant to go; although I would love to get to their fashion week. I think it would be fascinating; their style is always bright, creative and unique. How did you find the country? Did you feel quite safe?"

Lance settled further back into the couch as he relaxed.

"Yes and no. I mean: there are obvious issues there, but to think we don't have our own here in America is laughable. It is a beautiful country and, whilst I won't try to hide its faults, they certainly wouldn't stop me from returning."

"Hang on! I have wanted to hear that part of your trip, too." Gwen had stuck her head through the doorway, tea towel and a wooden spoon in hand. "I prohibit the continuation of this conversation until I am with you!"

"Next question?" Lance smiled at Genevieve, whilst silently irked at the evident eavesdropping going on from the kitchen.

God, please help me to walk in love!

Genevieve's attention was soon apprehended by Johnnie, who bore her off to watch him ride his tricycle around the back lawn. Lance went back into the kitchen with Gwen and Fiona until they finished the dishes, after which the three moved out into the sunroom.

Fiona called Johnnie away to change, relinquishing Genevieve of her duty.

Fiona rejoined them with the children a few moments before Jo. Ann was dressed in a purple frilly dress, and Johnnie in a smart, collared shirt and breeches.

Lance assumed Johnnie's placid behaviour was the result of a strict lecture from Fiona. All the same, when Jo arrived, Johnnie raced forward to greet him, Ann trailing in his wake. Picking one up in each arm he swung them around, placed them back down, and ended by giving each a kiss and quick hug as he did so.

"Rug rats!" he exclaimed fondly.

Jo was introduced to their guest before he packed his family into the car to drive to "A County Pig". Lance followed with Gwen and Genevieve.

The restaurant was an established family favourite. The grey stone building was designed to emanate an old country homestead. The inside was dimly lit; the atmosphere jovial. Families sat chatting across wooden tables whilst children ran back and forth from the outside playground.

Décor had been kept to a minimum; an American flag hung on one wall, chequered curtains had been drawn back from the windows, and disposable green paper placemats sat upon the tables.

"Okay, Lance, now you can share with all of us about your perception of South Africa," Gwen instructed as their starter plates of buffalo wings and cheese sticks were delivered by the waitress, who was dressed in an all-green outfit complete with leprechaun hat for the coming St Patrick's Day.

"We were talking about security in South Africa before you came home," Fiona explained to her husband.

"Right," he acknowledged her inclusion of him.

"To be honest," Lance started, "I fell in love with the country. There were times when I was given openly hostile looks – the colour of my skin being enough to condemn me – but they were minimal. Mind you, I didn't leave the Cape, which was reportedly one of the more integrated of the main cities during Apartheid. And I didn't visit any townships, which are where lack of job availability and close living quarters lead to some trouble."

To Genevieve he added: "I was based in St James, which is a beach-side town close to the city of Cape Town."

As he continued to share, Lance contemplated the drawing force South Africa continued to excerpt on him. It had become an automated response to say he loved his time in Africa; that he had fallen in love with its most southern nation. Whilst this was true, the hold was not of a superficial nature; he had felt a connection with the land and its people. There was pain and bitterness, festering wounds, and hardship; and yet, in seeming contrast, there was an inextinguishable hope throbbing under the surface.

Perhaps that was why he had loved the land. Perhaps, if he went back, it would not be the same. Perhaps it had simply called to him at time when their seasons aligned.

Both Jo and Lance had ordered prime rib steaks, which stole their attention upon delivery. The women smoothly upheld a steady flow of talk, and if each topic seemed to boomerang back to Genevieve, Lance chose not to notice.

The children received small ice-creams as part of their meal-deal and the family headed off once these dessert bowls had been emptied.

When Gwen invited Genevieve in for a coffee, Lance offered to bath the children and tuck them into their beds. He lingered over story time, judged it late enough not to return downstairs, and softly entered into the sanctuary of his bedroom.

* * *

When Genevieve took leave, Fiona went upstairs and gently tapped on Lance's door and was bid to enter. She did not appear surprised that he was awake, lying on top of his bed covers, reading .

"I'm sorry. I didn't mean to upset you," she said repentantly.

"Why would I be upset?" he returned, sitting up. "I'm sorry if I wasn't polite, it's just that I've been surrounded by people this week and I had kind of hoped for a quiet night out with Mom. I hadn't known we would be entertaining company."

"I'm your sister, remember? You can't fob me off with such shams! I truly am sorry. We sprang Genevieve on you without warning. I thought you wouldn't mind; that some company might help you –"

"– move on?" Lance finished.

"Sorry."

Lance shook his head to ward off the apology.

"It's like – you don't let a bruise heal by poking it," he tried to explain. "You protect it and give it the time it needs to heal. Only once it's healed do you return to using it normally. That's how it is with my heart; in time, I will start using it again."

"I understand. It's only . . . you've mentioned a Tammy a couple of times which led us to think perhaps you were getting ready to move on . . ."

"Tammy? Tammy . . ." Lance turned the name over thoughtfully.

"Not Tanya?" he questioned suddenly.

"Yes, that's the name."

"That's what I had thought, too," Gwen added. She had silently entered the room, stepping around Fiona, who sat leaning against the door frame, and joined Lance on the bed.

"You too? What did you think?" he asked.

"I thought Tammy signalled . . ." she trailed off, looking at her son.

Lance tried to remember an incidence involving both his mother and sister, about South Africa, where Tanya's name may have come up. His memory was blank.

"Tanya? Did I mention her on the phone in S.A.?" he queried.

"No. You've talked about her here, since you've been home," Gwen answered.

"Tanya?" Lance repeated.

Fiona was trying hard to hold back a bubble of laughter as she watched her mother and brother try valiantly to sort out their mutual confusion.

"Yes, Tanya. Look, it doesn't matter," Fiona interjected, having determined it to be time to intervene. "The only reason I brought her up was because that is why we thought you may have been ready to start meeting some of our more – available – acquaintances. I guess Mom and I both read more into this South African girl than there was to it."

"Australian."

"Sorry?"

"She was from Australia."

Lance saw a baffled look on his sister's face.

"It doesn't matter," he said hastily. "And it's okay – don't worry about it."

Despite his words, his mother and sister did worry about it.

* * *

Gwen joined Fiona for another pot of coffee, leaving Lance to prepare for bed. They shared their night time respite at the kitchen table, away from the stairwell, so as not to disturb the slumber of those upstairs.

"I hope he isn't upset by it," Gwen steered them back to Lance. He seemed to have unwittingly become one of their favourite topics of conjecture.

"I think he understands we only had his best interests at heart," Fiona reassured her.

"Who do you think Tanya was?"

"I don't know. By the sounds of it she may have only been a friend, or acquaintance. Maybe she was part of the business contingent."

"Yes, you are probably right. And yet . . . I was sure he had formed some type of connection to her."

"If he did, let us hope it helped his healing process. I didn't realise how deeply he was injured by the divorce. I knew it affected him, particularly at the start, but it has been well over a year –"

"I know. I guess neither of us can actually relate with what he is going through. I can't imagine the pain which must come when one tears themself from their spouse. There is a reason that the Lord declares: **"what God has joined together, man must never separate"** [9]. Let us pray that God helps him through this time . . ."

* * *

Meanwhile, Lance stood brushing his teeth before the mirror wondering when he had mentioned Tanya. He certainly hadn't been aware of it; in fact, he couldn't remember thinking about her since his return. However, now she had been recalled to mind, he couldn't help missing their easy conversations. He also missed her enthusiastic ways and ready laugh.

You're a fool, he told himself. Who was he to be thinking of someone so untainted by life, whilst still grieving his divorce? It would bring him no benefit.

Lord, keep me safe from burying my pain a second time. It would be easier to do as Fiona believes and simply "move on". However, I know that such a course would not solve anything. I certainly do not want to hurry into a relationship before I am ready. The harm I have done to myself would still be sitting there: simmering away under the surface, waiting to boil over.

Lance walked back to his room and slumped down by a sudden onset of longing.

Oh God, this is a lonely place! All the arguments of your eternal love do not shut out the emptiness inside when I consider that I may never know the joys of partnership again.

Please protect me against these longings, brought on by loneliness. May my focus solely be on you and your desired path for my life. Teach me your ways and keep me safe in your love.

The ache remained as he switched off the bedroom light and tumbled into bed.

CHAPTER 2

"Lance, do you have any set plans coming up?" Fiona queried as they sat with Jo on a park bench, watching the children joyfully climbing on the playground.

"No. Why? Is this the polite "you've overstayed your welcome" speech? If it is, I totally understand."

"No, of course not! Actually, it's exactly the opposite. Jo and I were wondering if you would be interested in extending your stay here for, oh, let's see, six months?"

"Six months? Fi, I love being here – don't get me wrong – it's just: I am really hoping God will give me some form of direction before then!"

"Still, would you think about it for us?"

"Okay, I will honestly consider it. So, why do you need me to stay?" Trying to think of a reason, he exclaimed excitedly: "You're not pregnant again, are you?"

"No! – Jo, did you want to share the news?"

Jo gestured for his wife to continue as Lance waited in perplexed expectation.

"We're going to Australia!"

"Australia?"

Fiona nodded.

"We leave in three weeks," she added.

"What? Why?"

"Jo's job. He was offered a short-term transfer and the timing fits in well with the children; their schooling won't be interrupted and John, at least, is old enough to appreciate a different place and culture."

"We prayed about it and Fiona felt a peace from God," Jo said with a smile at his wife.

"Wow! I mean – congratulations! What an opportunity for you and the children . . . they will have a wonderful experience."

"Yes, we hope so."

Lance remained silent as he tried to absorb the news.

"Which is why we need a house-minder," Jo added. "We figured it would be easiest to ask you."

"I will think about, I promise, but no guarantees."

Lance felt a lull in his spirits. Surely God wanted more from him than to play house-minder? He was pleased for his sister; and yet, he could not repulse the thought that God was giving her all he desired – closeness to Him, a chance to combine faith and travel, purpose . . .

He wistfully wished he was the one going. Fiona had a beautiful family and a blossoming faith whilst he was trapped in idleness and (soon), isolation.

When will my time come, Lord? Is this the consequence of my choices? What of your forgiveness? Will I always carry this loneliness within me as the result of the choice to walk away from my marriage? What about Amanda? Does she also live with this heartache?

Lance prayed about Fiona's request knowing that, if he accepted, he would be faced with greater loneliness than he had hitherto experienced.

* * *

Fiona looked out of the window as the plane approached their destination. The sea was calm beneath them; its vastness was all she could see.

It was difficult to believe the little map on her personal television screen, which showed that in less than an hour they would touch down at Sydney Airport, where they would complete customs prior to boarding a second plane to Brisbane, their new home.

There were those butterflies again!

Glancing across the aisle, she smiled at Jo, who was sitting beside their sleeping son. Soon Johnnie would be up and clambering for her seat by the window to watch the landing. She couldn't help smiling.

Ann was with her, sleeping soundly like her brother. Fiona was grateful the children were getting some sleep. They would have some challenging days ahead as they searched for a new home, a school for Johnnie, and a church, not to mention the task of establishing new friendships.

You asked me to give up my plans; asked that I trust in you. Here I am; I have done that. Please be faithful. Please take care of us, particularly the children. Even if this is a difficult transition for us, I believe it is your will and that gives me confidence. Continue to be our confidence.

"Mom, Mom, can I look out the window?"

Ann stirred beside her as Johnnie jostled to climb past.

"Okay, hang on! Give your sister a chance to wake up," she shooed her son back into the isle. "There isn't anything to see at the moment."

Fiona helped her daughter to sit up, before making her way past into the isle, allowing her son to duck into the vacated window seat.

"Make sure you allow Ann to look out, too, if she wants to," Fiona instructed.

"Come on, Annie. You can come up onto my lap. You will be able to see better."

Fiona glowed with pride. That was her boy! She tried to engrave the beautiful moment into her memory. Perhaps she would regale her grandchildren with the image one day . . .

"Put the brakes on!"

An hour later, Johnnie's scream broke into the silence of the cabin at the sudden deceleration after an otherwise smooth landing had startled him.

The surrounding passengers glanced around, laughing at his out-burst. A beaming smile broke on Johnnie's face.

"Why is everyone laughing?" he asked his mum.

Fiona was lost for words.

"It's alright, son. Next time we will put you up with the pilot," Jo assured him, smiling fondly at his son across the aisle.

Johnnie beamed back and squeezed his little sister's hand.

"We're here, Annie!"

* * *

Jo commenced work in his new position within eight days of their arrival, leaving Fiona to look to the domestic arrangements.

Fiona was struggling with the stress. With an initial stay of six months they had decided that they didn't require an ideal house, merely a reasonable one. It had to have three bedrooms, be close to Jo's work, and have a weekly rental price within what his company subsidised.

Jo partook of the house hunting during their first week in Brisbane and that had been their sole focus. Unfortunately, they hadn't found anything suitable with a six month tenancy contract.

At the end of their second week in Australia, Fiona came to tears. The children had been put to bed in the adjoining room of their hotel suite. She sat on a plush single seater lounge chair, wine glass in hand.

Jo came and knelt down before her.

"Honey, it's okay. There is no rush to find a rental. If we don't find one this week, we shall simply continue in the hotel until we do. Don't worry!"

"I know! I know! I just keep thinking how hard it will be for the children to settle down; the longer it takes to find a house and a kindy, the longer it will be until they can adjust."

Fiona's selflessness moved her husband. He looked upon her with tender adoration and respect; a woman who had given up friends and family in a hair's breadth of time to allow him this opportunity and her only concern was for their children.

"God will provide," he reassured her. "He promised us He would. We need to trust in His promise."

Fiona knew he was right. Only, she wanted to see how God was going to fulfil His promise. She knew her fretting wouldn't stop until she had seen His provision. Did that make her unfaithful and distrusting? Great, she thought, all she needed was to add guilt to her already frayed nerves!

Jo grasped her hands in his own and brought them to his lips.

"You know what? I'm going to ring and cancel our first house inspection for tomorrow morning."

"What?" Fiona asked, glancing up.

"We can rearrange it for the afternoon and it will free up the morning for church. That was one of the important items on your to-do list before we left: find a new church, A.S.A.P."

"Yes, which we can't do until we've found a place!"

"Nonsense! We don't have to stay at a church because we visit it!"

Faithful to his word, Jo began altering their arrangements. Once he had called the real estate agent he rang down to reception to investigate whether they could recommend a local church.

The receptionist found a church half an hour's drive away, which would be close to their scheduled house-inspections. Leading his family into a pew the next morning, he estimated the large hall to have the capacity to seat one thousand. Given the bodies already seated he guessed there were roughly nine hundred in attendance at what was the second service of the morning.

Jo had been impressed by the church though he was loath to admit it. In general, he preferred small churches with a congregation not surpassing a maximum of a hundred members; nevertheless, he sensed that the large Baptist community managed to create the same family-like bond, sharing together in times of both joy and hardship, whether on a Sunday morning, or at midnight on a Wednesday.

Jo was glad they had made the sacrifice to attend worship. He squeezed Fiona's hand as they met in the morning tea area, hoping she felt the same way; she deserved a reprieve from the tension.

She did.

* * *

Fiona couldn't comment on the preaching, having accompanied her children out to Sunday school and stayed with Ann. She was, however, aware of a warm atmosphere of fellowship, and had been impressed by the devotion they gave to their children's ministry.

An expectant mother reached out and gently touched Fiona's arm as she left the crèche with Ann in tow.

"Hi, I don't believe we've met?"

"No. No, we haven't. I'm Fiona."

"Nice to meet you. I'm Diana. Are you here visiting?"

"Sort of – actually, my husband and I have just moved from America."

"Oh, lovely! I could hear you have an accent."

Fiona smiled.

"Will you be staying for a cup of tea? I'll come over with you," the expectant mother continued.

"That would be lovely, thank you. I need to collect my son first, though."

"Okay. What will you have: tea, coffee . . . ? I'll fight the crowd while you find him . . ."

Fiona proceeded down the corridor from the crèche to the Sunday school area. John was full of excited banter about his new friend, Tommy, and their morning activities. He proudly displayed a mobile of stars – they had been learning about the first day of creation.

Tommy's mother was going to move outside with a few others supervising their children on the playground and offered to watch Johnnie whilst Fiona socialised indoors. Thanking her profusely, Fiona went back out to the church fellowship area with Ann beside her.

Looking around through the crowd, Fiona spotted Diana coming towards her holding two mugs of hot tea.

"Thank you! I'm impressed you were able to navigate the maze of bodies with such ease!"

"Believe it or not, it gets easier with the added bulk," Diana chuckled, patting her stomach. "The seas part before me; the power of a pregnant woman, I suppose."

"Yes, I had the same treatment! I suppose we must receive some perks during the nine months of waiting. Is this your first?"

"Is it that obvious?"

"No, no I didn't mean anything . . .!"

"Sorry, I was just kidding. I shouldn't joke about it. Perhaps I can blame my inexcusable and unwelcoming behaviour on the hormones?"

"Of course you can. Blame away!" she replied, feeling herself relax.

Fiona liked the young woman. She had a humble smile and loving eyes. Fiona felt certain Diana would make a fine mother.

"Have you bought in the area?" Diana enquired.

"Oh no, we aren't planning on staying. Jo, my husband, has a six month exchange contract. Unfortunately, that doesn't mean we escape house hunting – we are currently trying to find a place to rent . . ."

Jo came over and was introduced to Diana before shuffling his wife out to their first appointment of the day.

* * *

Four houses later, Fiona longed to join in with the children's disheartened melodies and whining shows of impatience. Her spirits had soared with the warmth she had felt at the church. How could her mood have dropped down again in such a short space of time?

What she wouldn't give at times to be fifteen again with the cares of a young woman worrying about sport, careers and boys; now it was houses, children and a new country.

Oh God! A new country. No friends. No family. Two children and a husband – but no home, no connections, and no school for John.

"You have a family. You have a home."

Yes, God, and the last time I looked this wasn't it! Where are they? Back in America! How is that supposed to help me?

We never realise what we rely on until it is taken from us. I can finally see what a blessing it was to be able to call up Mom for advice, or my friends when I needed a pick-me up, and just recently with Lance living with us . . .

God, I think we made a mistake moving here. I was the one pushing for it. Did I hear you wrong?

"We need to go back to the hotel," Fiona directed suddenly.

"Darling, we're nearly there. I appreciate that you are tired, and that the kids have been tired since the second house, but we're nearly done for the day. Maybe this one will be the right one."

"I know Jo, but, please, we need to go back to the hotel. I can't do this."

Jo pulled the car over to the side of the road, and turned off the ignition.

"Are you serious, Fi?"

"Yes. Let's go back and call it a day. Please? It sounds absurd, I know, I just have this freezing sensation about going to the next place."

"Okay. Okay, we'll go back."

"We're going home?" Johnnie asked.

"No sweetheart, not home." Fiona was on the edge of tears, overwhelmed by the need to go back to the hotel and out of the car.

"Yes, son, we're going back to the hotel," Jo said calmly.

Jo looked at his wife in utter bewilderment. Nevertheless, he called the real estate agent to apprise him of the change, before turning the key again and starting their trip back to the hotel.

When they arrived at the hotel, the children were unusually subdued and stayed close to Jo. They could sense there was something wrong with their mother and it scared them. Jo looked worried.

"Can you take them to the park? Please?" Fiona beseeched Jo. An urgent impulse to be alone and pray had overtaken her. She began to wring her hands, frantic to get back to their rooms.

"Okay, yes, of course. Only you have to promise me you are going to be okay on your own . . ."

"I promise. I can't explain it now. I'm not losing my mind! I just have this overriding need to be alone. I think I need to seek out God."

"Alright. Well, you call me if you need anything. We won't go far."

"Thank you."

Kissing the top of her head, Jo unpacked the stroller in case Ann had to rest on the way back, and informed the children that they were going to the park.

"Is Mommy okay?" Ann asked, apprehension showing through in her soft voice.

"Yes, Annie. Mommy will be fine. She's gone to ask God some questions, that's all."

"She isn't in trouble with God, is she?"

"No, she isn't in trouble with Him. In fact, she is very much in His favour and He has asked to have some time alone with Mommy. That's why God is treating us to a trip to the park: so He can talk to Mommy."

"Oh! Mommy is special."

"Yes, Mommy is special."

Jo thought his daughter was probably more right than she could comprehend. He was baffled by the special relationship his wife seemed to have found with God. It left him in wonderment.

* * *

Fiona's skin registered the warmth of the hotel foyer as she walked through the glass, automated doors. She was strangely more aware of her surrounding as she crossed the polished marble tiles. The cool steel of the elevator frame proved a calming sensation as she ran her fingers across and pressed the button.

"Ding."

The lift arrived and the doors swung open. Stepping inside she leaned back against the rail and waited as it slowly began its ascent.

Fiona's nerves were set on edge as the lift jarred to a halt on the fifth floor. The doors opened to an empty hall.

She pressed the button to close the doors. Only ten more floors to go.

God?

What was she meant to do? When she arrived at the room . . . then what?

The ascent was starting to make her nauseous.

Was this a bad idea? What did God want from her?

The doors parted again at the fifteenth floor. The carpet beneath her feet made her stockings rub against her shoes in a way resembling gritty chalk. She ground her teeth.

Striding purposefully towards her door, she jiggled the key card and pushed down the handle.

Well, now, or never.

Stepping inside, the heavy door swung shut behind her. Fiona remained barely inside the threshold, alone in the room.

No flash of lightning. No loud, quaking voice.

God?

It was a tentative question. Fiona wasn't sure whether she wanted God to turn up. What was she expecting? Lightning bolts in the hotel room? Who was she kidding?

All that anxiety for . . . what? All she had found was an eerily quiet room and an easing of anxiety. She certainly would look the fool when Jo came back with the children.

* * *

Jo walked into the room to be met by his wife's tear stained face peeping up from between her hands.

"Fiona?"

Wiping her eyes, Fiona attempted a smile and welcomed Ann into her arms.

"I'm fine – honestly! – simply tired and a little stressed," she reassured her husband.

"How was your time with God?" Johnnie asked curiously.

Fiona looked over at him. "Sorry, darling?"

"Daddy said you were special and God wanted some alone time, just with you."

"Did he now?" A genuine smile lit her face. "Well, He did want some time with me, except we didn't have any adventures this time. We just sat quietly together, in silence."

"Oh."

Johnnie lost interest and went to turn on the television.

The children occupied, Jo went over to comfort his wife and pry out of her what had truly caused the tears.

"Look at me, beautiful. What's happened? It appears to be more than a little tiredness."

Closing her eyes, she leaned her head onto his shoulder as he perched on the arm of the lounge chair.

"I'm being silly, that's all. I thought – I'm not sure what I thought." Fiona felt uninclined to talk about it. Lethargy had come over her. Her body felt deadened.

"What happened in the car today when we were approaching the last house? You seemed to become panicked at the thought of stopping there."

"Yes. That's why I feel so ridiculous now. I had a strong urge we shouldn't go to the last house. And I was also certain God wanted to tell me something about our home and that He would reveal the details to me once I had made it back here."

"And did He?"

"No. Nothing."

Amidst disappointed hopes, Fiona charged God with letting her down; although, she would not admit to it. Faithful Christians did not go about professing that God had failed them, and she certainly shouldn't speak such secret thoughts in the presence of her children, even when their eyes were glued to the television screen.

"Turn the sound back down, please John. Thank you," Fiona instructed automatically as she noticed the slowly-creeping increase in volume.

"Should I see if the agent is able to meet us at the final place again? I could meet you and the kids there on my way home tomorrow."

"Hello?" Fiona said. Her phone playing the tune of "Amazing Grace" had interrupted them.

"It's Diana, from the church," she mouthed to Jo.

"No, you haven't interrupted us. Jo and the children have just arrived back from the park."

Fiona maintained eye contact with Jo as she listened.

"Umm, I haven't gotten as far as tomorrow . . . Jo will be working so I will have the children."

Fiona paused as Diana moved forward to the point of the call. Would she like to meet with her tomorrow? She could come over for coffee in the morning, or perhaps Fiona and the children would prefer to come over for lunch?

Lunch sounded nice. One less item to attend to and it would likely keep the children occupied for a time. She accepted the offer.

CHAPTER 3

Fiona awoke under a haze of hesitation. Why did she not want to get up? The reason came flooding back as she recalled her plans with Diana. The young woman seemed lovely, which made it worse. Fiona was overset by the prospect of having to interact with people already established in their friendships whilst she knew no one. Every relationship would be brand new and this placed her far outside the bounds of her comfort zone.

She considered pulling out of their lunch date except Jo would not hear of it. If he had to abandon her to the office, it would help him to know she would have company! And who knew, he reasoned, she might even make a friend out of it!

Fiona wished he hadn't said the part about friendship. It added extra pressure to the meeting; pressure which she did not currently need with all her other stressors.

As noon approached, Fiona hustled the children into their blue Toyota Camry hire car – cars being one more thing to sort out! The drive to Diana's house was mildly stressful for Fiona as she navigated without assistance, to an unknown destination, in an unfamiliar city.

She was used to winding roads but the windy, constantly inter-crossing streets of Brisbane were a completely different hurdle to the familiar ones surrounding her hill-side home. How she missed driving past the rows of pines, oaks and maple trees!

She must be home sick to be missing trees! Fiona chided herself for sentimentality. She was simply in a new place and needed time to adjust and settle in, she told herself. It would get better, it had to get better, and this lunch would be the start!

Fiona thought Diana's place was charming. It was a quaint little home. Its age was told by peeling paint and creaking front steps. There was a small, unkempt front yard to the left of the driveway.

Walking up to the door, Fiona hunted unsuccessfully for a doorbell. As she lifted an arm to knock, she was startled by the darkened security screen moving outward. Diana appeared in the doorway.

"Hi Fiona!"

"H-hi Diana! Sorry, I was looking for the door bell . . ."

"Yes, we really must inform our land lord about that! It stopped working a few weeks back so Chris took it out. I'll have to remind him to chase it up next time he speaks to the real estate agent. Anyway, here I am prattling on; please, come in, come in!"

Ann and Johnnie followed in their mother's wake, making Fiona claustrophobic.

"Children! Give me a little space, please!"

"It's Ann and John, isn't it?" Diana asked, bending down to their level.

When they nodded she went on: "There is some orange juice at the table over there, and some pens and paper. Why don't you go and draw your Mum a picture whilst we get some lunch ready?"

John nodded once again and led his sister over to the designated table.

"I hope they are as easily occupied by colouring as my nieces; if they are, there should be enough there to keep them busy at least until lunch."

"Yes, I am sure it will. Oh, we brought some cookies, too."

"Thank you," she said, taking the proffered choc-chip biscuits as she led the way into the kitchen. "We have a rather simple lunch, I'm afraid; all the same, it will warm us up."

"I think you might be fibbing because it smells delicious! I hope you didn't go to any trouble . . ."

Diana was too polite to tell Fiona the thought she had applied to planning their lunch. She loved to entertain and was naturally dedicated to the role of host. For the children, she had gone with the ever-safe chicken nuggets with a few potato wedges and fresh juice. Perhaps it wasn't the healthiest option, but she wanted them to be comfortable. As for the ladies, lasagne was chosen with a small, simple side salad. The salad made the plate colourful whilst the lasagne was hot and easy, being leftover from the night before.

Fiona was set at ease by Diana's friendly narrative as she swept around the kitchen. The pair were soon chatting away across the kitchen counter about moving house, hard-working husbands, and pregnancy.

Fiona was glad of Diana's warm-spirit and grateful to be welcomed into the bubbly woman's life. She was put at ease and gained the courage to share about her growing anxieties. She even told Diana of the "disaster" that occurred during house-hunting the previous afternoon.

"Oh, that's exciting!" Diana answered in response. "Maybe God wanted to see you walk in faithfulness. I am sure He already has your home and your children's school in mind; He only wants you to trust Him for it."

"I wish I had your faith!"

"It is easy to have faith when you aren't the one waiting for something to happen! Are you looking in this area?"

Diana served and handed Fiona a plate and cutlery. Fiona waited to answer until they were seated at the table on the high-backed kitchen chairs.

"We don't have a set locality in mind, and having such a great sphere of options is making it harder rather than easier! Our main restriction is: it has to be within half an hour of Jo's work, making this area amongst the ones where we've been looking."

"In that case, I'll have to introduce you to my sister. She has two girls a few years older than Johnnie, and I know she's has been happy with their school. I am sure she would be only too willing to tell you about the various options she explored in the area."

"Oh, you don't have to go to all that trouble . . ."

Fiona was hopeful that Diana would, all the same, go to the trouble, even if she couldn't bring herself to say so.

Thankfully Diana mustn't have seen it as any trouble because Fiona received a call from her that evening to arrange an introduction to her sister, Maggie.

* * *

"Thanks for coming. I know it was rather late notice," Diana greeted her eldest sister, Maggie, with a hug the following evening.

Diana was only younger than Maggie by two years, but her sister's world-wise expressions added five years to her true age, making her appear in the mid-thirties.

"Mum said there was going to be a little girl and boy here to play with," Kate exclaimed excitedly whilst peering around, as if to determine whether the said little boy and girl were hiding in a cupboard, or behind a sofa. Maggie's oldest girl was a rusty-haired nine year old with a lightly freckled face and strong personality.

"That's right, Kate. They're not here quite yet. They'll probably be another half an hour," Diana responded to her niece.

"Half an hour!" Kate whined as if half an hour was a whole year away.

"Oh hush, Kate," her mother chided. "I'm sure Aunty Di will set you up with an episode of Vegi Tales if you ask her really nicely!"

"Can we?" Wendy was clearly enthusiastic about the prospect. Younger than Kate by two years, there was little to hint in her chestnut hair, or big brown eyes, that the two were sisters.

"Sure, hang on."

Kate and Wendy followed their aunt into the living room and took over the bean bags in expectation.

Fifteen minutes later, Kate's hopes for playmates were again disappointed as her uncle walked in. Diana's husband, Chris, appeared in a dusty suit having had to conduct an unplanned site visit for his company's major contractors. He was a head taller than his wife and was rather handsome when his pensive brown eyes weren't underlined by blue craters, which conveyed his tiredness.

Diana greeted him with a warm embrace and his shoulders relaxed slightly under her tender care. He took to the shower and re-emerged ten minutes later, looking somewhat more alert. Not long after, a gentle, excited tap was heard on the door and Chris moved forward to greet the guests on his wife's behalf, as Diana was busy in the kitchen. He opened the door to be met by a beaming Johnnie, standing in front of his parents. Never shy, Johnnie marched in without a word to Chris and headed straight for the activity table of the day before. Ann squirmed out of Jo's arms to follow in her brother's wake.

Fiona gave an embarrassed apology for Johnnie: "Sorry, he is always biting at the bit!"

Chris brushed the apology aside, introduced himself, and shepherded them inside to meet his sister-in-law, Maggie. Fiona was planted down on the couch with Maggie whilst Chris took Jo outside.

Diana moved backwards and forwards from the kitchen table, bringing out steaming dishes as they were ready, and was pleased to see her sister conversing easily with Fiona on the couch. To her eyes, Chris and Jo seemed to be bonding unobstructed as they looked over the outdoor entertainment area with beers in hand, discussing Chris' new barbeque, which had come complete with a small roasting spit.

Over a scrumptious dinner of baked barramundi, mash, and steamed vegetables (the children had fish fingers with their mashed potato), Diana introduced the subject of local schools.

Maggie was passionate about her girls' school and willingly began to highlight its attributes.

". . . the school was chosen for more than its convenience (it is an easy walking distance from our home): The teachers are marvellous. Kate has been there for four years and has a firm friendship group. The music and sport program focuses on participation and emphasises sportsmanship over competition . . ."

"Sounds like you're sold! It has a good culture then?" Jo asked.

"Yes, definitely. I'm a single parent so it was encouraging to find a school that wants to be involved with the home life, too. Teachers socialise with patents; I'm acquainted with all the parents of Kate's class and a fair few in Wendy's; I've found it easy to find offers to mind the girls if I'm going to be late home . . . I would have liked to have sent them to a private Christian college as public schools aren't allowed to affiliate with religions; however, the school does have a marvellous R.E. program, which is run by members of a local church."

Chris was exhausted and was grateful to be able to enjoy some company whilst not having to uphold, or even overly participate, in conversation. His wife, meanwhile, played hostess marvellously, allowing Jo and Fiona to uninterruptedly ask Maggie questions whilst she kept the four children occupied, cleared the plates, made hot drinks, and shifted the party into the entertainment room.

It was an open-planned house meaning the move from table to lounge wasn't far, yet during the transition, the conversation also underwent a shift as it moved from schools on to local real estate.

Jo and Fiona conveyed to one another by a look and a hand squeeze that they were close to persuaded on the school, meaning they were solely looking for houses in this area. In addition, Fiona felt a growing peace that she had found her home church and it was where these two beautiful ladies attended. This week had shown her that it was more than a comfortable Sunday gathering; it was a family of believers, and she wanted to be part of its faith community.

Maggie pulled out her mobile and gave the house-hunters the number of a work associate whose husband was in real-estate.

"He'll find you something appropriate in the area. Make sure you tell him that I gave you his number. He'll take care of you; he's a great guy!"

"Great, thank you so much!" Fiona replied with gratitude.

"No worries. And you should drop the children off at my place in the afternoon if you want to go looking together, without them under foot."

Maggie's offer was genuine. She liked this young couple and prayed they would find a rental place in the area. She also hoped she would be given the opportunity to know them more.

"Oh, no, we couldn't. You've already done more than enough."

"It wouldn't be any trouble," Maggie smiled reassuringly. "I have to look after my own girls and truthfully it will keep them occupied. You can see for yourselves how much they love looking after younger children."

The truth of her statement could be seen as Kate directed activities at the craft table, hovering over the three younger children, helping them with their cutting and gluing, and praising their colouring attempts.

The party broke up a little after eight P.M. with the families needing to take their children home and to bed. Diana thanked God for a successful evening and prayed, for Fiona's sake, that her new friend's would find a house to rent by the end of the week.

* * *

Sitting in a low wicker chair looking out over the small backyard now scattered with Johnnie's toys, Fiona was shocked when she calculated their time in Australia to have reached the two month mark. Although in some ways it seemed they had been here forever, settled as they already were in their rental home and at church.

It saddened her to think that they would be leaving in such a short time. She had already begun to entertain thoughts that perhaps Jo's contract would be extended. This sunny nation had become associated with God's faithfulness and a sense of wellbeing and she was not in a hurry to leave.

Moreover, Fiona was eager to be around when Diana entered motherhood. She smiled as she thought of the young woman who had quickly found a way into her heart. Fiona wanted to be there in support of Diana just as Diana had been for her.

In fact, Diana's entire extended family had embraced the McCarthy's as an extension of their own; Johnnie and Ann had found themselves with foster grandparents, three aunties (one with children, giving them cousins), and an uncle.

Nevertheless, it had been hard to be away from her mother; even with the modern technology, which enabled them to keep in touch more readily than the old system of snail mail.

She was looking forward to Lance's trip to Australia, and was excited about the whispered rumours coming through from Dave that perhaps, just maybe, her dear big brother would be over sooner, and for longer, than initially anticipated.

Fiona didn't have to wait long to have the rumours confirmed.

CHAPTER 4

Lance was sitting on the kitchen stool, looking out the window at a dreary, overcast sky, when a boy raced down the street on a bright red bike. Merely a kid with no agenda; perhaps ten years old.

What would it be like to be that age once more? He wondered. Would he be destined to make the same mistakes a second time? Would the same fool-hardy choices be made? Was it possible he would choose a different path?

What silly thoughts! he chided. What use was it to dream of days gone by? Better to move on and keep one's chin up. Nevertheless, it did not stop the past from hurting.

Turning back to his Bible, lying open in his lap, he tried to engage in the words of First Corinthians, chapter thirteen. He remembered the verses spoken by the pastor on his wedding day as he had smiled lovingly at Amanda.

Lance shoved the memory aside. It was too painful to think on.

He didn't want to remember her glowing face, or the way her eyes had sparkled. Neither could he bear recalling the hope within his own breast on that occasion: a hope for a long and happy marriage.

All of that had gone. Only heartache remained.

He looked down again. "1 Corinthians 13"; the famous passage on love.

Lance closed his Bible and, standing up, he dumped it on the bench. He didn't want a bar of it. Not now. Not when he had seen what actually came from it.

"What fruit came from it?"

The thought nagged at him. It begged him to take another look. The passage had had much spoken on it . . . and it was in God's Word. If he believed the Word was powerful and contained truth, then he could not dismiss the passage out of hand.

Oh God, help me here! You placed this passage in Scripture. I know it speaks truth; and yet, the love spoken of in this passage does not equate to what I have experienced. If this passage speaks truth, why did the marriage sink into a mire of distrust? Where did we go wrong? Where did I go wrong?

I need you to show it to me. I need you to reveal how these words are truth.

Lance sighed. He couldn't do it; he couldn't force himself to read the passage. It was as if he had developed a mental block to the words, not allowing them to penetrate past his vision.

He left the kitchen and paced restlessly around the house. Eventually he changed into his sporting clothes and went for a fast paced run through the oak- and maple-lined streets. Half an hour later he stood back at the base of the driveway, leaning over and breathing heavily.

Successfully exhausting his body physically had only served to intensify the ache within by weakening his ability to fight against it. Defeated, he walked slowly up the drive and returned to where his Bible sat neglected on the counter.

Once more he opened to the heart-rending passage, forcing his eyes to read it. He sat on the cold, hard tiles with his back against the bench. It took willpower to go slowly, allowing the words, and their meaning, to seep into his heart.

Revelations dropped heavily as a sudden torrent of rain. Implications he had not seen before were standing out from the page as clearly as if they were pictures in a pop-up book. He saw the practical commands held within the passage; he saw that the attributes spoken of did not flow out of emotion, but rather, that love came from practising these actions; he saw how "1 Corinthians 13" was a call to demonstrate love by one's deeds.

"Love is patient and kind . . ." [10]

There wasn't patience in our marriage. Perhaps if she had been kinder to me . . . No! Let's look at me: I wasn't patient and I wasn't kind.

"Love does not envy or boast . . ." [10]

Envy. I know all about that; I was envious of her career and how she seemed annoyingly **content** *with where she was and in what she was doing. I don't think I boasted overly, did I?*

"It is not arrogant or rude . . ." [10]

I was never humble. I started arguments. I thought I was right. I never gave in. I broke her down. I **purposefully** *hurt her!*

"It does not insist on its own way . . ." [10]

I'm sorry, Lord! It was my way – full stop. I used emotional manipulation; I yelled when I knew she hated heated arguments, and then left her alone until she gave in to my will.

Oh God, this is my fault, isn't it? My marriage was loveless because I chose not to love.

"It is not irritable or resentful . . ." [10]

I was always irritable and I held grudges for a long time.

I am truly sorry, God. Change my heart. Change me. Release me from this selfishness. Teach me to release the hurts I received.

Lance paused in his reading, numb. Looking out upon a vista of grey skies did not alleviate his bleak state of mind. He continued in the grief of disillusionment.

"It does not rejoice at wrongdoing, but rejoices with the truth." [11]

I rejoiced in winning arguments unfairly. I chose to break down rather than strengthen. I not only rejoiced in wrong doing – I was the one doing wrong. I hurt your beautiful daughter.

"Love bears all things, believes all things, hopes all things, endures all things.

"Love never ends . . ." [12]

Our love ended. It ended because I let it. I didn't love as you call us to love. You call us to love as you loved us. When have I ever loved another more than myself?

I have not loved as I should have. It isn't a matter of when I became selfish; it is a matter of why I remained so after your Spirit touched my life . . .

Lance knelt forwards, his forehead touching the cold tiles as tears blurred his vision.

Melt my heart of stone. Give me a heart of flesh, instead.

Teach me to love as you would have me love. Show me how to love those whom I have hurt, particularly – I don't even want to say her name! Bring healing to her life. I know I caused the divide between us. I did not love her as a wife should be loved. I did not cherish her as a daughter of the King should be cherished. Bring healing into her life.

Lance thought back to the first verses.

"If I speak in the tongues of men and of angels, but have not love, I am a noisy gong or a clanging cymbal . . ." [13]

He felt he was the clanging symbol; he was the nothing; he had gained nothing.

Tears were flowing from his eyes in earnest, making a little puddle on the grey slate tiles.

All he had done and said in the marriage was meaningless because he had not done it with love. He had been proud of his ability to provide for them. He had been boastful, he could see that now; boastful of his abilities, his promotion, and their lifestyle. None of these things mattered! Why had he ever taken pride in them?

He had not sought the ways of love and so love had not upheld him . . .

I failed at love in the past. I can't go back in time and love Amanda as I should have . . . Help me to do better in the future. Make it a compulsion for me to love. Teach me how to love, to truly love: as you demonstrated through your life and teach us through your Word. Teach me what it means to love in practise and restore those I have injured.

Lance remained on the hard floor, lost in misery of soul, until his knees ached and his feet tingled from pressed nerves.

* * *

Lance spent the following week reflecting on "1 Corinthians 13". He considered what it meant to pursue the call of Christ, walking in the love God had bestowed upon him.

He incorporated his reflections into his morning exercise routine. Before his run, he would read through a passage in the Bible about the call to Christ-like love. Afterwards, his jog would take him down to the pine forest in the hills behind Fiona's house, letting his mind ferret over the passage and its implications.

The smell of the pine and the crisp air kept his body going as he tested its ability, pushing himself up hills and sprinting around bends. He enjoyed exploring the forest paths. It was his own private world where he explored Kingdom principles in the midst of God's glorious creation.

Six days into his new practice, Lance fell upon "Ephesians 5". It commanded believers to follow Christ's ultimate example of love, giving oneself as a sacrificial offering before God. His life was no longer his own. He wanted to live a life pleasing to the Lord and was eager to live a sacrificial life, compelled onwards by the love of God.

However, as he continued in the passage, he became confused and uncertain of what the words meant for him in his current circumstances. How was he to apply talk of sexual immorality and loving one's wife? He was divorced so did the passage still concern him? How should he walk in relation to Amanda after their marriage had ended?

"**Husbands, love your wives, as Christ loved the church and gave himself up for her . . . Husbands should love their wives as their own bodies. He who loves his wife loves himself. For no one ever hated his own flesh, but nourishes and cherishes it . . .**" [14]

Fine commandments, he was sure, except . . . what about him? Amanda wasn't his wife anymore. Did these commands still apply?

It was a relief to step out into the freshness of dawn. Sitting on the front step of the house, Lance pulled on his shoes with anxious eagerness. His insides churned with confusion as he tried to squeeze application from Paul's commands, written so many years ago.

Starting down the street, Lance pushed the passage aside and said a prayer for the day. God was faithful. He knew from experience that releasing such muddled thoughts to God was better than chasing the tail of a circular argument.

Sweat was beginning to form on his body when he passed a fallen, moss-covered oak tree; the half-way land marker of his usual route. He decided to extend his run by taking an additional side path, revelling in the sweet pain of physical exhaustion as his muscles tightened. A pleasant burning sensation radiated from his calves, thighs and gluts.

Lance found his spirits rising as he praised the Lord for the beauty of nature.

Leaving the forest, he stopped at the local park to do a trio of sit ups, chin ups and push ups. Fifteen minutes later he rose from a final set of sit-ups to be overcome by a sudden sapping of strength. He decided to walk the rest of the way home.

"For no one ever hated his own flesh, but nourishes and cherishes it . . ." 14

What am I supposed to do with this now? he wondered.

Rage shook within him as he put the heated question to God.

Too little and, by far, too late. Why could I not have been shown this two years ago? Maybe then I would still have a wife. Maybe then I could have been the husband she deserved.

He paused to do three quick tuck jumps; after which, he shook out his limbs in an attempt to dislodge the unfounded anger.

Lord, as per First Corinthians, we are commanded to keep no account of wrongs. I choose to walk in forgiveness and grace. I release all the hurt Amanda did to me. I pray you will release from my heart any grudge it embraces against her.

I thank you for draining the poison of unforgiveness out of my blood stream. I thank you for opening the wounds I allowed to fester. I pray you will help me to heal the wounds that lie between us.

I don't know what you are calling me to do. I have a growing desire to contact Amanda to see where we could go; to see if we can mend the brokenness in both of our lives. What the future holds I do not know; however, I do know that I want to seek her forgiveness. It will be hard, though; she doesn't even want to talk, let alone look towards reconciliation. Show me how I am to go about this.

If this is your will, I pray you will lead us to it. Prepare her heart and prepare mine. Bring us to a place of reconciliation, forgiveness and healing.

Lance closed the front door as he entered the quiet house, praying God would open Amanda's heart to reconciliation.

* * *

No trace of dawn's grey light had appeared when Lance awoke with an overwhelming urge to pray for his baby sister. He sat up and pushed a plush pillow behind his back, swallowing a lump of fear.

God, please keep her safe. If she is lonely, stressed, or afraid, I pray that you will be there for her. Comfort her at this time. Help her not to doubt you, or her choice to obey your call. Please give her the courage she needs to step out boldly at the sound of your voice. Whatever her circumstances, please meet her in her place of need.

Lance paused, listening. He sought whether further was required of him. It would be delightful to crawl back under the sheets and collapse into the blessed abyss of sleep . . .

Alas not. A weighty need to pray continued to hover over him. Lance reached over to switch on the bedside lamp and grasped for his journal as he waited upon God.

Writing the date at the top of a new page, he began to doodle down the side margin in an attempt to keep his mind idle and open to the Lord's directing.

Thinking of little Ann brought a smile to his face. The days couldn't go fast enough until he was able to sweep her up into his arms once more. He missed them. It had been a joy to watch his niece and nephew daily as they learnt new skills and mastered their existing ones day by day.

Changing pens from black to blue ink he began to colour the loops of his scribbles. His smile broadened as he looked upon his artwork: even Ann coloured more neatly than he did!

"They're not your children", the thought fluttered across his awareness.

Well, no; not directly. But they are family.

"They're not your children."

I know they aren't, but I wasn't given any of my own, was I?

His mood sank. He put the pen down.

Didn't he know he hadn't been blessed with children? Didn't he know that his marriage had failed and that he would never have a beautiful family like his sister? He didn't need God to remind him of it! Why wake him up if only to taunt him?

"You'll get your family."

He sensed God calling him to lift his chin and look to the future.

No.

Lance shook his head.

"You'll get your family – (He had to be imagining this! It would be impossible) – **except, first, your sister needs you."**

What is wrong with my sister, Lord? Why are you having me pray for them? What is so important it can't wait? Please keep them safe.

Lance felt as if he was being urged to go to Fiona.

What about their house? I can't simply pack up and follow them having promised I'd take care of this place.

"Go to her. Go where I send you."

Lance saw that his role was only to obey; to go faithfully and leave the provisional aspect to God.

"You'll get your family . . ."

Slumber returned to Lance with the promise echoing in his dreams.

* * *

Lance became obsessed with the thought of calling Amanda. First Corinthians had given him a vision for reconciliation, whilst God's promise had given him a hope for a family of his own. He longed to make amends with her. He hoped for a second chance. There was an aspect of fear, too. The unpleasantness hanging between them resembled a thick, sticky spider web and there seemed no way to progress past it without becoming entangled.

Nothing is impossible with God. He repeated this truth to himself almost hourly.

For three days he wandered the house, moving from room to room ceaselessly and without purpose. He was in a state of anxiety, near panic, from overwrought emotions: Should he call her, or shouldn't he? Was this consuming obsession from God, or of his own making? Would he do more harm than good trying to establish some form of communication between them? And what was his role when it came to loving her as Christ would post divorce settlements? Would it be loving to re-establish communication?

The never ending flow of questions ate away at Lance's sanity until he could bear it no longer. He picked up the cordless home phone. His fingers hovered over the buttons. Would he? *Should he?*

Lance flung the phone onto the couch.

Dashing off, he climbed the stairs three at a time, making his way to his bedroom. Collecting his journal and a pen he returned to the living room and sat upon the floor.

Using the couch as a table he penned an entry:

God,
I'm not sure if I am doing right by this. You're not giving any answers to the questions plaguing me so I will step out in what I believe is the right thing. I pray I am moving in accordance with your Word.
Even now I know you can close the door if this is foolishness. If not, I ask you to give me words of love and healing as I speak. Be with both of us and help us to act wisely.
Amen.

Lance picked up the phone and pressed the number sequence of Amanda's mobile.

It was ringing . . .

* * *

Lance brought his head to his knees. The phone dropped from his slack hand. A muffled "thud" resounded as it hit the carpeted floor.

His head was in a whirl. He could not believe he had spoken to Amanda! It had seemed nearly normal; like speaking with an old acquaintance . . . until she brought him up short, inquiring as to the purpose of his call.

Amanda had replied with polite sweetness whilst making it absolutely clear that getting back together was simply not an option – ever. Nonetheless, the call had contained one positive: she responded openly to his request for forgiveness.

He was emotionally drained though not without hope that healing could occur between them. He would trust God to bring restoration.

The telephone began to ring. Lance nearly hurled his face into the low coffee table in his eager attempts to clasp it. Surely Amanda wasn't calling him back? His heart began to flutter in anticipation . . .

"Hello?"

"Hi there!"

"Oh, hi Dave." His heart fell with his voice.

"Gee, I'm sure glad to hear from you, too, mate!" was his brother's bitingly sarcastic reply.

"No, you know I didn't mean it that way."

"Expecting a call?" his brother chuckled.

"No, no. Just thought perhaps it was Fi. I had a question I wanted to ask her about the house."

"Alright then. That's actually why I'm calling. I was talking to Fiona this afternoon and she told me to run it by you."

"Oh yeah? Run what by me?"

"Well, knowing how much you like children . . . Amy and I were wondering whether you would mind us moving in there with you. It would be a few months leading up to the baby and for a few months after, too."

"Umm," Lance paused, remembering what God had commanded of him less than a week earlier.

No, surely not, God?

He could not understand why God would want him to move to Australia to join Fiona and Jo. His attempts to reason it out had failed. And here God seemed to be providing him with a solution to the home situation.

"You said Fiona is alright with it?" he responded at last.

"Yeah, that's right – although we will completely understand if you'd prefer a baby-less house," he hurriedly assured Lance.

"No, of course not. It's only . . . well, it is good timing, is what it is! I've been contemplating moving forward my trip to visit them. The house sitting has been the factor stopping me. Plus, I imagine the two of you would prefer an empty house."

"But, you would only be over there for a couple of weeks, surely?"

"Actually, I'm not sure. That had been the plan . . . I just have an impression that my time there might become somewhat – extended."

"Oh, right. But Amy and I are welcome? Even if you do come back?"

"Yes, yes, of course you are! Another little niece or nephew to dote on? I'd love to be a part of that!"

"Great! I'll tell Amy and call you back about dates. It would be fairly soon though . . ."

"Perfect!"

"Great! Catch ya, mate."

Lance couldn't wait. He went on-line and booked his ticket immediately.

He did a quick calculation and worked out it was seven A.M. in Brisbane. Johnnie would definitely have Fiona out of bed by now!

* * *

He was right – she was in the kitchen pouring a bowl of Frosty cereal for Johnnie when she answered the phone. He could faintly here Johnnie exclaim in the background: "Uncle Lance? I want to talk to him! Moooom!"

Lance smiled.

Johnnie missed out on talking to his uncle. It was only a short call to relay the fact that he was coming out on a plane that same Friday and would e-mail her a copy of his itinerary, pronto.

Lance sat back to process all that had occurred in a mere hour: he had talked to Amanda, relinquished house-minding duties to Dave, booked a flight to Brisbane, and talked to Fiona.

Joy broke through the shock. He was going to Australia! He was going to see his dear sister and her beloved family!

CHAPTER 5

Lance's arrival in Australia was not as he had anticipated. His mouth felt dry, he was sure his breath smelt, and his eyes felt chaffed by sand. None of which would have mattered if Johnnie and Ann had been there to welcome him.

Images of a delightful niece running into his arms, and a naughty little nephew regaling him with stories of recent mischief, had been the anticipated scene. However, when he walked out of Gate 22 at Brisbane Airport, his two favourite little people were not present to meet him.

After an exhausting trek he emerged to be met by a lone Fiona, who looked equally depleted of reserves.

"Hi Little Sis. All right?" Lance greeted his sister with a hug.

"Mmm. You?"

"Yes. Tired and in need of a shower – but, other than that, I'm fine."

"The children were all anxiousness to be here until Johnnie had a little tumble last night and ended up in emergency with a broken arm."

"No! What happened? Is he okay?"

"Yes, after scaring his poor mother half to death! He managed to fall climbing out of the bath," she explained.

"Don't wear yourself out worrying over him! We boys store up our tumbles to brag about later."

Noting her fatigued appearance, Lance suggested: "I'm assuming it turned out to be a late night?"

"We didn't leave the hospital until five A.M.! It was a nightmare: There was a waiting line at the hospital, and a couple of rather more urgent casualties to be attended. After that there were x-rays to be done and a scared little boy to fight into submission."

Lance smiled. "Royal tantrum?"

"Yes. He managed an almighty fit. I barely credited it from one in his amount of pain, but I have a tender bruise that will bear testament to the fact!"

Fiona pulled up a sleeve of her t-shirt to display a purpling bruise on her toned upper arm as they began to walk towards the elevator, heading towards the basement car park.

"Anyway, how was the flight?"

"In a word? Long!"

"Try doing it with two children!"

"I'll pass, thank you."

Fiona chuckled, enjoying being in her brother's company once more.

* * *

Lance liked the rental home immediately. It was in what appeared to be a quiet suburb. Grand, white Ghost Gum trees stood tall up and down the street, well above the power lines. There was a small lawn dotted with a couple of shrubs. It wasn't an elegant house by any means, which was of no concern to Lance; it looked homely and that appealed to him.

A plain cement drive curved slightly to the left leading to the two-door carport. The house had been constructed from light coloured bricks. A shabby wooden fence ran from the garage to the edge of the property, separating the backyard from the front.

Lance stepped through the internal door leading from the garage into the main house. His entry was more subdued than his airport welcome. All the lights were out, although it was only early evening and a grey-light still shone through the windows. Even Fiona was surprised when all three of her family were found under their bedcovers.

The ringing of the telephone broke in on the silence.

"Oh!" Fiona exclaimed. "Oh, that scared me."

She rushed across the room to answer before it could wake the sleepers.

"Hello, Fiona speaking."

"Hi Fi. It's Diana here. I'm s – "

"Hey Di!" Fiona cut in delightedly. "How are you?"

"Yeah, well. And you?"

"Very good!"

"Great. Look, I'm sorry to disturb you at the dinner hour – "

"No, that's okay. I've just arrived home to a sleeping house so you're not interrupting anything."

"What?" she responded in startled amusement.

"I hear a night in the Emergency Department will wear out even the most energetic of boys," Fiona informed her friend with a tinge of emotion not dissimilar to pride.

"Emergency!" Diana exclaimed.

"Nothing serious! Nothing serious!" Fiona added hastily. "He broke his arm and, since it was after hours, we had to go to Emergency."

"Is he okay? I mean, apart from being understandably tuckered out?"

"I believe he is. He was a little shaken today and I believe he is frustrated with the cast."

"Poor little man!"

"I know!"

"And how is Mum doing?"

"I'm okay. I was rattled last night and, (now my nerves have settled), I'm ready to collapse into bed!"

"And so you should! I won't keep you long. I was thinking your brother must be arriving soon and – "

"Yes, he flew in this afternoon. He is looking at me as we talk."

Fiona smiled at her brother, who had taken over the sofa whilst waiting for his sister.

"And here I am holding you up! You should have said something!"

"No need to worry. We are all very casual in our family. Sorry, keep going."

"So, yes, I was ringing to see if you would be up for an Aussie Barbie whilst he's here. Chris tells me he must experience one as part of his "Australian cultural experience"."

"That sounds great! I'm sure Lance will be up for it."

She mouthed "Barbeque" to her brother who nodded back, happy to go along with any of the family's plans.

"Let me run it by Jo when he is up on his feet again. When were you thinking?" Fiona enquired.

"Saturday? Say two o'clock?"

Fiona took down a few further details regarding what they could bring before farewelling her friend. At the end of the call, she relayed the invitation details to her brother who replied that he would love to meet some of his sister's new friends. Jo added his willing acceptance of the invitation to the mix when he materialised later in the night, apologising to his brother-in-law for his tardy appearance.

A secret hope formed in Fiona's breast that Maggie would attract Lance's attention. Despite knowing she shouldn't attempt match-making a second time, she thought the pair would make an excellent match. Fiona had spent considerable time with Maggie since their first dinner and had since discovered that Maggie's husband had been caught in an affair and, subsequently, they had divorced. It had happened two years ago. Fiona hardly credited it when she'd first been told; she thought Maggie would make a charming wife and could not conceive how a man could do that to her . . . And now, Fiona decided, would be an excellent time for the attractive Maggie to meet a man worthy of her love.

Smiling at her private hope, Fiona resolved not to make any hints to Lance – or anyone, for that matter – she would simply wait and see what eventuated come Saturday and beyond . . .

* * *

Diana went busily to work planning the barbeque and was quick to gain the help of her younger sister. As her belly grew so did her need for rest and Tanya's energy and enthusiasm would be greatly welcomed. She asked her sister the favour as they were gathered around their mother's dinner table for the weekly family meal.

It was Chris who introduced the topic: "Fiona's brother is here on holidays and we planned an Aussie Barbie to introduce him to good old Aussie culture."

"Yes, and we were hoping you would be able to join us?" Diana expanded from her husband.

"Sounds lovely, darling. How many will you be having over?" her mother asked. Tina was a pleasant, matronly woman. She had a tender heart and was generally soft spoken, yet decisive. All three of her daughters had inherited her compassion, if not all of them her gentleness. Streaks of auburn could be seen amongst her softly greying hair.

"It would only be us and them. Maggie is bringing Kate and Wendy, too; I've already asked her."

"Oh, right. It'll only be a small gathering then?" her younger sister clarified.

"I thought they would probably only want a quiet Saturday afternoon. From what I gather, Fiona has a full schedule planned for them next week."

Tanya laughed. "She seems the type!"

"Tanya!" Tina chided.

"What? I didn't say it was a bad thing. I'd want someone to fill my schedule, too, if I was visiting them in a foreign country."

Turning to Diana, Tanya enquired whether she desired help with the preparations.

"Yes, please! I was hoping you wouldn't mind!" Diana gratefully accepted the offer.

"Of course! Just let me know when you need me and what I can do."

Conversation moved on to their mother's garden and how she was to keep it alive during the upcoming visit to Canada she had planned with her husband. Tina was right not to entrust the duty to Tanya, her only child left at home, who had not inherited her green thumb!

* * *

Tanya was in the kitchen preparing a large tray of sliced onions when the doorbell rang. She quickly washed the juices off her hands and brushed a forearm across her eyes before drying her hands on her floral apron.

She was in a bubbly mood, feeling beautiful in the antique-style apron and expectant for a day spent in good company. Springing forward she skipped out of the kitchen. She heard voices in the living room and inferred that her sister had beaten her to door duties.

"Hi Tanya," Fiona greeted her on the way through to the kitchen in order to unburden herself of a home-made caramel tart.

Jo followed in his wife's wake, carrying a bottle of wine and a couple of soft drinks, the later being tucked under one arm.

"Hi Fi! Hi Jo!" Tanya greeted enthusiastically.

The next instant Tanya's movements came to a dead stop. Her chin fell and her mouth formed a small "o".

"Lance?" she questioned breathlessly.

Lance, who had been bent over talking to Johnnie, stood before her and a quick smile leapt to his face. A laugh was in his eyes as he gave out a delighted: "Tanya!"

"Hi!" Tanya said, still somewhat perplexed. "What are you doing here? I mean, wow! I, – this is – unexpected! You and Fi – ?"

""Hi" back at you." Lance was grinning from ear to ear and put his arms out slightly.

Tanya responded in kind and moved towards him. The next instant she felt herself in the grips of a strong embrace and her arms moved to grip him a little more tightly around the neck. They remained there for slightly longer than necessary until Tanya, recalled to a sense of place, pulled away.

She cast her eyes downwards knowing the gaze of her sister and Fiona to be upon them.

Diana broke in on the momentary silence: "What – do you two know each other? How's that?"

Tanya allowed Lance to explain their meeting in South Africa. He tactfully stated they had met through a local church in Muizenberg. As he continued, she quietly murmured an excuse and retreated to the kitchen to continue preparations.

Ten minutes later she had made her way into the newly finished nursery and it was here her sister found her.

"Tanya?"

"Down here," was the muffled reply.

Diana had to push the cot out a little from the wall in order to make her way into the narrow space between it and where Tanya sat with knees wedged up and her back to the wall.

"What are you doing in here?" Diana sounded amused until she was given a glimpse of the tear stains on Tanya's face. "Tanya! What's wrong, sweetie?"

"Nothing." It was a pitiful reply.

Diana draped an arm around her sister.

"That's him, Dee."

Perplexed, Diana waited.

Receiving nothing further, she prompted: "Him?"

"Lance."

"Yes? What about him?"

Understanding came upon Diana and she let out a soft "Oh!"

This received a sad chuckle from Tanya. "Precisely," she said.

Upon arriving home from her semester abroad, Tanya had confided in her sister, telling of a handsome and strapping man she had met during her final weeks in South Africa.

Diana was caught by a sudden urge to laugh.

"Why are you hiding in here, then?" she questioned in perplexed amusement.

"I don't know what to do! I don't know what to say to him. I want to run away, except, in all politeness, I can't!"

"Tanya, I hate to tell you this, but you already have run away from him . . ."

"How am I going to get through today?" she wondered miserably.

Diana gave her sister's hand a squeeze, not knowing how to reply. They sat there for a moment in silence before Diana gently guided her sister to stand and shuffle out from behind the cot.

"Come on," she said, giving Tanya a tight hug.

Tanya nodded and made her way out of the room after Diana.

"I'm going to go into the bathroom first," Tanya said.

"Okay."

Diana released her sister's hand at the bathroom door. "No more hiding, though!"

Whilst Tanya didn't seek to escape from the party again, she did manage to avoid Lance. Being the guest of honour he found himself monopolised by one person after another until lunch, whilst she played with the children outside. He glanced at her from time to time through the glass doors and made one venture outside to her, which was frustrated by Tanya's father who promptly drew him over to the barbeque, much to Tanya's relief.

Lance formed bonds with Chris and Ben almost instantaneously upon being introduced. Confused over Tanya's behaviour, he had at least found interesting company with the men. Chris was a senior engineer for a large civil-construction company. Lance ploughed him with questions relating to the industry, always fascinated by the multitude of careers available. Lance could understand why Chris did well in his industry: the guy was astute, calm, and likeable.

Meanwhile, Tina's husband, Ben, had impressed Lance before they had ever exchanged a word. Fiona had highly praised both Diana and Maggie on nearly every call she had made to Lance during her first two months in the country and, of course, he already knew Tanya was a faithful young woman of God. Any man who raised three god-fearing, intelligent and caring women was worth looking to for wisdom.

As they became acquainted, Ben's love of anything mechanical came quickly to the forefront. His weathered hands bore many light scars from accidental run-ins with his beloved tools and the only shirts he owned that weren't stained with grease, or rust, were those his wife hid in their linen closet for special occasions.

The easiest way to draw Ben out was to ask him about his latest project. Chris employed this tact and moments later Lance found himself in Chris' shed being shown the workbench Ben had fitted for his son-in-law. He was only retrieved by an amused Chris, tongs in hand, when lunch was ready.

Tanya returned to the adult group for the meal, but if Lance was hoping the meal would provide a chance for them to talk, he was wrong. He was hurt to see her remain as close as possible to Diana. Surely this was not the same friendly, open young woman he had known in South Africa?

Fiona and her troop made movements to leave as the light began to fade. Tanya was no longer able to avoid Lance. To the side of the group, as the two families congregated by the doorway, Lance had gently taken her hand.

"Hey?" he enquired gently, compelling her, with a squeeze of her hand, to look up into his face, filled with gentle compassion. A question lurked in his eyes, demanding to be answered.

Tanya felt a lump come up into her throat.

"I missed you," was all she could, quite breathlessly, say.

Suppressed emotions threatened to escape from him. He longed to whisk her up into his arms and was grateful for the presence of the others, which prevented him from acting rashly.

"Did you?" Leaning back a little, Lance looked at her intently, trying to come to a decision.

"Of course I did! Why do you sound so startled?"

"I didn't see you before I left, we didn't exchange contact details . . ." he trailed off. "I missed you, too. And our discussions."

It was all they had time for as Diana came over to say goodbye.

"It was lovely meeting you, Lance. I hope we see more of you during your visit," Diana said.

"Yes, so do I," he replied, stealing a glance at Tanya.

After Lance and the McCarthy's had taken their leave, Tina began to talk of how small a world it was that would have a friend of Tanya's turn out to be the brother of Diana's new friend. Tanya made small of the topic stating they hadn't known each other well, not meeting until the end of her time overseas. She changed topics as quickly as possible and was soon confirming the overall success of the barbeque with her mother.

Tanya was glad when the day's events were over and she was back at home where she could retreat to the safety of her bedroom.

* * *

Fiona had been plagued with the nagging suspicion that she was missing a connection ever since hearing her brother proclaim Tanya's name in greeting. Her mind continued to worry away at the problem as she rubbed shampoo into Ann's hair during bath time. All she could think was: "He knows her. He knows her from South Africa".

It wasn't until she made her way down the corridor from Ann's room that realisation struck:

"Tanya!" she thought suddenly, and a small laugh escaped as an image of Genevieve flashed into her mind. The horrible matchmaking episode had all started by Lance mentioning a bubbly young Australian woman!

Walking out into the main living area she forcefully stifle the feminine giggle threatening to surface.

Lance was sitting on the kitchen bench staring blankly across the kitchen table and out into the black night. Fiona stood torn between a desire to satisfy curiosity and a protective instinct, which suggested to her that he needed time alone. After a moment's pause, she quietly made her way over to where Jo was watching a movie in the lounge room and snuggled up beside him on the couch.

* * *

Left alone in the kitchen, Lance was confused. From his perch, he reviewed the events of the day, trying to fathom what had passed behind Tanya's pretty face.

What had kept her at bay throughout the afternoon? Had she truly missed him, or was that a polite remark, given out of kindness? No, surely the look of tender affection she had given him gave the truthful answer. He had read in her eyes love and confusion, hope and fear. Not too dissimilar to his own emotions in the moment.

His own emotions – they were something he did not want to dwell on! Only a week ago he had talked to Amanda wondering if reconciliation was possible. And now . . .

His heart felt as if it was being squeezed. Joy had leapt up within him at the sight of Tanya and the sound of her voice, her Australian accent having deepened since coming home. He recognised it as a joy that sprang from hope; a hope he must suffocate.

She deserved a godly man untainted by the world. What could he offer her other than brokenness and pain? How could he ask her to love a man who could not love himself? He was not fool enough to believe his heart was asking for friendship. Nevertheless, friendship remained the only option, if kindness compelled her to extend it.

God, give me strength! I can't do this alone, I do not have the character. I need you to keep me safe from harming her. Put barriers around her heart. Protect her from the wretch that I am. Let her feel nothing towards me.

My own pain I can bear, I even take comfort in it at times; however, I could not live with myself if I hurt her. She is your precious daughter, whom you love, and therefore I can entrust her into your care. Keep her safe. Amen and Amen!

Lance soon retreated to the isolation of his room. Despite his mind being full of processing, his heart did not have the strength to journal. He lay on his bed staring up at the ceiling as he was bombarded by the dispiriting weight of insufficiency.

CHAPTER 6

Diana arrived at her family home early the next morning. Abuzz with excitement, she gently tapped on her sister's bedroom door and entered without waiting for the reply, eager to discuss the bizarre events of the previous day.

She found Tanya mindlessly occupied on the internet.

Tanya turned off the screen and joined her leaning against the side of the bed, before looking at her with an amused smile, making Diana broach the subject that was clearly on both of their minds.

"So . . . Do you think this is God giving you the green light?" she prompted.

"I did at first," Tanya answered honestly. "I couldn't believe it when he came into view at the Barbie!"

"But now?"

"I just don't know! My heart quickens when I think about him and I get butterflies – although these aren't exactly new experiences in the guy department!"

"Where does that leave you? You can't keep ignoring him and, being Fiona's brother, we are bound to see more of him, especially as it sounds he is here on an indefinite visit!"

"He's what?" Tanya exclaimed in alarm.

"I thought he would have told you? Fiona said he's changed his plans; instead of a short visit, he will probably remain with them for the remainder of their six month transfer."

"But . . . but, that is at least – what, three more months?" Tanya was near despair.

Diana thought through the calculations.

"Perhaps a little more . . . I hate to be the bearer of bad news, but Fiona's talking about extending their time, too."

"Oh dear."

Tanya was disheartened. She could hide from him for a week or two – that was reasonable – but four months?

"Tanya, why are you afraid of this?"

Tanya thought over the question. What was she afraid of?

"Dee, I don't want to be afraid. I am. But I'm not sure why I am."

Tanya needed time with God to think. She needed to pray about the qualms churning over in her heart.

It was not until the afternoon that Tanya found a moment alone as her mother had seconded her from Diana in order to help clean the house before her monthly book club meeting, which would be held in their house that evening.

When she was at last free to take her leave, she retreated into the quiet seclusion of the bathroom. Soaking in a tub full of warm water and essential oils, Tanya's apprehension began to flow away.

Why have I been anxious? It doesn't matter that Lance is here if I abide in you. Guard my heart. I don't know where all this is going. Is it a mere coincidence, or is this strange meeting of you?

Tanya slid down to immerse her head. Water trickled pleasantly down her back as she re-emerged. She could do this. She would simply have to wait to see how events would transpire.

* * *

With Tanya's re-entry into his life, Lance had begun a fresh struggle with the grace of God. He had thought himself to be on the path to healing until she brought back all the old emotions of brokenness, sorrow and guilt.

In the backyard, Lance played idly with the tassels of the hammock as he lay considering his past. It was hard to look back on a broken relationship and consider your own failings.

He longed to be able to embrace the love God had for him. He knew God had forgiven him; except, sometimes – it was easier to accept the forgiveness of God than it was to forgive oneself.

Lance could not break free from condemnation. It was not from God; rather, he cast it upon himself. Guilt for a failed marriage; deserved pain for a broken covenant; sorrow of heart for causing God's daughter anguish. If God would not punish him, then he would punish himself.

Lance stared grim-faced up at a cheery blue sky.

When the marriage ended it had been easy to justify their incompatibility. He had been ready with answers as to how Amanda had brought them to the point of separation and how it had been her that had left, leaving divorce papers on the table.

Lance sighed.

Blame was the easiest game to play. Now it was over, an ever-growing conviction had appeared telling him that his marriage disintegrated as a result of his selfishness.

I was quick to put the blame on her. I was focused on my unmet needs. It was my choice not to love. It was my choice not to put her needs first.

Lance's jaw tightened. He squeezed his teeth together against the emotional pain.

It was bittersweet to chastise oneself for past failure.

Fiona brought out a glass of ginger beer, momentarily breaking his reflections. He gave a pained smile and thanked her.

As her back retreated into the house, Lance tried to convince himself of what he had received through Christ:

I am worthy of your love.

I am worthy of your forgiveness.

I am declared righteous.

I will be holy.

I am redeemed by the blood of the Lamb.

I am a chosen one of God.

I am a saint.

I am beloved of the Father.

On and on went the list. So did his low spirits.

Unable to be convinced of his identity in Christ, he tried the path of praising God and offering his gratitude:

Thank you for loving me. Thank you for teaching me to love. Thank you for showing me the meaning of love. Thank you for showing me how love is more than an emotion, or a desire.

Love is actions. It is the showing of kindness. It is having patience . . .

I am sorry I did not apply these lessons during my marriage. Heal me of this brokenness. I have been content in self-pity and the comforting sting of brokenness. Let this be so no longer.

I do not want to remain in this place of brokenness. Bring me healing. Bring me into a place of redemption, of freedom. Bathe me in your grace.

Fiona joined him once more, this time empty-handed.

"Hi," she greeted quietly.

Lance sat up, throwing his legs over one side, and she scrambled up beside him.

"Do you want to be alone? I can go . . ."

"No. You're okay."

"When I brought out your drink . . . you looked – grieved."

"I haven't been the most cheerful person these past few days, have I?"

"No; not if I'm truthful."

"I'm sorry."

They sat silently for a moment.

"I talked to Amanda before I left," Lance confided.

"Oh?"

"I thought – this is going to sound stupid – I thought God was leading me to build a bridge. I still think that; only, when I called I had expected . . . I thought He might bring us back together."

"Is that an option . . . ?"

"No. She was kind about it. Distant, though. Not that I blame her . . . She said she was open to forgiveness, in time, but one hundred percent against an attempted reunion, ever. I don't know, Fi . . ."

"What do you hear God saying?"

Lance shrugged, a look of hopelessness on his face.

"He isn't."

Fiona gave his back a gentle rub of compassion.

"Before I rang Amanda, I was certain He promised me a family – of my own. That's what led me to believe He would do a miracle between Amanda and me."

"Amanda's response doesn't exclude you from having a family . . ."

Lance looked over at her, before nodding once.

"Although, I wouldn't be worthy of such a blessing," he said simply.

"Oh, Lance." Fiona was looking at him with pained compassion.

"Like I said – I'm not a fun person to be around at the moment."

"Can I ask you something – ?" Fiona queried tentatively.

"Mmm?"

"Tanya . . . is she . . . was she . . .?"

A sad chuckle broke forth from his lips. "Always said you were a bright one! Yes, she is the woman that I – at some point – mentioned to you and Mom."

"Did you two . . ."

"We were just friends. Barely that – we only hung out a few times."

"Sorry, I didn't want to be nosey . . . I just wondered, was all."

"I don't mind. She's an amazing young woman. Her husband will be a very lucky man, indeed."

Lance did not share any further insights into his emotions. Fiona offered a cup of tea and the pair moved inside. Already breaking her vow not to match-make, she began dreaming up possible invitational opportunities to extend to Tanya.

* * *

The following Saturday, the families met again. Fiona had returned the barbeque invitation with one for a park picnic. The day dawned overcast, threatening rain. Fiona was nervous they would have to cancel the picnic and prayed for the rain to hold off. Thus far the weather was complying.

The McCarthy's were the first to arrive at the J.C. Slaughter Falls' picnic area. They chose a shaded patch of grass and began unfolding camping chairs, spread out their brand-new picnic rug, and opened a packet of sea-salt potato chips.

Chris and Diana were the next to arrive, followed five minutes later by Maggie and her two girls. Wendy and Johnnie were on their way to a fast friendship, both being lovers of bugs, spiders and other creeping animals. The pair were soon chasing after butterflies and tracking trails of ants.

Kate had just settled down to read a picture book to Ann when the remaining three picnickers arrived. Tanya had accepted the invitation willingly, determined to be the epitome of distant amiability. She would be friendly without becoming personal. Her stomach betrayed her, fluttering nervously, as they walked across the grass to the rest of their group.

However, Lance seemed disposed to act out her intensions of distant friendliness. He greeted her with a smile and slight hug, just as he did Tina – and Diana and Maggie before them – and then joined Jo, Chris, and Ben playing cricket. The game had to be dulled down when the children opted to join them.

Tanya joined the women chatting about the four children whilst making mugs of tea in plastic cups out of a stainless-steel thermos. She didn't mind for she loved the children, although part of her would rather have been out amidst the action of the game.

Thankfully Kate and Wendy soon became bored with cricket and pulled her over to dance with them. She picked up each girl in turn, twirling them around with her in a waltz. Ann toddled over, hovering at the edge of the group.

"Would you like a turn too, Annie?" she asked.

Ann nodded.

Tanya set Wendy back on her feet and bent down to Ann. As she picked her up, her eyes caught Lance watching her. She smiled shyly before continuing her activities. His eyes remained on her as she swung Ann around, who was giggling with delight.

It wasn't until after lunch that Tanya's armour was put to the test. Lance offered to take the children for a walk around the scrub trails in search of wildlife. All four were delighted by the prospect. Lance looked at Tanya, eye brows raised in invitation.

"Want to join our exploration?"

"Ah . . . I would . . . only, I should help clear up."

"Don't be silly," her mother said. "We can manage here and you love your walks."

Tanya was caught and so readily gave in. The six of them trooped off on a nature hunt. Johnnie took the lead until his first animal sighting caused him to squeal in excitement. The bearded dragon he had spotted took fright and ran off into the underbrush too quickly for the others to see more than a passing sweep of the little guy's tail, after which Kate decided to take to the front.

Kate's leadership was more conducive to everyone seeing the various animals along the way. She had a sharp eye, spotting a laughing kookaburra, a koala, and, the more frequent butterflies and white-and-black magpies. Upon observing an animal of note, she would stop, put a finger to her lips, and point to the spot of interest whilst the three remaining, younger children crept up to peer around her.

Lance had gently taken Tanya's arm at the beginning to keep her with him at the back, since which time they had kept pace contentedly behind the young adventurers, talking softly.

"It still amazes me that you're here," she uttered again.

"Me too. God is incredible in that way. He knows what we need."

"Yes," Tanya couldn't think of anything else to say.

"I needed a friend and here He has brought me to you again. You always seem to pop up at such a time!"

"I'm handy that way," she laughed.

Lance smiled. Kate had halted once more and they followed suit.

"I missed your laugh. It is life giving; so joyful," he said.

Tanya gave a nervous half-laugh.

"Dee mentioned you were here long-term?" she enquired to change the focus.

"Yes."

"What will you be doing?"

"Ha! Good question; I have no idea! I'm currently trying to discern what God has for me. South Africa has remained on my heart, and going back there to do some form of mission's work is a possibility. I have always had a heart for missions. It was a passion I gave up when I married. I think God might be preparing to call me back."

"Though you aren't certain?"

"No, not at this stage. What about you? You'll be done with your studies soon, won't you?"

"This is my final year, yeah. I want to use my degree overseas. I would love to go to India! There is a project running with Christ's Hope. Have you heard of them?"

Lance shook his head.

"Never mind; they're only a small organisation. Well, they have a project in India at the moment needing another community developer to come on board. I'm talking to them about it. I'd have to do their training course down south for a few weeks in January, as well as raise financial support, which frankly daunts me! We'll see . . ."

"Plenty of time yet."

"Yes."

Lance asked Tanya questions about Christ's Hope and they fell to discussing various mission organisations. Tanya said she had also been impressed by the care Operation Mercy gave to their staff and the preparation assistance their missionaries received. Being a people-person, administration skills were not her forte.

Their walk lasted forty minutes, the last twenty of which Ann spent a-top Lance's shoulders, and at length they returned to the larger party.

Tina stole Lance's attention, wanting to discuss more of his past travels. She had discovered earlier in the day that he had once made a trip to the Philippines, a place she strongly desired to visit. Tanya had at last shed her shyness and remained sitting with them, enjoying listening to Lance's accent.

The day wound down gradually. Ann curled up in Lance's lap and was beginning to nod off to sleep, the air was cooling down, and the crowded grassy clearing began to empty of people. Fiona made murmurs of heading off, Maggie added her voice to the suggestion, and the party packed up.

The strength of Lance's arms still lingered around her from their parting hug as she sat in the back of her Dad's blue Ford Fiesta. Tanya shivered in a pleasant way, and a secret smile broke upon her face. Unfortunately her contented frame of mind was not of long duration.

* * *

By the time they arrived home, Tanya was already upset at having allowed her heart to run in front of her. She was a woman of quick passions, yet reason always followed close after them. She was annoyed at her natural emotions. She did not want to be swept up over a man. She had dreams of conquering India for Jesus.

She determined once more to quell her affections. She spent the evening sending a much delayed e-mail to Becca and Sam, telling them of her studies and her dreams to make a trip to India at year's end, where she had volunteered with an organisation called Christ's Hope during the previous year's summer holidays. A bubble of excitement grew within her as she wrote of her hopes to return to Christ's Hope Ministries to rejoin the team working on a safe water project.

India! Her heart swelled when she thought of the overcrowded, humid nation. People with thin wallets and large hearts. She longed to walk along the Swarnamukhi River, spend Wednesday afternoons walking around Srikalahasti Temple in intercessory prayer, play impromptu soccer games with the street kids, and worship with her family of fellow believers at Christ's Hope Community Church.

The rancid smells and oppressive crowded living spaces had not slipped completely from her memory; however, they were distant enough to be remembered with fondness. She smiled, knowing that the old feelings of exasperation would return upon returning to that nation.

India certainly did not offer the luxuries of Australia; nevertheless, it had stolen her heart.

She left the news of Lance until last, knowing Sam and Becca would be able to think of little else once she let out that juicy piece of information.

Tanya enjoyed picturing the response her e-mail would receive at the other end. Becca would unceremoniously run into Sam's dorm room the minute she finished reading the update – if she bothered to read the final few sentences.

Tanya waited anxiously for their reply, staying up later than she had intended knowing the eight-hour time difference between them. She eventually turned her light off at one A.M.

No message was waiting in her inbox when she awoke and hastily signed into her account on the Sunday morning. She would have to face church unstrengthened by their advice.

* * *

The McCarthy's and Lance merged into one with Tanya's family for the service. They took up two rows between them, appearing as a large, extended family. Somehow Tanya found Lance beside her as the congregation rose for the first hymn.

She was vastly aware of Lance's broad profile beside her, which reached a full head taller higher than her own.

God, please bring my focus back onto you this morning. Consume my attention. Capture me. Overwhelm me as I sing your praises.

Tanya closed her eyes. Tranquillity descended upon her as she sang each verse of the song with intentionality. As they began to repeat the chorus, she stopped singing to allow the words to wash over her and used them to formulate a prayer:

Lord, reign in me. Let the words of this song become truth in my life. Reign in me. Oh, reign in me. Take my dreams. Take my fears. Take my burdens. Reign in me, reign in me, reign in me!

Tanya lifted her hands high and listened as the worship band continued to sing. She began to nod her head in time to the tempo. Her face was radiant, reflecting the overwhelming love she had for her Lord. Her desire was purely to be ruled by the Holy Spirit. She desired Him to mean more to her than any riches, family member, or earthly thing.

Lost as she was in worship, Tanya managed to hit Lance with her left arm before knocking her right arm into Diana. Her praise momentarily disrupted, she squeezed past her sister in order to gain the space of the aisle for her dancing.

* * *

Lance was thankful when she moved as it enabled him to turn his attention onto the Lord. Having Tanya standing next to him had not been conductive to worship. He was compelled to sit as the words of the next song penetrated past his barricades. Words reflecting God's loving grace swept him up in amazement and wonder. How could he respond to God? He was nothing when considered in the light of the great universe and yet God had turned His eyes upon him. Even as a sinner, God loved him. Overwhelmed, he prayed:

Regardless of my sins you love me. What amazing love. What amazing grace. I live in awe of you.

Lance knew that he could do nothing to make his God love him more, and likewise he could do nothing to make his God love him less.

Let this truth permeate my inner most being. Remove the guilt I bear; I know it is not of you. Your Spirit convicts; it does not condemn. Enable this broken man to accept your healing grace.

Lance slid forward off the chair to kneel on the carpet. His feet poked out under his pew into the row behind him and his chest was uncomfortably close to the pew in front.

I am yours. I belong to you. Take my life. Take all of me.

During the sermon the family sat, faces towards the guest speaker; a tall woman who taught at the local Bible college.

Diana, whose baby was beginning to ruthlessly kick and wiggle inside the womb, was in a distracted state of mind as she enjoyed the blessing of a growing child. Chris was soaking in the words so that he could share them with his wife at a later time. She would enjoy discussing the sermon's theme of plans with him; sticking to God's Plan A for their lives, and that of their family. A smile of pride lit his face.

Ben was thinking of his back shed, which consumed the days of his retirement. The speaker was saying how God does not want his children to settle with ordinary; but rather, to seek the extraordinary. Perhaps, if Tanya's plans to make it to India worked out, he would volunteer for a few weeks on one of Christ's Hope building projects. She was always sounding the need for tradesmen on the frontline. Tina was satisfied she was walking in God's "Plan A" for her life, and she was uplifted to hear the message.

Fiona smiled up at her husband as her petite hand found his larger one. Jo had signed on for a further six months exchange. Her only hesitation over the extension had been due to missing her mother. Jo had suggested they fly Gwen and his parents over for a short visit.

The radiant expression had not left Tanya's face since worship. Excitement bubbled within her. "Extraordinary life" . . . where would that take her? She wasn't sure, which provoked even greater anticipation. Surely with God, life was an adventure!

"This isn't to down play the need to grieve certain occurrences in our lives," the speaker added. "When my husband of seventeen years walked out on me I went through a dreadfully bleak winter season. I could not imagine a way out of the pain, hurt, and brokenness of my soul. The water was up to my neck and I longed to drown."

Tears gently fell down Maggie's face as she symbolically placed her hands forward, offering God the pain of being left by a husband. She could resonate with this woman's experience: She had been abandoned with two young children. She knew what it was to lose the ability to trust. She, too, felt robbed of the opportunity to live out God's "Plan A" for her.

Maggie's spirit soared as God showed her how He had not left her to drown. God had held her safely in the lifeboat of His arms until she regained the strength to swim. A fresh glow of life appeared on her cheeks. Tears ceased to fall. Her eyes were left brightened by the added moisture; sparkling with joy as God promised her a future surpassing her ability to envision. He would be the Father her children needed. He would be the support for which she longed, and her strength when she was weak. God was worthy of her trust and hope. He was holding tightly to her hand.

Lance was the only one in the group who did not find the message uplifting. He sat jiggling his legs in agitation. Plan A? He had stepped off that path long ago! Did he step off it during his engagement when doubts had plagued his mind about the marriage? Or had he stepped off it when he allowed resentment and bitterness to root in his soul? Or was it when he signed the divorce papers? The "when" wasn't important – at some point he had stepped from the path. Nothing extraordinary remained for him.

"There is a season for grief and during these times we need red-shoe friends around us. Every woman should have a pair of red shoes!" the speaker went on. "You don't buy red shoes to go with an outfit; you buy outfits to go with your red shoes! And they aren't to be worn on just any day of the week . . . We pull them out of the closet when we need a boost of power; when our mood is low. Walking out in a bold pair of bright, cherry-red shoes transforms the down-cast frame of our mind.

"Red-shoe friends are those close few who help us through the winter seasons in our lives. We all need red-shoe friends. They listen and empathise when we share of our pain. They can also be relied on to give our faces a gentle slap if we begin to tell the story for the eighth time, in one week, three years on from the unpleasant event."

Lance felt that God was calling him to step out of his winter season. Fiona and his mother were his "red shoe friends". Hadn't they tried to bring him out of his despair? Hadn't they tried to cue him that it was time to move on? Who was he not to accept God's grace?

"We have to grieve painful events," Lance listened to the speaker. "But we can't allow heavy snow fall to trap us in those winter seasons. God wants more for our lives than to wallow in bitterness, or pain. It becomes unhealthy when we begin to replay scenarios, imagining the revenge that we could take, or replaying them as a form of self-punishment."

Sure, his mother or sister hadn't been through a divorce, he thought, but that did not mean they hadn't suffered through painful events of a different nature. His hurt was no more than that of his mother's when she lost her husband; it was only tinged with bitterness and regret, where hers wore the cover of sorrow and the question of "why?".

Help me to start treading the water. Help me start fighting towards a goal as I move towards the tide-line. It is time to come out of the icy sea of winter and into the bright, life-giving sands of summer. Bring me to the shore.

I choose not to replay events as self-punishment. I choose not to condemn myself for what you have forgiven. I choose not to poke the wound you have healed.

I praise you for Fiona who has been a "red-shoe friend". I ask for you to bless her as she walks along the path of your "Plan A" for her life. I don't know what plan I am on – "E" or "F", perhaps? – but I ask you to bring me back to your "Plan A". Enable me to believe for the extraordinary. Your Spirit abides in me as a seal of your promise. I can not claim to be lost when I am found. Bring me into the sunshine.

Lance thanked his sister after the service with a tight embrace, lifting her gently off the ground. She laughed in delight.

"What was that for?" she asked.

"For being a "red-shoe friend"! I'm going to start treading the water until God gives me the direction to the shore. You have permission to jab me in the ribs any time I start moodily dwelling on the past!"

Fiona impulsively returned his embrace, praising the Lord for answering her prayers.

The families separated in the morning tea throng. Lance found Tanya when he went outside to check on Johnnie in the playground. Tanya was talking with an older mother, who appeared to be of Korean descent, as she kept an eye on Wendy and Kate for her sister.

The mother gave Lance a smile of greeting as he approached before moving off in response to her son's entreaty to be pushed on the swing. Kate gave Lance an enthusiastic wave from the cubby house. He returned the gesture as he came in line with Tanya.

"Babysitting duties?" he enquired.

"Not really – Kate dragged me out to show me a routine of cartwheels and handstands."

"You were privileged to a show!"

Tanya murmured agreement.

They stood in silence for a moment looking over the twelve or so children enjoying their various games.

"What did you think of the sermon?" Lance initiated.

"Good! Just what I needed!"

"How so?"

"I felt God confirming my next step after uni' finishes. I've been asking whether I could return to India and I felt Him giving me the green light this morning. I'm stoked! I'm going to e-mail the director of the community development program tonight!"

"Wow! That certainly is exciting news!"

Tanya looked as if she was hard-pressed not to start jumping up and down like a kangaroo from excitement. "Yep, yep! How about you?"

"Seeking God for the next step. I mean, I have been for a while . . . but today redirected me to ask Him to reveal "Plan A" to me. I'm no longer content with a "Plan C" – or anything less than His "A". Who knows . . . perhaps I'll find myself in India, too."

Tanya turned her head sharply to look over at him. What did he mean? Was the comment intentional, or idle? Was he inferring he wanted to be where she was, or that he could be sent anywhere next?

"Yes, perhaps!" she laughed the comment off and turned the focus to Kate, who was currently hanging upside down from the monkey bars.

* * *

Lance went home with his sister and brother-in-law for a Sunday spread of cold-meats, gourmet cheese, and fresh bread.

Fiona gently brought Tanya up in conversation once the children had gone off to play in their outdoor cubby house. She asked a score of questions all at once, leaving Lance with the task of trying to gather them together: Did he love Tanya? What was changing within him? How was God moving? and Was he gaining a sense of release from the past?

"She makes me – hopeful. That is the best way I can describe it. When I went to South Africa I had no hope. Since then, God has slowly been restoring it to me. Hope: it truly is a beautiful thing."

"What restored it do you think? What was it about Africa? Or was it through Tanya?"

Lance paused thoughtfully. What had occurred in South Africa to change him? He knew God's hand had been in it. Perhaps He could have done it anywhere and St James was simply the place He chose. Although, there was something about that country . . . In the face of its problems, it continued to ebb with a profound hope, and that hope was in one extraordinary dream. Any nation that had eleven national languages, even more tribes, and was still able to dream of a united future had to have a large heart, which refused to give up. The people of that land may speak differently, look dissimilar, and not even share favourite sports, but they all held a fighting spirit; a spirit that refused to die. God had infected Lance with the same spirit, and from that spirit his hope to dream was reborn.

He tried to express this to his sister: "It wasn't Tanya – she came later. It is hard to define what it was exactly, Fi. I fell in love with the country. I mean, America will always be "home" and will never lose its place in my heart, and yet, South Africa . . . South Africa has a heart beat that pumps its blood into your own system. The land calls you to dream, to hope, to hold on to love. Yes, that's it: God showed me what it is to trust in His love again."

"The way you speak of it pulls at my heart! It must be a special place."

"It is, Fi, it really is."

"Have you considered whether South Africa might be where you should go next? Don't get me wrong – I love having you around – but, maybe, it's worth considering going back to South Africa since that is where God started everything?"

"I would be okay with that! I'd love to go into missions. Though, I can't do anything until I hear His voice for direction."

"And Tanya? Does she know you have a heart for missions?" Fiona asked her brother.

"Yes. She is actually planning to go into the field next year."

"Well, then, at least we know she isn't after his money!" Jo quipped.

Fiona gave her husband a stern look. "Honestly, Jo."

"What? Older man – Younger woman. It's the classic stereotype: the man is after her youthful beauty and the woman is after his money - hard-earned, or otherwise. They both get what they want out of the bargain, making them both happy; however, their family isn't. So, in my reasoning, if Tanya knows Lance is planning the life of a poor missionary, then the scenario allows not only the couple to be happy, but we, as the family, can be delighted, too!"

"You are unbelievable!" Fiona exclaimed, shaking her head in disbelief.

"What? Lance thought it was funny."

Lance had indeed found his brother-in-law's insights, if not funny, certainly amusing and was trying his best not to laugh.

"It's okay, Fi. I'm not easily offended and I can see Jo didn't mean any harm by it," he reassured her with a smile.

By no means appeased, Fiona nevertheless let the comments slide.

* * *

Diana, Tanya and Maggie were lying on the back lawn beneath a low, golden moon, heedless of the dew's wetness as it seeped into their clothes.

Maggie had entered into Tanya's confidence after the family barbecue at Mt Coot-tha and she was guiltily relieved. Fiona had given Maggie the sense that she was once again about to become the target of well-meant match-making.

Yes, she longed for a praiseworthy man to come into her life and walk the path with her, and she did not resent the efforts of those who tried to pair her off with available men (it showed their love and care for her), she only wished they would leave it to happen naturally and in God's timing.

The sisters had been discussing God's glorious creation as they looked up at the night sky, brimming with stars, many light-years away when Diana introduced a more personal tone to their reflections. It was what Maggie had been quietly wondering about, but hesitant to ask:

"Are you and Lance . . . have you guys talked about where you stand?"

"No!" Tanya answered in exasperation. "He has only hinted at it."

Maggie laughed. "You could bring it up, you know."

"I don't want to! He's the man. He's the one meant to pursue."

"He looks to be pursuing you from where I stand," Diana said. "And I think that clarifying where you stand doesn't fall into the same class as pursuing if he is sending confusing messages."

"You're right. Perhaps I should say, rather, that I don't want to broach the subject until I've worked out where I stand."

"What makes you uncertain?"

"I think part of me sees that he is striving to find his next step. He needs to know where he is going to end up. I'm praying God uses this time to give him direction."

"And this causes fear in you . . . because you don't know what he wants from life?"

"No, it isn't that. I do think he needs more certainty in his calling, but that isn't what holds me back. I only mentioned it because I think a relationship might confuse him as he tries to discern God's directing voice."

"And not for you?" Diana teased, knowing her sister was also fighting with God, seeking an impression for the following year, post graduation.

"Sorry?" Tanya replied in confusion.

"It was barely a few days ago when you were frustrated at God for not having given you any direction for next year."

"He has today! I'm going back to India!"

Tanya's announcement caused a brief disruption as Maggie and Diana asked for more details. Tanya shared how she believed God had confirmed the destination with her during the morning church service and that she had already written to the project director about opportunities to return (longer-term), to their team.

Diana turned slightly to give Tanya an awkward embrace, made clumsy by her expanding girth. Maggie squeezed Tanya's hand.

"We'll miss you, of course, but I'm happy for you, honey," Diana said.

"Yes," Maggie agreed. "But, getting back to Lance . . . If you've only just received guidance, and have a further six months until you finish your course, why is it such a big deal that he doesn't know, at this stage, where he's going next?"

"Neither Chris nor I knew where we were heading when we started dating, or even during our engagement," Diana added.

"That's different."

"Why?"

"It just is!"

After further encouraging their sister once more to talk to Lance about her feelings, Diana and Maggie said no more on the topic.

Meanwhile Tanya, far from embracing her sisters' advice, was praying fervently for God to take Lance from her mind and out of her heart. She was beginning to realise it had been fear that had caused her to keep a distance from Lance when she left South Africa. She could have asked for his contact details, or even found them out after arriving home, and had chosen not to. She feared how a relationship with him would develop, what she'd have to give up, and, most of all, she feared sinning against God.

It had been the reply from her friends in South Africa, received after church, that had opened Tanya's eyes to see the deeper questions in her heart. Becca and Sam had typed their reply together as Tanya had anticipated they would. Overall it had been an encouraging e-mail: they liked Lance well-enough from what they knew of him, it was good that he could see her in her home environment where she was less emotionally-vulnerable, they were praying for her, and they expected to be kept up to date on any developments. However, there were two questions (she was sure that Becca had written), which Tanya could not shake off: How did she feel about divorce? and Did she think that she could marry a divorcee (because if she couldn't, then the matter was simple: she couldn't move forward with Lance)?

Unfortunately, Tanya was unable to give a simple answer to these questions. She would need to give them considerable thought and prayer. She was confused about divorce and where God stood on the issue. Could she marry a divorcee? She didn't know. The question began to haunt her; awake and asleep she wrestled with the unspoken fear that to marry a divorcee was to commit a sin against God.

CHAPTER 7

A land mine exploded on the side of the dirt road to her right, a small chard barely missing the side of her cheek as she crouched as an instinctive response. Huddling over, and keeping close to the ground, she began to duck-walk forward. She knew the position wouldn't keep her safe from mines; nevertheless, the noise of gun fire around her caused her senses to reel and she found herself physically unable to stand. Her sensory system was in shock. She wanted to stop moving, to given in, to find a ditch by the road side to lie in and wait for it to be over. Would the firing never cease? Would a peace never be established? Would the conflict always continue?

Tanya's emotional conflict pulled her out from the day dream the warm sun had drawn her into. Sitting on the small, stone bench in the backyard, surrounded by her mother's prized rose bushes, she absently reached down to pull up a weed. The image was an apt picture for her mind's state, which she presently saw as a battlefield.

Questions and scriptural quotations chased each other around in her mind whilst conflicting thoughts vied to be cemented as the truth.

She thought on "Genesis 2:24" and how, right from the get go, God made it clear that man and woman became one in marriage. One man. One woman. For life. But what now – in this time after the fall? she wondered.

In contrast to the verse in Genesis, she saw the book of "First Peter" declaring love to cover a multitude of sins[15]. And, of course, there was grace; Tanya could not pass by God's beautiful, wondrous, far-reaching grace, which removed sin from sinners as far as East is removed from West.

Ah, she thought, but one could not easily forget the very words of Christ condemning as an adulterer any who married a divorcee[16]. Neither could one forget Paul's words when he proclaims to the Corinthians the same condemning circumstance[17]. Where was the grace there? Surely, grace is sufficient? She had so many questions, doubts, and fears. It was enough to give anyone a headache!

The paper illustration she had heard many times during her days in youth group came to her mind. She began to pray as she sought God for guidance:

God, I recall the illustration of gluing two pieces of paper together. They begin as separate entities but once joined by the glue, you cannot neatly pull them apart; the two sheets of paper will come apart with pieces of the other attached, if they don't tear, completely.

This is how I see the separation that comes with divorce. Your Word tells us not to separate what you have joined together. The pain it must cause when two souls, which became one in marriage, are later ripped apart by divorce! I can't imagine it. The papers can never be restored to their original states, but is this true of our hearts and spirits?

Can't you bring healing and restoration? I've heard friends testify of how you've restored them after they've fallen into sexual sin before marriage. If a young person who has had multiple partners can be healed, why not someone who has been married?

I do not believe this is too big for your grace. In fact, I can trust you for it and would argue with anyone that you do bring complete restoration to those who have suffered the pain of divorce. So why am I finding it this hard for myself? Am I truly that proud (to believe I shouldn't marry someone who's been divorced)? If they have truly accepted your restoration, then surely it is no longer sin to marry them because they are a new creation in Christ, whole once again?

Tanya was now pulling up the weeds from the rose bed with rough determination.

Lord, heal Lance! Bind him up. I sense he has been fighting this restoration. Does he desire to be restored? Is he content in the safety of brokenness? Show him this is not the freedom you call us to! We don't have to hide in brokenness to protect ourselves from falling into sin!

Give him freedom, Lord! Bind up his wounds. Mend his heart. Restore his soul completely. Make him one; make him whole again in you.

I am convinced that, until he accepts this restoration, he is still bound to his ex-wife in spirit and it would be a sin to marry him. As it is said in Matthew – it would be adultery[18]. *But if he has been forgiven?*

Oh Lord, I don't want to be wrong on this! Help me, I pray, to walk in righteousness! I think if he accepts your forgiveness then he is cleansed, pure and holy, and therefore free to marry again. Am I wrong? Please tell me if I am! To be wrong in this doesn't fit with my picture of your grace, which seems to break all bounds and rules.

Tanya continued to pray for God to reveal the truth to her and asked Him to show her the way. She believed God could heal and restore Lance. She was confident this was what God was doing. However, that was to deal with past sins. To marry him . . . wouldn't that be to intentionally commit a sin? And yet, she could not accept that He would extend grace over a whole multitude of sin, only to hold it back from the one who married a divorcee.

God, I do not understand at all! My head aches with the conflict. It seems you are promising me that your grace is sufficient.

You say we are made righteous by faith and have been made pure, made white; that we are cleansed and restored. But then your Word also says: "he who marries a woman divorced from her husband commits adultery"[19].

If I was to marry Lance, surely that would be to commit adultery? Although if he has repented, and you have cleansed him, then isn't he free from the sin of adultery? And if he is free from adultery, then surely it is no longer a sin to marry him?

Ah, Lord! Teach me of your grace! Give me a greater understanding of it.

Tanya had made noble promises to herself not to be found in Lance's company whilst her heart wrestled with God and sought His guidance. It was one she found herself unable to keep.

With Diana nearing the end of her eighth month, she had stopped working and Fiona was often to be found in her company. And where Fiona was, her children and brother would also be. Tanya wanted to spend time with her sister during this exciting phase, but was finding it challenging to see Lance frequently when her own heart was in turmoil and was struggling with God's grace.

Frustrated by the circular tone of her prayer and thoughts, Tanya escaped inside, where she began chatting with her mother, who was working away in the kitchen on their dinner.

* * *

God, me again!

Tanya was sitting in a comfortable sofa chair at the Coffee Hut. The local café was brimming with people who had opted for an indoor location to escape the chill outside on the sunny winter's afternoon.

Tanya prayed quietly as she waited for her ordered soy-chai latte to be delivered. As was becoming annoyingly common, she found herself praying about her ever-growing regard for Lance.

Why can't I be free of him? He haunts my dreams. He isn't anything like how I would have pictured my husband to be. He doesn't fit neatly into the box I had drawn for the man I want to marry and yet he seems to surpass my mythological creation.

Seeking to distract herself from the image of his thoughtful, loving eyes, Tanya opened her Bible. Given the restlessness of her mood she decided to read through a small book – perhaps one of Paul's epistles.

The pages fell open to where her bookmark sat in Psalms. She remembered Sam had given her the bookmark, which had a picture of two friends hugging. Her gaze fell upon the words:

"I thank God every time I remember you – Philippians 1:3."

You have got to be kidding!

Disgruntled, Tanya turned to Philippians to see how the verse actually read. She was convinced the bookmark's designer had taken artistic liberties.

To her disappointment, she read the words Paul had written to the church in Philippi and had to repent of her initial disgust – the words were the same: Paul had told the Philippians he prayed for them every time they entered into his thoughts.

Contemplating the verses, Tanya wasn't sure what God wanted from her. She had come to believe the books she had read on purity that said she could pray against the emotion of love and God would take such emotion from her. Now it seemed God wanted her to use this same overpowering emotion as a reminder to pray for Lance.

God, I don't understand. It is painful thinking of him. Why do you ask it of me?

It's a romantic notion and all – thinking that perhaps I am praying for the man I will one day marry – I'm just unsure whether I can do it . . . It HURTS when I think of him. To keep praying for a guy I love and yet may never have . . .? It doesn't seem fair. And I know life doesn't have to be fair, although I do wish it didn't have to be quite this painful.

Tanya's prayer was momentarily disrupted as a waiter placed her drink onto the two-seater table.

You could still call me to pray for him whilst removing the burden my heart carries!

Tanya knew the petulant end of her prayer was not true. Whilst she had a heart for intercession, it was geared towards those who she cared most about and the issues for which she was most passionate. She found it difficult to pray faithfully for something when there was no emotional connection.

She petitioned God for the strength to use thoughts of Lance as a cue to pray for him and turned to read through Philippians.

Muttering the words under her breath in an attempt to focus, she began to utter for Lance the same prayer Paul had written for the Philippians:

"Paul and Timothy, servants of Christ Jesus, To all the saints in Christ Jesus who are at Philippi, with the overseers and deacons: Grace to you and peace from God our Father and the Lord Jesus Christ.

"I thank my God in all my remembrance of you, always in every prayer of mine for you all making my prayer with joy, because of your partnership in the gospel from the first day until now." [20]

[Well, I will try to.]

"And I am sure of this, that he who began a good work in you will bring it to completion at the day of Jesus Christ. It is right for me to feel this way about you all, because I hold you in my heart, for you are all partakers with me of grace . . ." [21]

[He is my brother. I hold him in brotherly affection and therefore care for him and what becomes of him.]

". . . both in my imprisonment and in the defence and confirmation of the gospel." [21]

Tanya took a sip of her coffee. Its flavour went unnoticed.

"For God is my witness, how I yearn for you all with the affection of Christ Jesus." [22]

[Make it with your affection, God. That would be easier.]

"And it is my prayer that your love may abound more and more, with knowledge and all discernment, so that you may approve what is excellent, and so be pure and blameless for the day of Christ, filled with the fruit of righteousness that comes through Jesus Christ, to the glory and praise of God." [23]

[Yes, Lord, grant him your love. Touch him with your healing love. Show him to love again.]

Tanya reached down to draw her maroon journal and a pen out from her rucksack. Opening her journal, she penned:

God, why is life turning out so differently to how I thought it would?

I remember when Dad used to tell us stories as girls about Cinderella and Snow White and the rest. I dreamed of such a tale for myself. I don't even want to be a princess – I'm your Princess and that's enough for me – but I wouldn't mind a loving man and the "happily ever after"!

Maybe I need a time of "adversity" before the ending. Each of the fairytale princesses had to go through some sort of trial, or misadventure . .
.

What's the one with the frog? Lance doesn't look like a frog (he's gorgeous; you made an incredibly handsome man in him), but he does have baggage.

Then again, I guess we all do. But divorce is such a heavy load! It certainly wasn't the sort of baggage I was expecting my prince to come with. I knew neither of us would be perfect, but I thought, I don't know what I thought my prince would be fighting with, I just didn't expect I would be the "second woman".

And maybe he isn't "the one" for me. But this is revealing to me just how little grace I have on others in some areas. I never would have thought it, but I really do think I look down on people who have had a divorce. And why? Lance puts me to shame with the devotion he shows towards you. He seemed to revel in devotional times and meditating on your Word. I have to push myself to read one of the smaller epistles!

What is that fairytale – the one about the man that comes as a bear? The girls fear him at first; however, he is kind to them and ends up protecting them against an attack by a cranky dwarf. He turned into a prince when the dwarf (who had enchanted him), died. I can't remember . .
.

Anyway, maybe Lance is my bear. His baggage seems daunting at first, but you will free him from it and he will become my prince. In the meantime, will you free me from this weight of fear?

Ah, the disillusionment of life! It never turns out as we dream it will as children, but I think I am with Dee – with you, it will be better! Help me to trust you with this.

Love you Lord, Amen.

PS – The story I was thinking of was "Snow White and Red Rose". What a classic!

Tanya's latte glass stood empty by the time she had finished her journal entry. She remained at the table a little longer, lost in thought. She loved that God and His ways remained a mystery to her. Life would be boring if the jigsaw puzzle was too easy to put together!

She knew Lance had healing to undergo as a result of the divorce. Moreover, she had growth of her own to undertake before she would be comfortable broaching the topic of a relationship with him, as Maggie and Diana continued urging her to do. And whilst she waited, she would continue to entrust her heart to the loving guardianship of her heavenly Father.

* * *

It was possibly a good turn of events that Tanya was left unaware that Lance had begun to accept God's healing. She put up new walls as Lance began to let his towards her crumble. Whilst his heart remained broken, he was finally allowing God to touch the shards; permitting God to gather them into his hands and begin the reassembly.

Lance was resting in a rather flimsy deck-chair on the back patio reading "The Screwtape Letters" by C S. Lewis when the phone rang. He had the house to himself, having opted out of a family stroll to the local park. He had to dash inside and scramble under couch cushions to find the cordless phone, which was edged into the ridge under the left chair arm.

"Hello?"

His mother's voice answered his greeting. Delighted, Lance took the phone back to his recently-vacated spot in the weak sunshine.

"You've caught me alone, I'm afraid. The others are down at the park," he said.

"That's okay; Fiona and I were able to catch up with the littlies via Skype a few nights back," Gwen replied.

She asked how he had been getting on and listened as he gave her a run-down of life amidst the McCarthy-chaos before coming to the objective of her call:

"Darling, I hope this doesn't upset you . . . I had a call from Amanda yesterday wanting your address over there. I didn't think you'd mind if I gave it to her as she mentioned you'd had a talk and she wanted to send you a letter."

"Oh?"

"She didn't expand; although, I was given the impression you'd understand what it was about. She mentioned the need to clarify her position . . . ?"

"Ah – I had asked her for forgiveness and she said she'd be willing to consider it in the future," he explained. "I also asked if she thought there was any chance of reconciliation in the future and she said absolutely not. I suppose she wants to explain a little more about where she stands and why she doesn't want to go down that road."

"I'm sorry, dear."

"No, it's okay. It was awfully confusing at first. I don't know if Fiona has mentioned it to you – I talked with Amanda just before flying to Australia. I was certain God was leading me back to Amanda. In retrospect, I believe He wanted to close that season for me in a tangible way. At any rate, when I arrived here . . ."

Lance found his tongue at a loss to form words, and trying to think of how to explain Tanya to his mother only chased the words further from his mouth.

"Your sister did mention a young lady called Tanya . . ." Gwen prompted.

"Oh, good – she has."

Gwen was relieved he did not sound upset at his sister's disclosure.

"Will you tell me a little about her? Is it serious?"

"We're just friends. She is amazing: intelligent, lively, compassionate, and beautiful; she is completing a Masters of International Studies and Community Development; she's interested in missions; she loves God – you should see how her face lights up when she worships . . ."

Gwen was smiling. She joyfully praised the Lord in her soul as she listened. This son of hers, who had been broken, bitter and lost, was now restored to life, and it seemed that God was not content merely to restore, but was giving Lance hope for a second love!

Lance proceeded to share with his mother about how he met Tanya, their unexpected reunion, and how their friendship continued to grow and deepen.

Gwen was concerned Lance felt he was "not good enough" for such a "young, lively and innocent woman". It conveyed to her that he was still holding out on accepting the complete measure of God's healing and forgiveness. She would continue to pray for him.

Lance came to the end of his monologue and waited in silence.

"Will I get to meet her when I visit?" Gwen asked.

"Is that certain? Great! Yes, I imagine you will. I'd like you to."

"Yes, I'm flying over in less than three weeks! But only for a short visit. I didn't want to book anything until it was certain Jo and Fi were staying and, whilst Amy isn't due until late-August, I want to be home by the start of the month, just in case."

"How are the expectant parents doing?"

Gwen gave Lance a short update on Amy and Dave. Amy was now suffering from fatigue and was forced to nap for a couple of hours each afternoon. Meanwhile, Dave had quickly established himself in the New York branch of his firm, Maney and Jones Incorporated. Gwen visited them at least twice a week and Amy was allowing her to pray over the child.

Lance could tell that his mother was delighted to have the expecting couple living so close to her, and was loving being able to fuss over Amy in the late stages of the pregnancy. He didn't realise that she was as equally delighted over the news that he had a young woman of interest in his life.

* * *

Gwen was not the only one encouraged by Lance's friendship with Tanya. Fiona was another pleased observer of how Tanya's joyful person was causing new buds of life in her brother.

Maggie and Diana saw Lance's more taciturn disposition and business mind as equalising factors to their sister's outgoing personality and care-free generosity. They had also observed a greater blush to their younger sister's cheeks and an added bounce in her ever-buoyant stride since Lance had come upon the scene.

Those within the church had first harboured protective instincts towards Tanya, whom they had fondly watched grow from an inquisitive child into a woman with Christ-like compassion and Kingdom values. However, Lance quickly became amalgamated into the community and the congregation began to view him in the light of a treasured son. As soon as he had been accepted as "good enough" for their cherished Tanya, they had joined the ranks of those cheering for the match.

However, at least one person was apprehensive watching the interest and affection grow in each party. For Tina, the growing friendship between Lance and her little girl caused no small degree of uneasiness. She feared for Tanya's tender heart and fretted for her daughter's future.

As Lance talked with hope to Gwen about Tanya, Tina and Ben were in their white Sudan discussing her with great concern as they returned home from a shopping expedition to the local hardware store. It was a conversation they'd had several times in the past few weeks:

"Ben, I don't think she sees what she is getting into. She is going to get hurt."

"Love, try not to worry. I am sure it will fizzle out fast enough. Tanya has always been volatile with her affections. Not that I mind Lance. . ."

"But . . . Ben . . . he's divorced! I know I shouldn't be biased against him for it (for he seems to think less of himself due to it and is truly repentant); it's only – I'm afraid of how much more experience of life he has than her. She remains raw in matters of the heart."

Ben drew in a deep breath, considering his answer. His wife was not the only one prejudiced when it came to their daughter. He liked Lance. He just wanted the best for his little girl. Nevertheless, he knew the day would come when he would have to give over his baby to another man's care. He only prayed for the man to be worthy of his most precious treasure.

"This might give her experience without ending in hurt," he comforted his wife. "Lance is a decent guy; he won't hurt Tanya."

Tina muttered an unconvinced "maybe".

"You know, Tina," Ben added as a bright idea occurred to him, "I reckon Lance sees he isn't right for Tanya and that's why he has held off asking her out. I credit him to do right by her. He'll put her off him gently, you wait and see."

Tina could not be satisfied with her husband's optimistic outlook. As they began to unload bags of potting mix, mulch and chicken manure from the car, she made him promise to talk to their youngest child. She would not know peace until he had done so. Ben reluctantly agreed. He would not relish such a talk.

Ben put off broaching the subject with Tanya for two weeks when events went against the confident pronouncement he had given to his wife. It seemed the matter was destined to progress after all, causing Tina to increase her entreaties to him.

CHAPTER 8

Tanya, blissfully unaware of most of the speculation aimed in her direction, fluctuated between gratefulness that Lance had not sought dates with her outside those of family gatherings, or church, and irritation that he was not pursuing her.

She was surprised her university work was not suffering as a result of his distracting intrusion into her life. Butterflies emerged from their cocoon whenever he was close to her, her imagination had started to depict scenes of a life with him by her side, and nausea came upon her when she gave her mind leeway to wrestle back and forth with the theological questions surrounding divorce, remarriage, and the extent of God's grace.

Picturing him going about his day with his sister's family did not help in the least. She longed for Sunday to come when she would finally have a legitimate reason to see him again! Assuming he would attend church . . .

Indeed this fluttering inside would be wonderful, if only she knew he felt the same way! Why hadn't he called her? Fiona had their number. Did he not want to see her? Had he even thought of her?

Oh please, Lord, let them come to church! I am going to go crazy! This is ridiculous. What is happening to me? This can't be normal. It just can't be! I want to be free from the constant battle with my thoughts. Set me free from this tenderness towards Lance.

Deciding to wallow in self-pity, Tanya grabbed a tub of ice-cream from the freezer and a block of chocolate. With goodies in hand, she quickly ran up the stairs and sat promptly down on her bedroom floor. She began to break the chocolate into pieces, letting them fall into the ice-cream. She returned to the kitchen briefly to pull a few chocolate biscuits out from the cookie jar, before returning to her room, clicking the "play button" over the music list on her computer entitled "Girlie music", and sat down on the floor to enjoy her treat.

Half an hour later, she was ill in the stomach, with a sugar-headache to boot, and pitying herself more than ever, with all the old restlessness persisting.

She recalled the last time she had seen Lance at church. His broad face had reflected a man wrestling with pain, forgiveness and God's healing.

Her heart ached for him. It was bitter-sweet to love a man who was held a prisoner by his past.

She knew God was at work in his life. Moreover, she firmly believed that God's work, when completed, would see complete restoration, she was only impatient for the work to be done.

She longed to see him come to her as one restored; to woo her and win her over in a romantic pursuit for her hand. She put countless questions before God, but all the response she received from Him was: a call to pray for Lance, to love him, and to encourage him. She found it a hard ask.

Steeling her heart, she determined to walk beside Lance in his current journey. It was her prayer that, in time, she would see him restored.

"What if he is not being restored for you? Will you continue along this path with joy and praise?"

Her chest was compressed by an invisible hand as she considered the implications of these questions. What if Lance was healed only to walk away from her? What if she reminded him of this season and he had to cut her off at its end? What if he returned to his ex-wife – could she smile, and be glad, and hope to be lucky enough to win the heart of a man his equal?

Tears welled in her eyes and she hugged her knees.

Lord, even if his restoration leads him away from me I will choose to walk this path. I will choose to pray for him, love him, and be a friend to him. Give me the strength!

In that moment, Tanya knew the role God had set before her. It was no easy task. She certainly would be unable to complete it in her own strength. Regardless, she would attempt it in faith, trusting God to give her endurance.

Queasy, Tanya went to make herself a cup of peppermint tea. Perhaps it would ease her churning stomach. As she leant back against the laminate kitchen bench, waiting for the kettle to boil, Tanya reflected on her singleness. She made no secret to herself, or before others, that she had a strong desire for marriage and children; yet she remained single. Why?

People often asked her that: "Why?" Others tried to reassure her, saying she would have her time, if only she was patient. What they didn't see was it was her choice to remain single. She chose that way because it was what God had requested of her. It required the sacrifice of her desires for a season in order to be part of a bigger plan and purpose.

In her years of singledom she had been able to offer support to others, both practical and intercessory, in ways she wouldn't have been able to do if she had been married, much less married with a family. It didn't mean God had dulled those desires, which was why it remained a sacrifice, a laying down of self.

She poured the steaming water into her favourite mug, which depicted Little Red Riding Hood offering a bunch of flowers to a wise-looking wolf holding a walking cane.

Tanya blew out deeply. God was calling her to lay her dreams for marriage down once more. When Lance looked her in the eyes she knew he loved her back, yet mingled with his love was a wary guardedness.

Her mood was low as she grasped the squeezable honey bottle from the cupboard. Until his grief was healed she knew they could not marry – and until there was potential for marriage, she would not enter into a deeper relationship than friendship with him.

God had given her a fierce, compelling, and jealous love for Lance. She would walk beside him for as long as he needed, trusting for more in the future. She had hope for it. She felt she had God's promise for it. Nevertheless, she was all too aware that it could be an extremely long walk and that her feet would ache before the end of it. There would be days where her feet would swell in the heat, and her legs would become as jelly from the arduous journey. Yet in spite of such probable trials, it was a journey she was willing to make. She would carry Lance at times if need dictated.

She carried her brimming mug to her room and placed it on the top of her bookshelf, positioned by her bed, and took a seat atop her mattress.

God, it hurts. It hurts so much. Still, I am willing. Make me willing. I see a strength in my heart only you could have put there. This love is painful but it holds a hidden strength, championing me on to give out rather than hold back.

I long for the day when I look into Lance's beautiful grey eyes and see only love, and hope, and a future. In the meantime, I will walk beside him, hold his hand, pray for him, and encourage him. Even if this means I love him right back to reconciliation between him and his wife, I will do it.

I only ask that you give me the strength to walk out these affirmations. The spirit is willing but the body is weak. Provide your strength on this journey. Amen.

"The aim of our charge is love that issues from a pure heart and a good conscience and a sincere faith." [24]
The echoed verse was the limit of what she could take. Breaking down, Tanya's body gently shook with heavy sobs as salty tears ran down her cheeks.

* * *

True to Tanya's hopes, Lance did attend church that Sunday. He arrived with a sense of expectation, knowing God desired to meet him there; he only had to be open to what the Lord wanted to say.

It had become his habit to sit at the back. This way he knew he could stand during worship free from all observation and enter more fully into a private time with his Father. As the band began to sing, Lance stood, allowing the words to wash over him as he prayed:

It is true, Lord: you have paid the ransom. Who am I to reject a gift so pure, so beautiful, and so selfless? You came that I might live. You came that my sins would no longer condemn me. I have no debt and you have taken away my reproach. I fall to my knees at the foot of the cross. I praise you for your sacrifice. I am no longer marked with guilt and sin, but am pure, white as snow, forgiven. Oh what joy there is to be found in your love and mercy!

The musicians flowed from one song to the next and Lance knew the Lord had planned this service just for him. God was placing the final pieces of his shattered heart back into the whole; faithfully fulfilling His promise of healing and restoration. His fellow worshippers faded from his awareness as he entered into the presence of God:

I was guilty and yet you cleansed me of my sin. I am free! Thank you Father! Because of your sacrifice my debt has been paid. I am alive in Christ. My sins have been forgiven. I am a member of the Kingdom of God.

You were rejected by man. You were hung upon the cross. Your blood was poured out for me. You went through pain unimaginable, inconceivable, for me, for us, sinful as we were. Your love, undeserved and freely given, pours over me and cleanses me of my bloodguilt.

Lance sang out the words loudly with a tear escaping from the corner of his eye as God's words echoed across his awareness:

"You are clean. You are pure."

Who was he that God should love him so dearly? He had no answer, simply knowing it was true. The God of all creation cared enough about him to heal his brokenness and to free him from the pain of loss. Humbled, Lance sang the final song as a prayer to the One who had given all. All he could see was the cross, and he praised the Lord for His redeeming sacrifice.

As the music faded and the congregation resumed their seats, Lance found himself unable to engage with the voices he heard as a member gave the notices, ahead of the pastor standing to give the sermon, as he was still engaged with the Lord.

He sat quietly in his seat, head tilted downwards and eyes fixated on the floor as he processed what he felt the Lord was doing in his life: freedom and forgiveness, what beautiful words.

Sure, he had made mistakes in his life. In retrospect he knew that he could have and should have fought for his marriage. He never should have given up on it. He chose selfishness, and the harbouring of self-pity, over love and self-sacrifice. Be this as it may, he could not go back and change the past. He had grieved it, and now God was calling him to accept His forgiveness and forgive himself.

It seemed harder to forgive himself than to accept God's forgiveness. Didn't he deserve to be punished? Shouldn't he wear the cost of his sin for the rest of his life? Surely God's grace only extended so far.

Lance knew that what God was offering him was more than he could have hoped for, all he had to do was accept it. Could God truly wash him whiter than snow? Cleanse him so that he no longer wore the reproach of a sinner, the shame of the divorced?

"Yes!" That is the answer you give me! "Yes, my son, you are clean, you are pure!"

I cannot conceive the love you have for us. You are unfathomable. As hard as I try I will never be able to perceive just how boundless the extent of your grace is. It is truly unfathomable; oh, scandalous grace!

It does not make sense that you would give your grace so freely. There seems to be grace even for grace-abuse. But I long to live righteously because you saved me and now have healed me. You have freed me; therefore, I am no longer a slave to sin. The guilt of my past sin has been washed away, and I no longer need to let it dictate the path of my life. I thank you for freeing me from shame. I thank you for setting me back in line with your "Plan A" for my life.

Lance lost the track of his prayer as an image of him talking to Tanya after the service came into his mind.

Annoyed at his irreverence, Lance apologised to God, but the image remained. He felt drawn to take notice of what his imagined self was saying: There he was telling Tanya he was a pure, spotless bride of Christ!

Furrowing his brow, Lance sought an explanation from God as to what it was meant to mean. What did the image represent? He liked Tanya, he already knew that. Was God giving him permission to love again? Surely it would not come this soon? He was cleansed and forgiven, but wasn't there consequences for his sin? Yes, there were consequences. His interpretation of the image must be wrong . . .

Lance avoided Tanya after the service. Offering her an incoherent excuse, he had fled out into the street where he completed several circuits around the block waiting for Fiona and her troop to emerge.

Try as he might, he could not escape the image from the service. It resounded over and over in his mind, bringing with it thoughts of India, of being with Tanya in India . . .

* * *

His reply of calm assurance wasn't what Tanya was wanting! She longed to be heard not merely listened to.

Lance had called her on the Monday morning as she filtered through articles for her course's major research project. She had been glad to have the tedious work interrupted. Would she like to go out that afternoon? She had a lot of work to do . . . What about a short walk – refresh the mind? Yes! She'd love to. And thus it had been arranged.

Tanya had released her stress about her assignment upon Lance's listening ears as they walked through the streets to a narrow pathway leading into the Bush Reserve. They had then turned down a side path, which led them into a neighbouring estate, and, a few streets later, to a local park, by which time Lance was attempting to ease her agitation with soothing affirmations of her intelligence.

Lance had felt her tense beside him in response to his endeavours to be supportive. He found it hard to believe she could not see how gifted she was in academics. Moreover, he felt compelled to make Tanya realise how God had created her with unique beauty, both in spirit and looks.

He had startled her by taking her arm, calling her to stop. With gentle firmness, he turned her to face him and, looked into her eyes, maintained her gaze. He smiled as he brushed a stray strand of hair from her face.

Tanya's breathe caught within her. She didn't want to make a sound lest she break the moment. She prayed to be made a prisoner, trapped in the moment.

His hand lingered under her chin for a moment longer than necessary. His persuasive eyes remained fixed with hers, inducing her to believe all the beauty he saw within her.

Lance was the one to break the moment. He gently took her hand and led her to the swings. Tanya sat and Lance gently began to push her.

"I admire you, Tanya," Lance let out quietly, as momentum carried her away from him.

She gave no response. Lance wondered if she had heard. He almost hoped she hadn't.

A moment later and she replied in kind: she admired him, too.

Lance mustered his nerves, praying they wouldn't desert him, and hoping he was doing right by Tanya. He had decided she had the right to know where he stood.

"I have been convincing myself you don't care – and perhaps you don't – but I want you to know I find you incredibly attractive. You are gentle, love passionately, and have a grace about your being that in no way lessens the strength I see in you."

Tanya swallowed hard. She brought her feet down upon the ground, starting to slow the swing's propulsion.

Lance added his aid and the swing stopped its pendulum motion, before continuing: "I've been holding off, feeling unworthy. Yesterday God gave me an image of a white, spotless bride. I felt Him saying I was clean, and pure, and new. I'm slowly accepting this truth."

She turned her head to look up at him in questioning expectation.

"I know I come with baggage, and I don't expect anything, but you have the right to know where I stand," he concluded.

"So, you are saying . . .?" she prompted, nervous of his reply.

He came around to face her. Taking her hands tenderly, he guided her to her feet.

"I care for you, Tanya. I would like to know you more; to pursue you. I want to see if we can move beyond friendship."

A tremulous smile was upon her lips. Her eyes searched his; looking . . . looking . . . seeking some unknown confirmation in their depths.

"I do come with brokenness," he continued humbly. "God has not finished the healing work in my life. We don't need to rush anything. I am asking whether you, too, wish to build on our friendship in an intentional manner – and see where it leads."

"I would," she replied. "I would like that, too."

Emerald eyes twinkled mischievously out at him from between her dark lashes. He found it captivating.

"Where to from here?" she asked softly.

"Honestly, I have no idea! I'll admit to being a little scared! I don't know where we go from here. Let's both pray about it and see what God says."

They sat on the swings beside each other for a few minutes in silence until Lance suggested they not think about what they ought to do next; but rather, wait to see where things led.

Standing up, he offered his hand and helped her to rise. Continuing their walk through the park, he led them into light-hearted banter with the purpose of settling Tanya's nerves.

* * *

Tanya ran to answer the summoning ring of the door bell. Would Lance have driven over to surprise her? Surely not . . . Yet hope stirred in her breast.

She opened the door, aware of a sensation in her stomach as though multiple golf balls had been suddenly dropped into it, only to be greeted by a stranger. The short, youthful man was dressed in a red company polo shirt with a tulip insignia on the breast pocket. He sported a matching red cap.

Tanya greeted him curiously.

"Hi. I have a delivery for a Miss Tanya Woolston?" he said.

"That's me." Her gaze fell on the long, white rectangular box he held under one arm.

With his other hand he held out the paper work, attached to a clipboard board.

"Sign here, and here." He pointed to the required spaces.

Once she had signed, he held out the box and wished her to "have a good one".

Tanya skipped across to the table. If the box was what she thought it was . . .

Opening the lid she found six long-stemmed, orange roses! She had never been given roses before – unless you counted quite an unwanted single red rose given by classmate on Valentine's Day back in Grade Ten.

She picked up the envelope, which had been resting lightly upon the stems.

Opening the card she read:

Dear Tanya,

You are too unique for red roses.

May your day be blessed with the same sunshine you bring into our lives.

Lance.

Tanya set about trimming the stems and arraying them in a crystal vase belonging to her mother. Her father walked in from his shed as she was inserting the last rose into the vase, whilst humming the tune of "Great is Your faithfulness".

"Someone is in high spirits!" he greeted.

"Hey Dad."

"Aaah – and no wonder!" he added with a smile, observing the roses.

"Aren't they beautiful? Lance sent them over."

Tanya had anxiously confided in her father the previous night about her walk with Lance. He had listened in silence before giving her a hug and conveying his happiness for her.

Tanya had been relieved at his response to her news. She had been concerned her overly-protective father would handle it poorly. She had promptly conveyed Lance's intention to come and speak with him about the relationship sometime during the week.

"Tanya . . . ?" Ben queried presently.

"Yeah?"

Ben pulled out one of the wooden dining chairs and sat down.

"Can I talk to you for a minute?" he asked.

"Sure."

Tanya took a seat and waited.

Ever loyal, Ben owned his wife's concerns: "Your mother and I were talking and we are both concerned that, perhaps, you are running into things a little quickly with Lance."

"Quickly? Dad, we've only just talked about moving forward! – wherever forward is!"

Ben started fiddling with the secateurs.

"Maybe I worded it wrong . . . We simply want to make sure you'll go slowly and carefully. Remember that you aren't . . . you aren't his "first love", so to speak. We don't want to see you get hurt."

Tanya reached out to grasp her father's hand.

"I'm not in a hurry," she assured him.

Tanya tried to understand her parents' point of view. She knew it could not be easy to watch their youngest prepare to take flight from the nest. She also had a reasonable suspicion her mother had instigated the conversation, concerned about Lance's divorce, whilst her father merely was grieving the thought of losing her.

"To be honest, I need you," she continued. "I know he comes with baggage – as we all do. I need you to be my protector in this. Obviously, I would not consider dating a guy if I didn't think it had the potential to end in marriage, but I will remain open to ending it at any point if it becomes apparent it won't work out, or if other concerns arise."

"I don't want you to approach dating negatively . . ."

"I'm not, Dad," she assured him. "I just want to approach it sensibly, and keep a proper perspective."

"I know you will." Ben gave her hand a squeeze. "Your mother and I are very proud of you."

"Thanks Dad."

"Welcome. Now on to important matters – when do I get to interrogate the fellow?" he asked cheekily.

Tanya gave a gurgle of laughter.

"I'm not sure . . . but feel free to grill him! Seriously – please ask the hard questions. I need to know he thinks I'm worth pursuing."

"Too straight, he better!"

There was a momentary pause as Ben broke their hand hold.

"Dad . . .?"she asked tentatively.

"Yes?"

"What do you think about divorce?"

Ben frowned and gave his daughter a stricken look. He leaned forward and cupped one of her cheeks in his rough palm, before proceeding slowly: "Honestly? I do not believe it is ever in God's plans and I believe it grieves His Spirit. We know it is against His Law, and is therefore a sin. However, we know it was to call sinners that Christ came. He died for our sins, and rose victorious. I firmly believe that His grace is sufficient for all people, over all things. To suggest a sin is too great for Christ to forgive is to stand in contempt of His sacrifice."

Tanya nodded. Her father's words resounded with her own conclusions on the matter.

"Thank you," she said.

"Come here!" Ben called his daughter to him and the pair embraced.

He spoke quietly into her ear as he held her: "My fiery little red head! I'd be worried if he took his divorce lightly. However, I can see he doesn't; I can see how deeply it affected him. Trust God to heal Lance. Trust in His goodness and grace."

"Thanks, Daddy," she whispered.

Tanya went to call Lance and thank him for the flowers, whilst her father retreated into his office.

Ben could not bear the thought of losing Tanya; even so, if it was to a man she really loved, and who loved her back, then he would support the match. Sinking into his high-backed leather chair, he secluded himself away for the remainder of the morning.

* * *

As it came time for lunch, Tina went in to her husband to see what was wrong. She had determined that he must have spoken to Tanya, and was wondering what the outcome had been.

"Did you talk to her, Ben?" she asked.

"Yes. Come and sit down," he invited, patting his thigh.

He wrapped her in an embrace.

"Don't worry about her. She'll be fine. She's more than old enough to look after herself," he said.

"I can't help worrying about her! I look at her and see her as a child."

"Me too. Yet you can't deny we've been waiting for this moment for some years."

"That's true, I suppose. I only hope he's good enough for her . . ."

Ben gave his wife a kiss.

"Let's pray for them – it's the most fruitful thing we can do."

Tina agreed and leant further into her husband's chest as he led them in a prayer for the new couple. Following which, Ben gave her a full account of the morning talk with Tanya and reassured her with the information that Lance would be coming to speak with him during the course of the week.

When Tina suggested they invite Lance over for dinner, Ben concurred whole-heartedly. Such an arrangement would hopefully ease Tina's mind on the matter and would provide a less awkward setting for him to pull Lance aside for a quiet chat.

CHAPTER 9

Lance did not answer Tanya's call, or return it that day. In fact, it took three days for him to contact her. This left Tanya ample time to speculate on his silence. The result was many hours spent in agitated prayer, seeking her Lord.

She received copious confirmation towards India – and none whatsoever about Lance. Although disheartened, she continued to wait upon God, trusting in His timing.

* * *

Once Gwen had a chance to recover from jet lag, and was learning the house-hold routine, Lance felt his duties sufficiently over to allow him to turn his focus back over to Tanya.

Tanya was quick to forgive his silence (although she did mention he could have let her know), and it was arranged for Lance, Gwen and the McCarthy's family to join Tanya's family for dinner on the Saturday evening.

* * *

An unexpected nervousness descended upon Tanya when she awoke on the Saturday morning. Lance had visited once during the week, on the previous afternoon for a short walk, during which he had informed her of his intention to return to America come September. He wanted to spend some time with his brother when the new baby arrived, but promised to return within a month and expressed his hope to join her in India, giving them a chance to see one another in a mission's environment. This Tanya could understand, as she daily hoped to hear the news proclaiming she was an aunty to another niece, or nephew.

Tanya had not told either of her sisters her own exciting news. She wanted to see their faces when it was broken to them. As a result, her nervousness was compounded: not only would she be meeting Lance's mother for the first time, she would be making an announcement to the two families. Perhaps Lance could perform those duties . . .

In the end, no one had to make an announcement.

Lance brought his mother over at five o'clock, well ahead of the others. Tanya adored his mother from the moment Gwen greeted her with a tender hug and led her over to the couch for a cosy tête-à-tête.

Gwen set Tanya at her ease, regaling the younger woman with her own story of romance, sharing how Lance's father had first wooed her, many years ago.

Tina was out collecting a few groceries, leaving Ben and Lance free to wander into the study for a one-on-one talk.

Lance walked across the carpeted floor to lean against the window sill. Ben half sat and half stood against his desk. A potentially uncomfortable moment was prevented by Lance chancing to see an eagle flying low across the sky. Pointing this out to Ben, who was soon beside him looking out the window, the pair watched it soar in the wind's current until it descended into the treetops of the nearby bush land.

"Magnificent creatures!" Ben exclaimed in wonder.

""On wings like eagles" . . . Yes, they are beautiful, and are associated with such wonderful promises."

Both men were glad to keep watchful eyes focused on the sky as Lance turned their focus to more personal matters.

"I know Tanya has talked to you, but I wanted to personally seek your permission to court your daughter," he began. "I'll respect your decision in this regard. If you think I am undeserving of her, I will step back now – without putting any blame on you."

"Do you think yourself undeserving?"

"No," he answered slowly. "Not undeserving as much as . . . she is a very precious gem and I will make every effort to be worthy of her."

Ben put a hand onto Lance's shoulder in response to his thoughtful response.

"You're answer tells me all I need to know." He smiled: "It might not surprise you to hear that Tanya gave me permission to "grill you" during this talk – and I might yet, if you come wanting her hand – but, for the time being, I'm happy for you two to date. I'm confident you'll treasure her as I try to, and as God does. I could not ask for more."

Permission granted, they embarked into the field of American politics, one of Ben's interest areas, until Tina came to shuffle them out into the living area.

Ben engaged Gwen in quiet talk in the lounge as Tina continued meal preparations. Lance helped Tanya set the large, twelve-seater barbeque table outside. The children would sit at a smaller table, which sat off to one side.

The couple had returned inside, Tanya standing within the fold of

Lance's embrace by the entrance to the living room. They were talking softly when Diana unceremoniously opened the door and gave a startled cry of delight.

Lance stepped back as Diana moved hastily forward to give her sister an embrace: "I am truly happy for you, darling!"

"Thanks Dee!"

Chris shook Lance's hand, giving him a telling smile.

Maggie's response was slightly more reserved when she arrived, although she did give Tanya a fond embrace. Wendy was enthralled over the event and received amused smiles from the adults to her assertion: "My prince will be coming soon, too!"

Through the course of the evening, Tanya and Lance sat side-by-side, and hand-in-hand. They didn't speak much; an exchange of knowing smiles appeared to suffice the new couple. Whilst knowing that there was a long road ahead of them, and quite a few hurdles, they both felt a quiet peace for the relationship.

Tanya took back possession of her hand for the length of the meal, and Lance put his arm around her shoulder.

Having trouble concentrating on the flow of table talk around her, Tanya prayed:

Oh Lord, thank you, thank you, thank you! When am I going to wake up?

This can't be real; it can't be happening. I wasn't expecting this. Be with us as we move forward. Be with our families. Continue your work in both our lives. Work on my pride and judgement. Finish mending Lance's heart. Be the foundation of our relationship.

At the end of the evening, Tanya accompanied Lance out to the McCarthy's LandCruiser. They walked slowly, falling behind the rest of the group.

Beside this amazing woman, and with the peace of a loving God upon his heart, Lance felt truly whole. A glowing warmth spread outwards from his heart.

He gently touched Tanya's arm and she stopped beside him.

"Tanya . . .?"

"Yes?"

"Thank you."

"For what?"

"For loving me."

Gold embers sparkled at him from her brilliant green eyes.

"You're welcome," she peeped back.

Lance bent to place a soft kiss upon Tanya's cheek whilst quietly thanking God for leading him into the joy of spring.

ABOUT THE AUTHOR

Originally from Australia, Shannon now lives in the Central Drakensberg region of South Africa with her husband. She studied Occupational Therapy at the University of Queensland before entering the mission field in 2008 and completed the School of Biblical Studies with Youth with a Mission in 2010. She has worked with Christian organisations in East and Southern Africa teaching on Inductive Bible Study and co-founded the NGO Redefined Ministries International in 2011. Redefined Ministries continues its community development work in Mahagi Territory, Democratic Republic of Congo; Shannon completes administrative work for them from home, visiting as often as she can.

Shannon is passionate about seeing the Word of God lived out and combines this with her love of writing to make His Word known. She holds to the words of 2 Timothy 3:14-17: *"But as for you, continue in what you have learned and have firmly believed, knowing from whom you learned it and how from childhood you have been acquainted with the sacred writings, which are able to make you wise for salvation through faith in Christ Jesus. All Scripture is breathed out by God and profitable for teaching, for reproof, for correction, and for training in righteousness, that the man of God may be competent, equipped for every good work.*

In addition to *A Walk through Winter*, Shannon authored the biographical work *Congolese Grandpa*, which details the life of an extraordinary man still completing community development and medical work in his nation into his eighties. He has lived through many eras of the Democratic Republic of Congo, starting when it was still a Belgian colony. All author proceeds from this work go back into community development in the Democratic Republic of Congo.

Being released in late 2015 is Shannon's extensive Bible study resource to equip believers in the Word, entitled *The Bible Companion*. It is a resource for any believer or small group hungry to get beyond the surface when reading and studying the Bible. Additionally, she has written a number of contemporary Christian novels.

Read more about Shannon on her website: www.ShannonBuchbach.com.

www.ingramcontent.com/pod-product-compliance
Lightning Source LLC
Chambersburg PA
CBHW030226180626
46810CB00008B/2983